THE
STONE MEN

Book One

Kathy Lyons
Anna Argent

Cover by The Killion Group www.thekilliongroupinc.com
eBook design by eBook Prep www.ebookprep.com

August 2017
ISBN: 978-1-61417-977-1

ePublishing Works!
www.epublishingworks.com

CONTENTS

ROCK HARD

The Stone Men Series

Kathy Lyons

CHAPTER 1

"**W**elcome to Windsor Castle, Miss Myles. No need to unload your luggage. You won't be staying."

Jacqueline grinned at the elegantly stodgy butler, too excited by the idea of staying at a real castle to fully process his words through his English accent. And yes, she knew that he'd said *Winsley* Castle, not Windsor, but in her mind they were one and the same. Except that she was in Northern England, not London. There were no royal guards about in their big hats, just a zillion good looking footmen. And...and...

"Wait...What?"

"Please do step in, Miss Myles. His lordship would like a word."

His lordship! She forcibly stopped herself from giggling. She was about to have a word with a real life earl. The Earl of Winsley, to be exact.

"This way," he said gesturing deeper inside. She really had to stop gawking, but it was like stepping into the set of Downton Abbey, only grander. And older. There was an actual suit of armor right there in the marble hall!

"Thank you," she said, trying hard not to look like a tourist. "And please call me Jackie."

"I think not, Miss Myles," he said. She was adjusting to his accent and his tone, finally processing that despite his words, he wasn't being complimentary. Or even polite, especially when he added, "This is a proper English household. We adhere to all the rules of appropriate behavior here."

She blinked at him, quickly reviewing everything he'd just said, focusing more on his lifted chin, his sniff of disapproval, and the two statues of naked men holding platters just above their privates. It had taken her a half-second to know that they weren't the statue she was particularly interested in and that they were completely tasteless, Euro trash decor.

"You're a proper English household?" she said, trying not to gape.

"Yes, miss," the butler answered repressively.

"I'm here to participate in a Saturnalia," she said. She pulled out her print of the website, reading directly off the page though she'd already memorized every word. "A Bacchanal of Bliss, complete with lush food, naked men, and tasteful aphrodisiacs artfully prepared. Single women only."

"The website," the man returned, the words filled with loathing. "Master James intends to change it."

"Well he hasn't changed it—"

"And I'm afraid you won't be staying, Miss Myles. His lordship has complete discretion on attendees. That too is on the website."

Jackie felt her blood heat. After all the travel and the maneuvering just to get the time off? After all the research and work? After a fracking miserable flight? "Now you listen to me. I've paid the exorbitant fee, had all the medical certificates approved—"

"Master James," the butler interrupted, smoothly giving her his back as he turned to face a young man in designer jeans and a stylish polo. "This is Miss Myles. She is requesting an explanation for the termination of her visit."

"Visit? I haven't even stepped past the foyer—" she began, but the newcomer raised his hand.

"It's because you're a journalist."

Busted.

"No, no," she lied. "I work at a publicity firm doing press releases and the like."

"And publish travel articles under the name JK."

Really busted.

She mentally scrambled for something to say. A twin sister, an abduction by aliens, something, anything. Fortunately, before she leaped to her clone being the journalist, another car pulled up in the massive driveway. Master James flashed her an urbane smile that she didn't trust for one second, then grabbed her arm.

"Why don't we take this out of the foyer? My father wants to meet you anyway."

His father, the Earl of Winsley. And damned if those butterflies didn't tremble low in her belly. Honestly, this was ridiculous. She was an American. She didn't believe a monarchy was the way to govern anything in this day and age. And yet she couldn't seem to fight that little girl *squee* at the thought of meeting a real life aristocrat.

But she had to get it together. Because if she didn't do some fast maneuvering, a quick hello as she was being shoved out the back door was all the meeting she was going to get.

So she did what she always did when backed into a corner. She relied on her research.

"Master James. You must be James Addison, the second son of the current Earl of Winsley." *Down butterflies, down!* "You're the computer genius who created that app." It was a simple thing that managed a person's gift-giving list, online purchases, and delivery info. Best of all, it was launched with a spectacular campaign before the holidays and presto whammo, he's one of England's richest men. "But your real love is in gardening and MMO gaming."

He flashed her a rueful look. "If you were trying to convince me you're not a journalist, you just failed."

Right. Skip the research. Go with creative charm. "Please," she said trying her most I-am-clueless drawl, "you're like one of the top ten richest bachelor catches. Every female within ten years of your age knows your stats."

He sighed. "It's not limited to within ten years."

She tried to smile winningly at him. "Have you been hit on by randy octogenarians?"

"That's a horrifying thought," he said with a shudder. "I think the oldest was seventy-six, but she might have been lying about her age."

"Poor baby–"

"And you're still not giving me a good reason to let you stay."

Ah-ha! He'd softened in his throw-her-out-now attitude. Which meant she still had a chance to talk her way in. "You know publicity is a good thing. Brings in customers, lets you expand to more than one Saturnalia a year, opens up new—"

"There will only be one a year," he said firmly. And when she started to argue, he shook his head. "You have no understanding of our business—"

"But I can learn—"

"I'm afraid not." There were more words. Lots more if she had to guess, but she heard only noise. Because just as they were stepping down a hallway, she saw it.

The statue. A handsome man in a short Grecian tunic with a hand raised as if in hello. Or perhaps—looking at the rueful expression on his face—it was more of a goodbye. It stood on a pedestal next to a window which bathed it in the rose gold of the autumn sun. It was late afternoon, and he was situated as if he wanted to look out at the back expanse of garden and trees.

The material was marble, but the carving was exquisite. So lifelike, she half expected him to turn and greet at her. Instead, she forgot all decorum and went straight to him, ducking under the cordon and squeezing through the partially shut doors. She had to be in his sight line. She had to look at him face to face.

What an expression, she thought sadly. She'd expected rage. That was the emotion she'd found on most of the statues by this unknown artist. But this statue was resigned, though she definitely saw anguish. And maybe—if the quirk of his lips could be trusted—a bit of gallows humor.

"Miss Myles! You can't be in here!" James grabbed her arm, but she wormed her way free. She wouldn't let him drag her away.

"God, he's so sad," she said. "It breaks my heart to see it."

She stretched up and touched the face along the jawline. The stone was smooth and cold, but she stroked up the path, her gaze seeking its. His. Whatever. She'd never been able to shake the feeling that these statues were real. So damned human it scared her, but there it was. She caressed his face and brushed into the curling hair that was mere ripples in stone.

"He's looking down," she said. "Not quite out the window, but downward. At what, I wonder."

"Me, actually," James said but she barely heard him.

"What?" She wanted to look at him, but couldn't drag her gaze off the tiny ridge of a scar along the statue's neck. As if a chip had been badly repaired. She touched the raised line. "What happened to you here?" she murmured.

"Me again," James said though she hadn't been talking to him. "Or rather one of my drunken friends. We should have had a true stone mason fix it, but I was young and embarrassed, so I repaired it myself and botched the job. Now it'll cause more damage to fix properly, so we let it be. He says he doesn't mind, but I'll feel bad about it for the rest of my life."

"He?" she prompted, not really listening. But she knew that the longer she kept James talking, the more time she'd have with the statue.

"Kane. That's his name, though of course, we call him the Satyr for the weekend."

"Kane," she echoed and this time she stroked his uplifted palm. The detail was exquisite. There were raised calluses on his palm and long fingers with unusual pads. "What are these from?" Ridiculous to ask the question of a statue, but there it was.

"Archery and some swordplay, I'd imagine."

She stroked her hand up his muscular forearm, the bend in his elbow, and the bulging biceps. There was a bump on the back of his arm and she rubbed her finger over it twice before she could force herself to stop gazing at his front enough to look at it. She had to step around the pedestal, but fortunately, James didn't block her, so she could move freely.

"A mole. He's got a mole right here."

"Most women look at his muscles."

She smiled, her gaze sliding over the statue's physique. "Oh, I noticed those too, I assure you." Then she stroked the mole. "Why would an artist sculpt something so perfect and then add a mole?"

"Realism?"

"Yes, of course." The first statue she'd ever seen had had acne scars. "True realism, but do you know how hard it is to add something like that? When carving stone?"

"You have some experience in stonework?"

She nodded. "I'm awful at it, but it gives me enough experience to know what it takes to do something like this so perfectly. So real." She looked back up into the statue's eyes. "Kane, you break my heart."

"Why?" It was a different voice. An older one with more anger, less forgiveness.

Her back stiffened when she heard it, and she knew she was about to be tossed out. She needed to confront this newest threat and win him over to her side. But she couldn't look away from Kane. And then the man repeated the question, this time with a demanding tone.

"Why does he break your heart? He isn't even real. He's a statue."

"True," she said softly, her fingers sliding back up his arm to the statue's shadowed cheek. Even knowing he was stone, the coldness still startled her. The other side had been warmed by the sun. This cheek had nothing to give it heat except her hand. "Just a statue. And yet he's so real to me. I can't explain but..." She feathered her fingers across his mouth. "Just look at his face. Look into his eyes. Can't you see the despair in there?"

No answer. It hardly mattered. In the silence she was able to memorize every curve of Kane's features. Every ripple of his lips, even the odd bushy push of his eyebrows.

"You need to come down, Miss Myles." James said as he tugged on her sleeve. "Miss Myles!"

She blinked, startled out of her reverie. He grabbed hold of her elbow and jerked her hard. She stumbled, belatedly realizing she'd actually climbed up on the pedestal with the statue.

What the hell? She was wrapped around the thing like a lover. She'd all but humped it! Embarrassment burned in her cheeks as she half fell, half jumped to the floor.

"I'm so sorry," she gasped. "I don't know what came over me."

"The Satyr affects everyone differently," James said, his tone not exactly kind, but not harsh either. More filled with speculation, and her gaze jumped to his.

Unfortunately, the earl's tone was a good deal harsher. "You will explain yourself, Miss Myles, or I will call the Constable."

She looked to the man. He matched the pictures she'd found of him. Late fifties, bushy eyebrows, curly hair, and a jaw that was currently clenched in fury. The man was large with a paunch, but that was the only softness in him as he glared at her.

She swallowed. This wasn't going to be easy. "You're right," she said. "I'm a stringer. Er, that's a journalist that sells articles. I'm not on staff anywhere or anything."

"I know what a stringer is," he said. His gaze darted to the statue. "Why were you climbing on Kane? Do you think I will turn a blind eye to casual defacement of my family?"

"I...No, of course not." She had no explanation. And if she weren't scrambling for an answer, she'd take a moment to wonder why he'd called a statue "his family." As it was, she could only stand there mute. And in standing, her gaze inevitably slid back to Kane. She couldn't help it. She just wanted to look at him, talk to him. Something. She rubbed her hand over her face.

"Jesus, I'm insane," she said. "Look, I don't have to write the article." Though how she was going to pay for this particular trip, she hadn't a clue. If she couldn't sell an article on this most exclusive of weekend resorts, she was going to be paying off her credit card debt for the next ten years.

"Then why come?"

Did she 'fess up? Would it help or hurt her cause? "I've seen two others of these statues in my life. Same sculptor. Had to be. Perfect detail in every way. Such expressions on their faces."

In her peripheral vision, James stepped forward. "Where? Where did you see these statues?"

"My friend's house in Chicago where I grew up." She wouldn't tell them about the mystery there. Well, not the full mystery. "It's not there anymore. The house...um...it blew up."

"What?"

She shook her head. "Old story. You can look it up online. Happened eleven years ago on June 12th."

She saw James pull out his cell phone and start Googling.

"And the second?"

"Last year in a little naval museum for sailors lost at sea. It...I..." She was looking at Kane's face again, mentally comparing it to the other. "The other two were angry. Like really, really pissed. As a kid, I was frightened. As an adult..." She shrugged. "It still gives me the creeps. I have pictures."

Without looking away from Kane, she pulled out her phone, keyed in the passcode, and handed it over to James.

"And Kane?" James asked.

She tilted her head, stepping to the base of the pedestal as she looked closer. "I think he's past anger. That takes a man to despair. Maybe even self-destruction."

"It's a statue," the earl said coldly.

"I know," she said softly. And again she touched his cheek—the cold one—pressing her palm flat to warm him. A moment ticked by. Then another. And another. In the end, she realized two things. She couldn't warm stone with just her hand. And the other two men in the room were staring at her because she'd done it again. She was back up on the pedestal and staring into Kane's eyes.

She really was insane.

She forced herself to look away. And then another act of will to step back down and guiltily look at the two men.

"I'm not here to hurt you or your business, I swear. I've just been drawn to these statues all my life."

The earl's hands were planted on his hips. "I will not permit you to write anything about the statues. One word, Miss Myles, and I will have my legal team bury you."

She swallowed. She'd hoped that this would be her PhD thesis one day. Or an exposé. Or something. Her life's obsession ought to pay off somehow, right?

But that was a problem for another day. Right now, she just had to stay near Kane. She had to learn all she could about him. It was a need bordering on obsession. Or insanity. So she nodded, and when that didn't seem to be enough, she spoke.

"I'll sign anything you want. Just let me stay for the weekend."

James nodded, obviously convinced. But he clearly wasn't the one with the ultimate say, because he turned to look at his father. The earl just stood there glaring.

"If this is an act," he said, gesturing roughly toward the statue. "I will destroy you."

It didn't seem like an idle threat. "I'm not lying to you, sir. Er, my lord. And I'm the worst actor in the world."

He glanced at his son who shrugged. "What have we got to lose?"

"Everything," his father snapped. Then he stared hard at her. "I'm watching you. Every moment—even after you leave—I'll have people watching you."

Stalker much? But she'd take it.

"Come to my office in an hour. There will be contracts for you to sign." Then before she could ask, he narrowed his eyes. "Nondisclosure agreements. A lot of them. Wherein you forfeit everything you have and a great deal more that you might get if you record anything I don't like."

No journalist in her right mind would sign anything like that. No sane person would agree.

"No problem," she said.

CHAPTER 2

The woman was fondling his penis.

Kane allowed his mind to curse her for a skank, all the while grateful that he was still a statue. It wouldn't do to shrink when fondled, but there was no subtlety in women these days. In truth, he hadn't seen any gentility for at least a century. He didn't know if that was a change in the world in general or just the women his relations brought in for him. Either way, he was revolted by this girl and wished she would just move on.

Thankfully, she eventually did. Then she took her aphrodisiac-laced cognac and slammed it back like it was cheap ale. He didn't care that she was a statuesque blonde. A beauty with the manners of a field hand held no appeal to him.

Though, frankly, no one held much appeal these days and not for the last decade at least. Except for that one girl this afternoon. Where was she?

The parade of women continued. He was hours away from his release and the current earl was doing his duty, lining up women for Kane like they were dairymaids in a row.

The blonde field hand moved on, and the next woman sauntered in. She was bedecked in jewels, so obviously she had wealth, but she was young. Early twenties, he guessed, with a brown coloring that had been the fashion for at least a hundred years. Repulsive, he thought. But then no one had asked him.

Meanwhile, Hugh began the story, relaying it in exactly the same way he had for the last few decades.

"Once upon time--"

Actually, it had been just over two hundred years.

"There lived a handsome prince."

Nope. He'd been the arrogant second son of the Earl of Winsley. Hugh there was his ninth-great nephew. A solid sort as earls went. Serious minded, married to a stodgy German woman, and with the mind of a banker. That last bit was the important part. Kane hadn't been damned to hell for two hundred years just to watch his family fritter away his sacrifice.

"Sadly," Hugh continued to drone, "his family was on the brink of destruction. Poverty had claimed them, and they might soon starve."

That was an exaggeration too, but one that he'd believed when he'd been the ripe age of twenty-three with barely a copper to his name. In truth, the family might have made it out of the quagmire if they'd applied themselves. Instead, he'd thought of a cheat. A quick bargain with a powerful woman. It galled him to this day that it had been his own idea. This bargain-turned-hell had been of his own making.

"In that moment, the young son Kane thought of a brilliant idea."

Bloody idiotic one, more like.

"Calling on a goddess, he offered himself in trade."

A war bitch goddess. And he'd been a fool.

"In return for his family's survival--"

Two million pounds of gold, which back in 1813 had been more gold that any nation could amass. It had sat in their wine cellar to be sold for cash at a slow, steady rate to rebuild the family fortunes.

"He gave himself to the goddess in service."

To be trained in the art of war. Which meant beatings, slashings, whippings, and endless violence as he trained. Hs soul have been shaped under the war bitch's directions while his statue stood waiting for a moment's reprieve. A time when he wasn't being trained to rest quietly in this stone prison at his family's estate.

"His only escape is once a year for three days and three nights."

Seventy-two hours of desperate release. Of frantic couplings. Of aching disappointment.

"He must give a woman a moment of bliss to break the spell. True pleasure, sweet joy, sensuous ecstasy."

No. Just True Bliss. As an arrogant twenty-two year old, he'd thought a good orgasm or three would do it. All he had to do was get the woman screaming in release, and he'd break the spell.

Wrong. He'd been so wrong. For two hundred years, he'd been giving women great orgasms. He'd pleasured them every way he could. Every toy, every position, every pleasure imaginable. And at the end of seventy-two hours, he'd always returned here to his blasted pedestal to serve that bitch goddess again.

While another year went by.

"He is the Satyr," Hugh continued. "Go to him now. Touch his body and whisper into his ear what would pleasure you this night. What bliss do you wish for?"

The woman bounced forward. She was a redhead by the looks of her, though he doubted it was her true hair color. Her jewelry jangled as she awkwardly climbed up to stand on the edge of his pedestal. He really wished Hugh would not have them whisper in his ear, but it had been the custom for nearly two centuries. At the beginning, he'd been so desperate for a soft touch that any caress was bliss. Anything that wasn't a sword or a fist. If he was in his statue body, he wanted a woman's touch.

Not anymore. Not these women. Not these bold creatures with no subtlety and stupid ideas. Like this bedecked child who giggled as she stepped up. She slid her hand boldly down his statue chest, and yes—she reached under the fabric wrap to stroke his phallus.

"My bliss would be world peace," she said loudly, obviously for Hugh's benefit. "And a million pounds, of course, to give to the hungry."

Sure she did. If he were flesh, he'd be growling at her to get on with it. Then she did.

She leaned in tight to his ear and whispered.

"A threesome. Or more. I've always wanted many men pleasuring me at once."

Liar. He'd learned early that girls like her only enjoyed the idea of multiple partners. It was too painful in reality and it never, ever produced bliss. But girls like her were so self-absorbed that she thought more of the same would bring bliss. As a former self-absorbed idiot, he knew better than most that more of oneself just produced more self-revulsion. And boredom.

He would not be going to her bed tonight.

The girl child finally left. She would be serviced by any number of willing footmen or paid professionals that Hugh brought in for the weekend. Meanwhile, in came the next girl. Then the next.

Then the next.

Nearly thirty in all.

Bloody hell, when would *she* get here?

There. There she was, at last.

She'd cleaned up since he'd seen her this afternoon, the impetuous girl with the strange accent who'd run in here much to his delight. Her clothing was simple. A modest dress by today's standards, at least. Tight bodice to show her curves and a flowing skirt that fell to just above her knees. She had honey blonde hair that she'd clipped away from her face such that it fell in soft waves around her shoulders. Her lips were painted a gentle red, her eyes seemed a strange changeable blue-green, and her ears sported simple gold hoops that weren't really gold.

And he found her lovely.

Hugh stiffened and frowned. "The American journalist," he drawled.

She'd been looking at Kane, but now flashed his ninth-great nephew a glare. "I signed all the papers. I won't be writing any article, so you can call me Jackie or Miss Myles, thank you very much."

Forget him. Look at me. Look at me. Look at me.

Hugh humphed. Pompous ass. But he began intoning the words of the saturnalia. Kane didn't listen. Jackie did though, with her head cocked to one side and her hair slipping past its pins to shadow half her face.

Not him! Me me me me me.

Hugh droned on, and when he was finished, she just shook her head.

"How much of that is true?"

Hugh frowned. "If you're not doing an article, the truth hardly matters."

"The truth always matters," she shot back, and Kane wanted to applaud her impertinence. For two hundred years, his life had been defined by orders. One did not disobey a goddess who could control you—or obliterate you—with a wave of her hand. He'd forgotten how much fun it was to hear someone fight back with words instead of weapons.

Hugh scowled at her. "If the Satyr wishes, he will tell you the truth himself tonight." It was clear from Hugh's tone that he thought nothing more unlikely. Stupid him.

"Satyr?" she mocked. "His name is Kane."

How beautiful his name sounded from her lips. Her accent was strange to his ears, but his name came through loud and clear. And now, finally, she was looking at him again.

"Tell him your bliss," Hugh ordered.

"What? Like walks on the beach or puppies?"

Nothing sexual? How unusual. And yet suddenly, Kane was filled with lust.

"Whatever you choose, just tell him." Hugh was getting impatient. So was Kane. Especially now that she was finally touching him.

She had braced herself on his arm, and he was gratified that in his statue form she could let her whole weight swing from his wrist and he wouldn't break. He was less happy that he couldn't cradle her closer, but that would come soon. So damned soon he could almost taste it.

"Okay, Kane," she said, speaking her words slower. Softer. "You want to hear my bliss." She smiled as she moved directly before his eyes. She had freckles, he now noticed. And a mole partially hidden in her hairline above her right temple. "I want to hear your story. I want to know the story of all the statues. And…"

She swallowed, her words cut off. Then she looked away, clearly embarrassed.

No, no, no! Tell me what you want and I will give you everything.

Slowly her gaze lifted, connecting again with his eyes. "Look," she said louder, clearly for Hugh's benefit. "I don't want some random guy in a toga creeping into my bed tonight." Her gaze settled calmly on him. "What I want— what would really be my bliss—would be you." She touched his cheek and whispered, "I wish you really could come to life."

I will. Just wait. A couple hours more.

She stood there a moment longer, her gaze searching his. He wanted to catch her eyes. He wanted to hold her body and tell her that he was awake and aware. But he couldn't move, and in the end she flushed, and he thought even that motley blush of pink and red beautiful.

"Look, I don't care how," she said as she turned to Hugh. "Print, e, Sanskrit scroll—whatever. I want to know about these statues. I've already promised not to tell. I just need to know."

Hugh didn't answer, though his eyes narrowed and his nostrils flared. This was not the way the Saturnalia usually went, and nothing bothered Hugh so much as something different. Without a word, he gestured to a side table where the glasses of cognac waited. The last one there.

"This the tasteful aphrodisiac part?" she asked.

"All our guests drink. Or they leave."

No, no! Kane didn't want her dazed and hyper-sexualized. He wanted her this way with her searching eyes and sharp tongue. He wanted her…

She sipped the cognac delicately, then blinked her eyes. "That's…um…not subtle."

So she wasn't used to strong drink. He liked that.

"You will consume all of it, if you please," Hugh said calmly.

"All the better to discredit me later," she shot back.

"Yes," Hugh admitted, a smirk on his face. "If you ever have the urge to pick up a pen, do recall that you willingly drugged yourself before this night began. Anything you say—"

"Can and will be held against me. Yeah, I got it." She finished the drink with a grimace. "And come into the twenty-first century, *my lord*. I use a keyboard or my phone. No one under the age of sixty writes with a pen."

She set her glass upside down onto the table. Actually, she slammed it down as if she were playing a drinking game he'd seen on a movie Hugh's father had once played. Then she lifted her chin and called out.

"Okay, Carson or Alfred or whatever you name is. Come take me to the boudoir of lust. Er…bliss."

A moment later, the butler appeared and guided her out. Kane wished he could turn his head, wished he could follow her right now. But he remained frozen, barely able to see the door in his peripheral vision. Meanwhile, Hugh pronounced his judgment.

"Cheeky brat."

If Kane were flesh, he'd have grinned. As soon as he was flesh, he was going to see just how cheeky she would be with him inside her.

Another hour yet.

Hugh look at him. "I'll be back with my recommendations before it's time."

Kane didn't care. He'd find his Cheeky American if he had to ram through every room in this mammoth place. Fortunately, he knew each and every bedroom by heart.

Hugh left. Kane waited.

Another forty minutes.

Thirty.

This was torture. The last hour always felt like an eternity.

Fifteen.

Ten.

Five.

Three. Hugh returned to stand patiently by the cognac, though he didn't drink any.

Two.

One.

Tingles. How he loved the feeling of pins and needles in every cell of his body. Pricks and pain, the agonizing revitalization of stone into flesh. Ants on his skin. Electricity through his nerves. Pulse and power and life again.

Alive again.

And free.

For seventy-two hours, he was free.

He curled his fingers first then tried to inhale. It was the breath that took the longest. He'd feel his face move, his blood surge, and even his toes curl before he could draw breath again.

Soon.

His buttocks clenched, agony like fire replacing the cold numbness. The first time he'd animated, it had been with screams. Silent ones at first, but then the rasping screech when he'd found breath.

His knees bent, softening like soggy paper and his tenth-great nephew James was there to keep him from falling.

A thousand knife stabs rolled up his spine from base to brain. He arched without willing it, his heavy arms pulling back as he nearly threw the young man off the pedestal.

His ears came next, sound rushing in like a cacophony. He heard when he was stone, but it was nothing compared to the nuances he caught as flesh.

Sight too. Bold colors flared where before there had been only muted tones.

He felt the brush of his hair—individual strands—as a lock fell across his cheek and his skin screamed at the caress.

True sensation.

True pain.

True air.

The razor sharp cut of breath as it shredded his throat and made mincemeat of his insides. And yet he welcomed it. He loved it.

He was flesh again and…

Cold. So cold.

James was there, offering him a robe but he didn't even look at it. Instead, he focused on Hugh. "Wh—"

His voice didn't work yet. It would take a moment more. Meanwhile, Hugh lifted up two pictures of women, neither of whom was the American.

"I believe these are the most promising candidates this year–"

"No." His voice felt and sounded like rocks scraping together, but he got the word out. Meanwhile, James had set down the robe and offered him a glass.

He grabbed it and drank. Brandy. Sweet blackberry bandy that throbbed as it burned down his throat. But it helped.

"If you would but listen," Hugh said, his tone patient and condescending.

"American." Hell. He didn't even know her name. In truth, he didn't really know what American meant, though he had a vague guess it was that rebellious British colony that styled itself as the United States.

Fortunately, James was of a more compliant nature. "She's in the last room on the right."

The furthest away. He turned and headed in her direction, but then paused.

"Name?" he rasped out.

"Please listen—" Hugh began.

"Jacqueline Myles," James answered.

Good man.

He left the room and headed for hers.

CHAPTER 3

Jackie was hot and uncomfortable. Whatever aphrodisiac had been in that cognac, it was strong. Her skin was hyper-sensitive, her mind felt fuzzy, and most of all, yes, she was freaking horny. She'd put on her fuzzy bunny pajamas because she didn't own a set of sexy under-anythings. She had the occasional hot dress—both of which were in her luggage—but negligee? It had always seemed like a waste of money. Just as well because right now a filmy anything would have felt like too much.

The brush of the soft cotton against her skin was like static electricity sparking everywhere. If she stayed absolutely still, she was less uncomfortable, but damn it, she was restless. And desperate. And what the hell had been in that drink?

She was ready to take matters into her own hands—so to speak—when her bedroom door flew open. She bolted upright in bed, a scream in her throat, then her breath caught and refused to let out a sound. She saw who it was. The hallway was well lit, and her curtains were open. Between the light from behind him and the moonlight from the side, she got a pretty good look.

It was the statue come to life—or at least he was supposed to look like that. Same face, same curly hair, same bulging muscles though his frame didn't seem as massive now that he was off the pedestal. He was pleasingly large, and the sensual curve to lip and brow had her belly going liquid even as her heart was pounding in terror. Or excitement. Or aphrodisiac overdose.

"Stop," she said, the word shoved out of her throat. She didn't even know if she was talking to him or her own body, but she needed to get some control. "Just…stop."

He did, though a sound down the hallway had him turning to look. A lot of sounds, come to think of it.

"What's going on?" she asked.

He stepped back and gestured for her to see. She scrambled out of bed, the rub of sheets against her skin sending lightning bolts ricocheting through her body. The cool shock of the wood floor on her bare feet was a welcome relief.

He hadn't moved far, but it was enough for her to look out of her room. Though even as she stared, she was all too aware of him right behind her shoulder. Then she frowned. There were a dozen men in short togas coming down the hallway. All of them were dressed to look like the statue, though obviously not the same man. Some were blonde, others had a short buzz cut. Their bodies were big and small and all variety in between, though they all were handsome enough.

"My stand-ins," he said, his voice a gravelly mess.

She turned to look at him, more because of the grating sound in his words than what he said. And then he continued, his tone casual, but his body seemed to vibrate with intensity.

"I cannot go to every woman. I chose you and so the others—"

"Probably won't know the difference in their current state." After all, she'd spent much of the afternoon and evening with her fellow Saturnalia guests. Many had been drunk by the time they went giggling to bed. Others were just giggly and none too bright. She supposed it took a certain type of woman to sign up for three nights like this, and the profile didn't fit with cutting intellect. She didn't want to examine too closely what that said about her.

"Oh, right," she said as she stepped back into her room. He followed her. "Look, I'm sure you're very nice and all..." Damn it, her words were coming out all breathy. All that rippling male chest right in front of her. "But I'm not interested in a gigolo." Liar, liar, pants on fire. In her current state, she wanted anything that would get her off.

"A what?"

She gestured down the hallway. "A hooker. A prostitute. A whatever it is you're called in this country."

He reared back, obviously insulted. "I am not a slag!" Then he moderated his tone, clearly struggling with impatience. "You asked for me. You wanted to know about me." He spread his arms, but his eyes seemed to burn into hers. "I am here. For you."

She shook her head, backing away from him rather than throw herself into his arms. He looked so close to the statue. "The statue. The history. The..."

He caught her wrist, and she gasped as her flesh sparked beneath his grip. "You don't have to believe it," he said softly. "Just let me try."

That's when she saw it. The scar on his neck. The one from James' drunken friend. It was a lifted ridge in a straight line on his neck, and it was inches from her face.

"How did they make such an exact replica?" she asked. And she forced herself to flip on the light.

"I'm not a replica," he said.

"Not you. The statue. It has to have been carved like you." God, he was an exact duplicate to the statue. As in completely identical. Could the statue have been computer generated? She couldn't stop herself from stroking along that straight scar. It even felt the same. "How did you get it?"

"I wasn't there. It happened when I was in Idola."

"Where?" She tried to clear her thoughts, but he smelled so good. No perfume or cologne. Not even soap. Just man. And every breath seemed to make her dizzy with want.

He wrapped an arm around her. She felt the sizzle along her low back as he pressed her close. When had she fallen into his arms?

"No," she said as she nuzzled against his neck. And it was more of a "no, don't stop" kind of no. "Oh hell…"

She melted against him, her body flush with his. Soft planes against his hard rock of a body. His hands slid to her bottom, cupping her there before pulling her firmly against him. Oh, yes. Oh, nice. Pressed hot against her pelvis.

"This isn't what I wanted," she murmured as she grazed her teeth along his scar. But obviously it was what she wanted now.

He rumbled deep in his throat as he picked her up. He just lifted her, and she rolled her pelvis against him as he took the steps to the bed.

"Tell me about the statue," she said trying to marshal her thoughts. It was a losing battle as he settled her on the mattress. "Start easy. Tell me its name and how it got it."

"My name is Kane Byron Charles Addison, and I was named by my parents in the usual way."

He'd set her on the bed and stepped between her knees. A huge male figure in a sheet of fabric with an impressive tent in front. She couldn't stop looking at that bulge. She wanted to grab hold of it. She wanted to do such things with it, and didn't that shock her prudish Midwestern soul. She'd never wanted to do the things that were rolling through her mind.

"What is happening to me?" she asked, suddenly frightened. "I've never…." She blinked her eyes and tried to focus.

He was bending forward, his hands already working the buttons of her pajama top. But then he froze. "You're a virgin?"

She reached out and began to stroke his thigh. Hard muscles, wiry hair, and heat. Such heat. Then she realized what he'd said. A virgin?

"What? No. I mean, it's been so long I might as well be. But…"

He touched her chin, his hand so large he caressed most of her jaw with a single touch. "It must not hurt. Please tell me if I hurt you."

There was concern in his eyes. A worry that pinched his brow and thickened his jaw. And that more than anything eased her mind. Thanks to whatever she'd drunk, she was beyond horny. And he was here—her fantasy come to life—definitely willing to satisfy her. She might as well give in to the experience. It's not like her mind was fully intact in any case.

"You're not sick or anything? No diseases?"

His lips quirked at that. "None."

"And I've got the IUD, so no babies."

His expression shifted for a moment. A brief flicker of sadness, and then it was gone. She would have asked, but his hand had slid down her face to the neckline of her top. His knuckles left a brush fire in their wake, and what was left of her focus disappeared.

"Promise you'll tell me everything you know afterwards," she said as she closed her eyes. "Everything."

"I promise," he said, then she felt him unbutton her top.

He made quick work of it, and she relaxed back on the bed to enjoy the sensation. When he stroked the fabric away, she was exposed down to her navel and the cool rush of air was so welcome. Her nipples were already tight, her belly quivering, but when he put his hands on her, she released a sigh of sheer delight. Such large hands, rough with calluses. And when he shaped her breasts, everything in her came alive. Then he pinched her nipples and she arched while lightning shot white behind her eyelids.

Her legs were restless, alternately scissoring or gripping him. He leaned over her, his breath hot a moment before he latched onto her breast. He took his time with it, kissing around the nipple before nipping at the tip. And when he suckled, she cried out in excitement.

She reached blindly for him then. Slipping a hand under his tunic to find him. Large. Hot. He hissed between his teeth when she began to squeeze.

Then he grabbed her wrist and gently pulled her away. "Not yet," he said against her belly.

She really didn't want to wait, but he was obviously a man who liked controlling the show. And given how good he was at it, she was willing to let him lead. So she let go and he drew her arm up, up over her head. Gently, he wrapped her fingers around the brass bars of the headboard.

"Hold on, Jacqueline." He said her name in the French way, rolling the word in a way that was sexy as hell. Especially since everyone else called her Jackie.

"Kane," she said. She had no other thought. Just that he had said her name so she wanted to say his. Apparently he liked it because he grinned as he drew her other hand above her head.

"Why do you have rabbits on your clothes?" he asked as he lifted her hips to draw the pajama pants off.

"Don't you like bunny rabbits?" she said as she was stripped bare.

"They make a great stew."

"Eww!" she opened her eyes to look at him. Given how fuzzy she felt, she'd kept them closed to fully appreciate every sensation. But at his words, she looked at him and got the full view above her. Granite hard chest, rippling with muscles. Broad shoulders, narrow hips. And toga. Stupid toga.

"Take it off," she said. "Let me see all of you."

He nodded, then stripped the draping fabric away. And in the room light, she did indeed see everything. Smooth hard planes. Tight dark buds of his nipples. Jutting hips and the dark red thrust of his penis—large and wet at the tip. Really large. She'd felt him before, but nothing like seeing a well-hung man to start mentally thinking internal dimensions and all.

She bit her lip and looked uncertainly up at him. He was holding himself back, his eyes an intense amber as they focused on her. And waited.

"I…Um…" She shrugged. "It's been a while for me."

"I will go slow." Then he touched her cheek, drawing her gaze back up to his eyes. She hadn't even realized she was looking back down. "This is about finding your bliss," he said. "Whatever pleases you, Jacqueline. Tell me what you want."

She caressed his face, so like the mysterious statue. She could almost believe it was him come to life. "Love me," she whispered.

He pressed his lips to her palm. Clever lips, wet tongue as it drew an erotic circle on her skin. Her fingers spread, her breath caught, and he smiled. "How, Jacqueline?"

She quirked an eyebrow. She didn't know. She just wanted.

"Leave it to me?" he asked.

"Okay."

So he began to stroke her breasts again. Gentle caresses followed by a pinch. She gasped every time, her body arching restlessly. Then his hands slid lower. He rolled over her ribcage, then pressed into her waist. He seemed to touch every part of her as he made it to her hips and then lower to gently separate her knees.

She was lengthwise on the bed and he adjusted her better such that her hips were at the edge, her legs lifted up to…to…She swallowed. He settled her legs in the crook of his elbows and now she was spread out before him.

She thought he would penetrate her then. That was the usual way wasn't it? And her body was liquid and open, waiting for it. For him. But he didn't. Instead, his hands slid between. Large thumbs, calloused fingers. He touched her everywhere. He pushed inside her and he rolled his fingers over. At one point, he even pinched her clit.

She tried to be analytical. It was in her nature to catalogue experiences. Good features. Tacky toga. Useful information. Historically anachronistic. Words were her tools, and she wanted to use them now. But she hadn't the focus. She simply felt everything, and the categories were burned away. Good became amazing. Wet became wild. Pleasure became yesyesyes in a continuous stuttered gasp.

In and out, around, up and down. Everywhere at once and all of it building the tremor inside her. Tighter. Pulsing. Nearly there. Just…Oh god. Oh yes. Oh!

Peak!

Lightning shorted out her words. Orgasm expanded outward from him through her. Pleasure such as she had never felt before.

Yesyesyes

She floated. She sighed. She…

What?

Again?

No!

Oh!

Ahhhhhh.

He stroked her again. It was too much at first, but he was gentle. And when she tightened against him, there was nowhere for her to go. He still held her. And he still crooned her name though she hadn't even realized he was doing it.

"Jacqueline. Jacqueline. Sweet Jacqueline."

"Kane," she answered. And in her mind, she was saying, I am here. Take me.

"Do you want more?" he asked.

"You." It was all she had breath for with him stroking her more.

"Do you want to rest?"

"You." She tightened her legs, trying to draw him closer. He smiled and leaned down.

She thought he would press into her then, but once again she was surprised. Instead, he took his time with her nipples. He sucked on one, then the other. A steady strong pull, and it was everything she wanted except for more.

And she really wanted more.

She began to undulate against him. Her legs were high and wide. Open for him.

"Please," she gasped.

Then he was there, slowly pushing in. The tip spreading her. She was so wet, he slid easily, but too slow.

"Please."

He laved her nipple, then bit lightly. She cried out, everything in her rolling into orgasm. No "almost there." No "nearly" about it. Just want and then Oh my god!

And while she was crying out, he impaled her.

A slam inside and she was gripping him.

The lightning was everywhere, exploding inside her and around her.

He thrust and thrust. Faster. Harder.

She screamed with every glorious impalement.

She cried as she thrashed beneath him.

And she gasped in delight when his greatest thrust held her pinioned and he groaned.

Release!

God yes.

Sweet yes.

She was still pulsing, though slower now.

His body was shuddering on top of her, and she welcomed the weight. And then he was pressing his lips to her neck. Scraping his teeth just beneath her ear.

"Good?" he whispered.

"Oh yeah."

"But not bliss." There was an ache in his words. A despair that pulled her heavily into the present.

"What? Of course it was."

He shook his head, and his body seemed to sink deeper against her. "I would know."

"What?"

He closed his eyes. She knew because she felt the brush of his lashes against her cheek. "It wasn't bliss."

She didn't know what to say. He seemed so defeated. And after the glorious explosions that were still randomly sparking inside her, his sadness felt like a physical pain.

"Kane," she whispered. She stroked his hair, brushing the curly strands off his forehead. "Kane, it's all right. I'm blissful, I swear. Full of bliss."

He took a deep breath. She felt his ribs expand, his body tighten, and then his back arch as he slowly withdrew from inside her.

"No—" She began, but it was too late. He was out, and she was empty.

"Don't worry," he said. "We have all night."

She rolled her head to look fully at him. She was still too languid to lift herself up. "What?"

He smiled, the expression decadent. "We've only just begun, sweet Jacqueline."

"But—"

"Trust me?" It wasn't an order but a question.

They'd just met, and there was something very bizarre going on here. She was drugged and in a foreign country, and yet she didn't hesitate when she answered.

"Yes, I trust you."

His smile stretched into a grin. "Then let us begin."

CHAPTER 4

Kane let his head drop back against the back of his chair. In his lap, the iPad stayed bright for a few moments more before settling into sleep mode. Jacqueline was resting as well, her body well sated, her limbs a sprawl that he'd covered gently with a blanket.

Though he had the endurance to spend three days and nights in copulation, she did not. Usually, he would have gone on to the other women. Twenty-nine rooms down this hallway and the next. All filled with willing women who had been much more specific as to what would give them bliss.

But he'd lost faith early this time. The others were more of the same. Different shapes and ages, but all a variation on a theme. He'd spent two hundred years shagging those types. Jacqueline was different, and so he'd had hopes that he could give her bliss. A moment of True Bliss—with capital letters—then he'd be free.

But he hadn't.

So he lost faith.

Now he sat in her dark room with an iPad on his lap and counted all the ways the world had passed him by. Computers, airplanes, and cars were just a few of the technological advancements. On a personal level, his friends had all married, had children, and died nearly two centuries ago. His brother and his brother's grandsons, all gone. The monarchy survived, thank God, but Britain wasn't the power he remembered. According to some articles he'd read, his native country had gone through its greatest hours and declined while he'd been encased in stone. Or shagging as many females as possible in his seventy-two hours of yearly respite.

Funny how it didn't feel like a rest at all.

Jacqueline stirred in her sleep, curling onto her side as she tucked a hand beneath the pillow. She'd left the curtains open—cheeky girl—and so the dawn was coloring her face rose gold. A natural blonde with eyes the color of a changing sea. Blue, green, brown. He'd seen them all in her eyes those moments when he'd been stone and she'd been searching his face.

Now she was resting, and he was adrift.

There was a soft scratch at the door. He didn't even turn his head. He already knew who it was. His tenth-great nephew who was still young enough to hope on his behalf.

He didn't answer. He'd watched the hope die in nine generations of his relatives. He really had no wish to kill it in a tenth. But in time the doorknob turned and James peeked in. Kane had already made sure that Jacqueline was adequately covered, so he remained in the chair keeping still enough that he might as well have been stone.

"Well?" James asked in a breath that was more facial expression than sound.

Kane simply shook his head.

"The others have rested. You could wake one and try…"

"No." What was the point? Two hundred years of failure ought to be enough for any man.

"Don't give up now. You've just started." The young man eased further into the room. "Come have some tea. We'll talk about it." When Kane didn't answer, he tried a different tack. "I'll catch you up on the world. Did I tell you that Kate Middleton had another child?"

Kane frowned. Who the hell was—

"The Duchess of Cambridge. Married…"

Kane waved a hand in dismissal. He didn't care. Once upon a time, the births of the royals would have been of great interested. Now he barely cared about his own relations.

"Come on to breakfast. We'll figure this out."

"Figure what out?" came a muffled voice from the bed. Jacqueline.

"Nothing," he said. "Go back to sleep."

She rolled onto her back, and he was pleased to see that she kept an arm over her chest to hold the blanket in place. Still, a porcelain-white shoulder appeared as her hair fell away from her face.

"Tempting," she said, "but not going to happen. Come on, I love a puzzle. What are you trying to figure out?"

James came further into the room. "He's got to give a woman a moment of True Bliss."

"I had several last night."

"No, you didn't," Kane said as he watched for her to open her eyes. Something about that first blink in the dawn's light. It was a moment that he needed to see. What color would her eyes be today?

She smiled, her rose lips curving, her perfect teeth peeking through. "I beg to differ."

"I'd know," he said.

"*I'd* know."

Finally, he found the energy to move. He leaned forward, resting his elbows on his knees. And he watched her face, waiting for her eyes.

And he waited.

Eventually, she must have realized the silence. Her brows pulled together and then…open.

Blue.

Like a perfect summer day.

Beautiful.

"You're staring," she huffed.

"You're beautiful," he returned.

Her cheeks colored, but then she noticed James. He hadn't wanted her to look away, but she did as she frowned at the young man. "Once more, please," she said, her voice growing stronger. "For those of us who haven't had our morning coffee."

"He has to give a woman a moment of True Bliss."

"Mind-blowing orgasms don't count?" Then she flushed and pressed a hand to her mouth. "That probably wasn't a polite thing to say."

Kane smiled. Modesty. How unusual for a woman who came to the Saturnalias.

Meanwhile, James stepped further into the room which was not at all the direction Kane wanted him to go. "Well, if that was all that was required, he would have broken the curse decades ago."

Twenty decades to be exact.

"Got it. So bliss isn't just a physical sensation. Gotta be emotional as well. Maybe even spiritual."

Kane snorted. "Why do you think we started calling this a Saturnalia. Even in my day there were pagans. This was as spiritual as we could make it."

James nodded. "They even brought in a real high priestess."

"Several," Kane added. It had been his focus when Victoria had been queen. After all, his jailor didn't fit in his Christian ethos. The closest religion he—and his third and fourth nephews—could find was paganism. So they'd brought in priestesses and paid them and their followers well to have three days and nights of bliss. And not a one of them had managed to break his curse.

At least these days the women paid to come here instead of the reverse. Made it easier on the earldom coffers, though he understood from Hugh the price he charged in no way covered the expense.

Kane sighed and let his body droop in the chair. God, he was depressed.

Meanwhile, Jacqueline rubbed her eyes and finger combed her hair back. She had classic bone structure beneath the freckles. Lifted cheekbones, arched brow. Quite a beauty, even when rumpled first thing in the morning.

Especially when rumpled first thing in the morning.

His cock stirred, and he shifted forward again. "You can go now, James."

His nephew frowned. "But we haven't...oh right. Well then, see you later."

He was gone before Jacqueline had finished straightening up in bed. Then she noticed the boy was gone, and her brows drew together in a frown. But that was all the time she had because he abruptly stood and began prowling toward her. Not walking, but prowling. And since he'd been naked in the chair, part of him was leading the way.

"Um...wow. You're awake."

"Yes."

She smiled. "Are you truly that insatiable?"

Obviously. Except not obviously because in the last decade or so, he'd been far from aroused by morning. In truth, he was grateful to focus on the women's enjoyment because his heart—and his cock—often weren't up to the task.

Not so with Jacqueline, apparently.

"There are still a dozen or more ways—" he began, but she held up her hand.

"Stop! Look, I get that you want to break the curse and whatever." She stopped speaking a moment and shook her head. "I can't believe I'm buying into this."

"True Bliss," he said softly. "Yours. Roll over onto your stomach."

"What? Wait!"

He stopped, but not because she'd told him to. It was because he was already at her side and pulling the covers away.

Everything in his life had been stripped from him. His life, his joys, all of it were given away to a goddess of war. Even his skills were not his own since the bitch goddess declared what and when he practiced. Except for three days and three nights a year.

These moments were his, and he would take them. He would take Jacqueline and declare her his own. For whatever time he had left. She would be his because he wanted it. Because he wanted her. And in that moment when she screamed his name, everyone in the entire bloody castle would know this woman was his.

He put his hands on her knees and pushed them apart. He wasn't gentle as he maneuvered himself between her thighs.

"Kane. Kane—ooh! Oh Jesus, that's quick."

He'd put his fingers on her core. If she truly resisted him, he'd stop. If she were dry or tight, he would ease back. But she was plump and wet for him.

She bit her lip, tiny white teeth pressed into red flesh as she looked at him with her blue eyes. She was anxious, but she wasn't unwilling. He'd been gentler last night, in deference to her innocence. But since some women preferred dominance, he might as well try it now.

So he pushed his hand between her legs and worked his fingers into her quickly. Roughly. While she was still scrambling to fully wake, he was stroking her sweet honey everywhere.

"Um, you're a little different this morning," she said, her voice breathy.

Her lips had darkened and her back was moving, making her breasts bounce as she tried to adjust to his rhythm. He didn't allow her to. Every time she seemed to settle against him, every time her breath steadied, he moved. He changed. He kept her off-balance and off-tempo.

And when her legs had relaxed to him, he suddenly withdrew.

"Kane---"

He didn't give her time to ask. He grabbed hold of her hips and flipped her over bodily. She landed face down on the mattress with an oomph. And then he hauled her hips up, kicked her knees wide, and thrust.

Hard. Fast.

He rammed himself in her over and over, but he listened closely to her.

When she started to moan, he knew she was as randy as he was. But just to make sure, he pulled her up to all fours. He wanted to hold her breasts as he worked in her. He wanted to twist her little peaks as she took what he gave. And he wasn't going to stop until she screamed.

She did. Quickly, but not loudly enough. At least not for him.

Her orgasm gripped his cock, drawing it in and in and in, but he was a man of stone. He knew how to hold off his release.

He pushed his hand between her legs and worked her clit. Inside her like he was, he knew just when her orgasm was easing off and when he needed to pinch her just how she liked it. And all the while, he kept ramming into her. Using the thrust of his body into hers to move her how he wanted. She was his instrument and he was the master, playing her until she made the sounds he wanted.

Cries. Sobs. Even grunts—he took them all.

"My name," he murmured as he twisted her nipple. "What's my name?"

"K-kane." Her breath was stuttered. The word too soft.

"Who's inside you?"

"Kane."

"Who needs this?"

"M-me."

He pinched her hard. "No, sweetheart. My name. I need this. I need you."

She reared back, but not because of the pain. Her orgasm had just ratcheted up another notch. She gripped him tighter than a vise.

"Who needs this?"

"Kane!"

"Yes."

"Kane!"

"Yes."

"Kane!"

"*Yes!*"

He exploded. He threw himself body and soul into her while she was still screaming his name.

And in this way, they passed the morning.

But by noon, he knew that it hadn't worked. He was still a stoneman, and she was exhausted.

He needed to let her rest. She needed to recover, even if he was sinking deeper into despair with every passing second. But as she lay there in the torn up disaster that had been her bed, she blinked her eyes open and her lips curved into a sensuous smile. Green. Her eyes were green now.

"So, got any other ideas?"

Lots. None. He hadn't the heart. He shrugged.

"Good. Because I've got one, but first I need a shower and some food."

And with that she pushed up from the bed, gave him a saucy wink, and disappeared into the bath. He was so shocked that it took him another two minutes before he remembered how to call for lunch.

CHAPTER 5

Well, this place was getting a five star rating on Yelp from her. Jackie buried her face in the most luxurious towels she'd ever felt, inhaled a spring-fresh scent, and then got to the business of drying off from her shower.

If it was possible for a woman to experience True Bliss from sex, she definitely would have. Kane was both an innovative partner and a considerate one. The combination was devastatingly amazing, and she was halfway in love with the man already. Mind-blowing sex did that to a woman.

Too bad he didn't seem so pleased.

She came out of her bathroom and went to her suitcase, quickly pulling on jeggings and a stylish tunic. He was still brooding, not even bothering to dress while he watched her with hooded eyes.

"Are you allowed to wear anything other than that toga?"

"I don't know why you're bothering with clothing. What is your idea?"

"For True Bliss?"

"Yes."

She glanced outside at a beautiful expanse of lawn, greenery, and statuary. An English garden at its best. "Start by getting dressed, then we'll grab a picnic lunch and head outside."

"Pic-nic?" He said the word like he'd never heard it before.

She looked at him, enjoying the sight of the sun on his rippling muscles and the casual toss of his curls about his face. Damn, he was gorgeous in a brooding, curly, I'm-Byron-at-his-most-moody kind of way.

"Yes. Picnic. Eating outside. Enjoying the outdoors. It's lovely out there, and I want to go see it." Her stomach chose that moment to punctuate her statement with a growl. "And eat. A lot. I'm starved."

"I have called for food. It is coming."

"Then it can come outside."

He tilted his head. "You want to eat a la Grecque?"

"Like the Greek? If that means outside, then yes."

He nodded slowly. "I had not thought exhibitionism was of interest to you." He pushed to his feet. "But I can accommodate—"

"Whoa, buddy," she said as she put a hand to his chest. Like touching the statue again, only his flesh was warm. Actually, it was meltingly manly hot, but she tried not to get distracted. "We're both going to stay fully dressed for this part."

"But you said you had an idea. For your Bliss."

"Wow, are you really this one dimensional? Do you truly think that bliss can only be achieved through sex?"

He stared at her. Well, apparently so.

"Oh, come on. Even if guys are that easy, girls aren't."

He inhaled and her hand expanded with him. Like for a mile. God, he was big. Then when he released a breath, his shoulders seemed to drop about three feet. "Of course it has occurred to me. But I have three days. Less now. I cannot fill a woman's every need in that time. I've tried."

"So you're just going keep banging the same drum, so to speak?" She shook her head. "Look, you want to find my bliss? Then come eat lunch with me alfresco."

He waited a moment. He seemed to be studying her, thinking deep thoughts or judging her somehow. But in the end, he dipped his chin. "As you wish."

She chuckled. "Now I know you're not some two-hundred-year-old statue, oh Dread Pirate Roberts. You were born after *The Prince Bride.*" The phrase "as you wish" was straight from the movie which came from the book which wasn't even written until 1973.

He frowned. "I am not a pirate. Or named Robert."

"Too late! You already said it." Then she laughed as she headed for the door. He moved to follow her, his footfalls heavy, but he stopped when she turned to look at him. "You really can't wander the halls naked."

"I really can and have. For two hundred years."

She sighed and shot him a look that was her best version of Do you really think I'm that gullible?

In the end, he shrugged. "Hugh will have appropriate attire for me. I will go get it."

She nodded and stepped into the hall. There were noises coming from a good many of the rooms around her. At least one person was taking a shower, but all the others...She blinked. Well, apparently Kane wasn't the only one with sex, sex, and more sex on the brain.

"Follow me," he said as he stepped past her. Yep, he was still stark naked and walking as proud as could be down the hall. She just managed to glance at his crotch as he passed by her—semi-erect and quite impressive even in full light—before she flushed and looked away. He didn't notice. So she had two choices: she could turn around and grab his tunic out of her bedroom or she could just follow a step behind him and enjoy the view.

She chose the view. When in Rome, right?

She followed him to the Statue Room, as she'd come to think of it. They walked in, and she was startled to see the pedestal standing there empty. But of course that would be true. The whole myth behind the weekend was that the statue came to life in search of True Bliss. So they'd have to hide the thing during the weekend. Too bad. She'd like to do a side-by-side comparison to her Kane. They had to be a near exact match.

That's the version of the weekend that she'd decided to work with in her thoughts. Seventy-two hours of sexual exploits hosted by the guy who looked like the statue. Why he'd decided to focus on her this weekend and not one of the bustier, prettier or more lustful women, she hadn't a clue. But she was grateful and not about to look a gift stud in the mouth.

And while she pondered the statue base, Kane turned his back on it and headed for a chest in the corner. He pulled out tailored slacks and a white button down shirt straight from the nineteenth century. Jacket. Boots. Even waistcoat and hat, though he didn't put those on.

She watched him dress in stunned fascination. Especially the tie…er, cravat. He whipped it about his neck and managed the folds of it with stunning speed. He had to have practiced it for hours.

And with every motion, every new piece of clothing he pulled on, she felt her mouth grow dry and her insides wet. Holy shit, he was gorgeous. Move aside Darcy, Kane beat him hands down.

Twenty minutes later, he was fully attired and she was weak in the knees. Then he held out his hand and she mutely grabbed hold. But then she caught a flash of herself in the mirror on his arm. Tunic and jeggings? She didn't fit.

"Now I really feel like a crass American."

"Why?"

She glanced down at her attire. "You can't imagine that I fit in like this."

"On the contrary, it is I who am out of time. I expect you match quite well."

She bit her lip, unsure how to respond.

In the end, he drew her hand to his arm, showing her how to set it on the inside of his forearm. "James has suggested I put on more appropriate clothing. Your attire is simpler, to be sure. And as I am frequently undressed during my time here, all of this trapping can be tedious."

"So why put it on?"

He paused a moment, looking back at himself in the mirror. "You must understand, all but three days of the year, I am told what to do, what to wear, even what skills I am meant to master and how. Everything is prescribed. Anything that makes me feel like a man again—like the person I once was—is treasured and remembered throughout the long wait until next year."

"So you wore those clothes…um…two hundred years ago?"

"Not exactly. My body has matured some since I was enslaved. The muscles are thicker, the waist narrower. I'm not sure exactly how it works except that within two years of being turned to stone, my old clothing did not fit as well. But after the first ten years, I have not changed in size or shape."

"Right. Because you were a statue."

"Because I had the muscles required for what War demands of me."

"War?"

"The Goddess to whom I pledged my service. That is not her true name. I will not say that aloud. But it is an accurate description of her nature."

"And you're enslaved to her until you give someone True Bliss."

"Yes."

And there it was. The problem restated for her again. At least he was consistent. And while she was still mulling that over, he arched a brow at her.

"I believe your idea had us outside with food?"

"Uh, right. Food."

"This way."

He led her through the castle. How did they not get lost in here? Down stairs, around footmen and maids, until they made it to the back door. Or one of them. It was a large open doorway to a terrace that then had steps out onto the green.

The butler stood beside the door with a picnic basket in hand and two footmen waiting with blanket, wine, and umbrellas should the sky suddenly cloud over and storm.

She wasn't a native of England, but she doubted the pristine blue would suddenly change. Kane swept past them without even a sideways glance. Jackie looked, of course, and felt a little weird as the three servants fell into step behind them.

So much for a romantic picnic just the two of them. But then again, this was pretty cool too. Just like she was a real princess out on a date with the prince.

"What a perfect day," she said. Then she flashed him a wink. "Practically blissful."

Much to her surprise, he didn't smile back. If anything, he scowled. Okay, so he didn't like her teasing about bliss. As if she hadn't already realized he took his role seriously.

"So…um…tell me about yourself," she said.

He arched a brow at her. Damned if he didn't look just like an imperious aristocrat looking down on the American colonial.

"Well done," she quipped. "I'm thoroughly cowed. Now answer the question."

He grimaced at her. "You don't sound cowed. You sound cheeky."

She grinned at the British word. She rather liked the idea of being cheeky. Made her feel like a true American rebel. "I'm terrified," she said with a grin. "Now talk."

He shook his head. "In my time, women were much more placid."

"Back when?"

"I was born in 1789 and there wasn't a woman around who would speak to me the way you do."

She studied his face to see if he was actually put off by her forward ways. His expression was impassive, but there was a flicker in his eyes. A quirk to his lips. And most telling of all, his gaze skittered away from her.

"You hated every one of those simpering misses."

He shrugged. "They were rather boring."

"Preferred the bawdy ones, did you?"

"I didn't really care what the bawds said. It was more about how they—"

"Yeah, yeah, I get it. Hot sex for the randy teen."

He smiled and lifted his face to the sun. "Being the son of an earl did have its advantages."

Quite the profile there. Chiseled bone structure, curly brown locks, a poet's mouth. Too bad she wasn't into exhibitionism. Otherwise they might be doing something else right then. To distract herself, she pushed forward with the story. "So how did you become a statue?"

His face tightened, and she immediately regretted the question. Even knowing he was an actor playing a role, she didn't like hurting him even if everything they were discussing was make-believe.

"No money," he finally said. "Generations of wastrels destroyed us. Most of the coin was gone by the time my father inherited. There wasn't a prayer anything would be left for me as the spare."

"The spare?"

His lips quirked. "The heir and the spare. My older brother was to inherit. I was simply there—"

"In case something happened to him. How awful."

He shook his head. "It wasn't so bad. I had all the advantages without any of the responsibility. Until I left school, that is."

They had made it to a perfect picnic spot beneath a majestic oak in stunning red colors. October had the autumn foliage everywhere, but this was beyond anything she'd ever seen before.

"It's so pretty here."

"Yes. And thanks to my forebears, we had sold off much of this land."

While the servants laid out the picnic, he stood apart, his hands on his hips, his gaze surveying the property. A man looking over his kingdom, she realized.

"We bought it all back," he said. "Every inch, every tenant, every rock, bird, and deer."

"How?"

He didn't answer at first. He took his time looking into the distance, probably seeing his past instead. And then he started speaking. "They wanted me to go into the clergy, you know. Become ordained into the priesthood." He quirked an eye at her. "To give up wenching."

"Well, that would have been hard for you."

He chuckled. "I thought so."

There was an undercurrent in his tone that added, *I was an idiot.* Or maybe it was his expression. Either way, she had to know the rest of the story. Because it was the statue's story, and that's what she really came here to learn.

"I was desperate for a solution. I was a gambler, you see. Thought I could win at cards. Or dice. Or..." He shrugged.

"Didn't work?"

"It did. Easy enough to win when you know your opponent and you're not drunk. But it was hard work just to keep myself in coin. There was nothing left for my family or the estate."

"So what did you do?"

He turned back to her. She looked up as he approached, expecting a kiss, but his expression was dark, his eyes hooded. And when he reached out a hand, it wasn't for her but for the full wine glass the butler held out. He passed it to her and then took the next for himself.

She didn't drink. It was barely afternoon. But he had no problem with his as he swallowed half the glass. And when he stopped drinking, he pulled it away with a sad smile.

"We don't get wine in Idola."

"Where?"

"The goddess' realm. She drinks, of course, if she wants it. But we..." He sighed. "We train, we drill, and we serve her. There is no thought given to simple pleasures like food and drink."

He gestured to the blanket and she settled down where the butler had set out cold chicken, cheese and fruit, plus honey bread. She sat down and accepted a plate, but her eyes were on Kane.

"Tell me what happened." He wasn't a master storyteller by any means, but he had her full attention.

"I learned of an incantation from a gypsy girl."

And here was where it became fanciful. Well, she'd go with the mythology first then later push for the truth. "Right. A spell done skyclad on the night of the full moon."

"What the devil is skyclad?"

"Naked. It's a standard Wiccan term." Or so her romance novels said.

"We threw some spices into a pot, said her name three times, and asked for a bargain."

Oh. Well, that was disappointing. She'd expected at least some dancing around a bonfire or ox blood. He hadn't even had to sacrifice a rabbit. She was about so say exactly that, but then she looked over to where he was staring at his wine. He'd stretched out beside her on the blanket, but he hadn't eaten. Instead, he simply stared into the dark wine and brooded.

Damn, he was spending a lot of today brooding. So she touched his face, bringing his gaze up to hers. Even knowing this was a role he pretended to, she was moved by his appearance of pain. "You don't have to tell me if you don't want to."

He blinked. "This is your idea, isn't it? Your bliss involves knowing the full truth."

She nodded.

"So I'll tell you."

Easier said than done, apparently, because he didn't keep talking. Instead, he grabbed a slice of cheese and bit down. Then he blinked and his eyes seemed to roll back a bit in appreciation.

"Not had cheese in a while?"

"Eons," he said. Then he looked over the view. The tree, the grass, the landscape, and then back to her. "This was a brilliant idea," he said. "Thank you for bringing me out here. I haven't done it in years."

"Too busy shagging everything in sight?"

She'd been teasing him, but his nod was gloomy. She waited, and eventually her patience was rewarded.

"You recall I was the gambler? My brother, on the other hand, he was the moneymaker. My father was ashamed of it, of course. Felt it was too common a skill, minding all those columns of accounts."

"That sounds enormously uncommon to me."

"Me as well, but I'd never call my father a thinker."

"So it was the two of you with herbs and a brazier calling on a goddess."

He nodded.

"Which one?"

He looked up alarmed. "I told you, we don't say her name aloud. Ever. The last thing I want to do is get her attention."

"Right. You call her War." Her lips curved in a gentle smile. "You picked a mean one, didn't you? Couldn't have gone with Aphrodite or something."

"We tried. Didn't work. But we had her name, and she came."

Jackie leaned forward, grabbing some chicken as she went. She could eat and listen at the same time. And given how starved she was, she was going to eat every bite.

"So? What did she look like? Golden blonde hair, flowing white gown, blue eyes like fire?"

He shook his head. "Black hair. Endless eyes with no white. Naked, but made of black silver or stone."

"Ewww. She was wearing black armor?"

He frowned at her. "No. She was made of metal. And she had a wolfhound with her. At the time, it was the scariest creature I'd ever seen. Especially since she had it eat right in front of us. She'd been hunting, you see."

"That's Artemis, not–"

"It's what she'd been doing," he interrupted. "And the thing had caught a bear or something. It was covered in blood and gnawing on the thigh." He shook his head. "I thought that was repulsive," he said, his tone rather surprised. "I had no idea."

No idea that there were worse more repulsive things to see? She wasn't sure she wanted to know. "So this metal woman appears with her gross dog—"

"Wolfhound. Massive wolfhound."

"Right. And the two of you are—"

"Reaching for our brandy. Harry wanted more to drink. I was wondering if someone had put something in it."

"A drug?"

He shrugged. "I had some untrustworthy friends."

She smiled because his lips had quirked at the memory of his friends. "I'll bet."

But then he sobered. "She demanded to know what we wanted, so we said—I said—I'd be a stoneman for her on certain conditions."

"And how did you know to ask for that?"

"The gypsy girl. Well, her grandmother. I thought the woman was doing us a favor even though she despised the Englishmen." He sighed. "Turns out she knew what she was doing all along."

"What were you terms?"

"Gold. An unending supply."

She finished her chicken and started eating the fruit. "A classic."

"I promised her ten years. She bartered for ten thousand."

Jackie snorted. "And you settled on…?"

He sighed. "Ten thousand. The woman doesn't bargain, and she knew we were desperate."

"Ouch."

"But there's an out clause. This other goddess appeared. I don't know her name, though the other one said it. Something like Thea. She said I had to have an escape clause."

"That's the True Bliss part?"

He nodded. "Given to me by a third goddess Pyrenia."

"Not Thea?"

He shook his head. "Apparently not. I think Thea is the mediator in these deals, but she doesn't make the terms."

"So you get three days every year to give a woman a moment of True Bliss. If you do—"

"I am no longer a stoneman."

"And this all happened on what day?"

"October 2, 1812." He looked back toward the house. "Right in the room where the pedestal is."

"So why you and not your brother? He was the heir after all."

Kane snorted. "Because Harry was boring. He couldn't give a woman a moment of bliss if he'd been given a map."

"Ah. You were the libertine—"

"And I thought I'd be out of service after one year."

But it had been two hundred years and he was still searching. She flipped onto her back looking up at the canopy of leaves. "Have you ever thought that True Bliss comes with True Love?"

"What?"

"That's how these fairy tales usually work, isn't it? Your one true love, the kiss of destiny and all that?"

He sighed. "This isn't a fairy tale, Jacqueline. These goddesses are real."

Oooh, she loved it when he said her name. "Fine, they're real. But maybe bliss comes with love."

His expression went impossibly sad. "I can't make a woman fall in love with me. Certainly not in three days."

"Not by just shagging her. What woman falls in love from sex alone?" Her. Because frankly, it had been really great sex.

His expression grew intent. "And?"

"And what?"

"And what would make you fall in love?"

She opened her mouth, but instead of words, she made a mocking sound. Part laughter, part despair. Then at his stricken expression, she covered her mouth. "Sorry," she muttered.

"Don't be sorry. Answer the question."

She shook her head. "I'm sorry. I don't do love anymore."

"James said you were cynical."

She twisted her head to look at him. "How could he know that?"

Kane shrugged. "He read your writing. Said it had a distinctly cynical bent. Then he put it all in a file for me to read on the pad while you were sleeping."

"How thorough of him."

Kane touched her arm, stroking it and giving her shivers of delight. "What happened to turn such a beautiful woman cynical?"

She sighed. Since she'd forced him to tell his deep, dark secret—even if it was pretend—she decided to share hers. "I fell in love hard as a teenager. His name was Alan and he was intense and completely passionate." Kind of like Kane here, especially when he started brooding. "I made him laugh, he made me come." She winced. Nothing like being crass out here with the servants listening to every word.

"And then?"

"He used to do these grand gestures. Take me to Chicago in a limo for an expensive meal. That's a big deal as a teenager. He filled my locker with roses. He..." She shrugged. "He was completely overwhelming, and I loved every second of it. Until overwhelming became stifling and angry and..." She swallowed.

"Violent?"

She nodded. "He was a big personality with big flaws. He sucked me in and nearly destroyed my life."

His eyes narrowed. "How violent?"

"Put me in the hospital when he found me studying with another boy."

His jaw became impossibly tight, but he didn't speak. Looking in his face, she shuddered and her breath froze. Kane could definitely be violent, and that frightened her a bit. But then he looked away, and she could breathe again.

"What happened?" he repeated quietly. "To the boy. To you? How did it end?"

"With smart, really good parents. Mine. They knew I wasn't going to leave him. I had this romantic ideal about him. About us together. I was the only one who understood him, blah blah blah." God, she'd been such an idealistic fool.

His gaze shifted back to her. He had himself under control now. The anger was still there, but it didn't seem so near the surface. So she finished the story.

"We moved. My dad took another job in California. No way to continue the relationship when I was half a country away. And in time, I got over it. And the more I got my head on straight, the more I realized that epic love stories don't exist."

He tilted his head. "Not just for you, though. Now you spend your time poking holes in other people's stories. Isn't that what you do with your articles?"

She straightened, ready to defend herself from his attitude. "I expose lies, Kane. The real truth behind the myth. The romance shown for smoke and mirrors."

He took another drink from his wine. "And that's why you're here. To expose me as a lie."

She shrugged, unwilling to be dishonest. "There's some dark secret behind the statues. I mean to find out what it is."

He had no response, just a sad, frustrated expression. "Everything I've told you is the truth."

She shrugged. "Of course it is," she said, though her tone probably told him she didn't believe a word of it. Goddesses? Statues that come to life? But he was an actor and it was his job to maintain the lie. So because she felt sorry for putting an actor in this position, she let the history slide. She popped a grape in her mouth, lay back on the blanket, and smiled at the beauty of leaves above her. "So you keep having these Saturnalias as you try to find a woman who will fall in love from epic sex."

"Yes."

"Hmmm." And this year she was the lucky woman under the sheets with him. Cool.

He leaned over her, his face impossibly close, especially beautiful. "Does that answer all your questions?"

She smiled at him, anticipating his kiss. "Not even a little bit."

His brows arched. "What else is there?"

Everything. Nothing. There were so many questions waiting for answers that weren't rooted in mythology. But at the moment, all she could do was trace the curve of his cheek with her fingers while looking into the mink brown of his eyes.

The mink brown that was turning brighter as she watched. Like electric brown. Like...were his eyes glowing?

"Kane—"

He'd already straightened up, his eyes narrowing as he scanned the landscape. He was on his feet in a second, pacing away as he looked for something.

"Do you have any weapons?" he demanded.

"What?" she squeaked. "No!"

"Not you," he hissed. "Sambridge."

The butler blinked. "Er, no sir. I didn't think—"

"What's going on?" Jackie could hear the tension in his tone, but not the reason why.

He looked at her then at the servants. "There's another stoneman coming."

"What?" She was on her feet and still staring at his eyes. Damn, they really were glowing. Like amber beams of brilliance.

Then he suddenly whipped his head around in another direction.

"Two," he bit out.

He looked back at her. His jaw had tightened, his hands had become fists and there was power in every part of him. Then he barked out one word.

"Run."

CHAPTER 6

"Domina?"

Zeva, Mistress of All, frowned but did not look away from the field of battle. It was a basketball court where ten of her warriors were practicing battle. She knew the game was to put the orange ball through the opponents' hoop, but she didn't comprehend the purpose. Especially since everyone kept slipping in the blood. And one certainly couldn't dribble the ball on squishy intestines.

"Gravest pardon, Domina, but I know something that would be of interest to you."

She didn't so much as flick her eyes at Ares. Instead, she gestured to the blood soaked court. "I do not understand this game. Why do millions of humans lust after this prize?"

She watched as the one with the ball was impaled on a short sword and fell. She flicked her fingers and the next stoneman took his place, neatly decapitating the impaler before kicking the ball to his teammate.

"I see you have added weapons to the game."

"When they played without weapons, the best wrestlers won. They merely had to hold onto their opponents with one hand then throw the ball with the other." She shrugged. "It took a tediously long time, and I grew bored."

Another two players were disemboweled. Perhaps she should switch their weapons to guns instead of blades. Less mess fouling the footing.

She didn't make the change though, and she watched as three more warriors fell. They weren't gone in truth. Just off Idola, back to their statue forms on Earth until she needed them again. But she made sure they felt every cut, every jab, every impalement. In fact, she created them such that they felt such pain even more on Idola so they would become inured to even the worst agony.

That way, when the final battle came, they would be able to destroy their opponents without thought or mercy, barely registering their own agony. After all, they'd been doing it here in Idola for centuries.

"Domina," Ares repeated. "The time for my news is limited."

Now she did turn, the dark metal of her face flowing slowly because she'd created it to be extra hard. Then she arched a single brow.

He swallowed and bowed deeply.

"Only if it pleases you."

She said nothing. Let him choose whether to risk telling her his surprise or back away in cowardice. To her delight, he chose to take the risk.

"It is about your stoneman Kane." He waited a moment while she recalled the details of his imprisonment. Three days each year to…do something that Pyrenia had thought clever.

"Yes?"

"I think he may be close."

"No. He still has nine thousand eight hundred years to his term of service."

"Close to giving a woman True Bliss. He has found emotion with a woman."

She titled her head at an angle, the metal skin crinkling awkwardly as she moved. "How else is he to get near enough to kill her?"

"But he wishes to copulate with her. To give her True Bliss."

"Hasn't he been doing that for two hundred years?"

"Yes, Domina."

"This is not interesting to me," she said, making the words sound like metal tearing itself apart. And because she was about to turn him to metal such that he would experience being torn asunder.

"But this woman is different. This woman thinks."

She frowned. "She is a worthy opponent?"

"Yes, Domina."

Excellent! "Bring her here. I wish to—"

"You cannot. You cannot interfere during Kane's seventy-two hours."

She growled at him. It must have been enough to frighten him because he rushed his next words.

"Which is why I dispatched two of your warriors to attack him. I did this completely without your consent or knowledge. Therefore you have not interfered and cannot be seen as violating the terms of your contract with Kane."

"Destroying one of my stonemen does not help me win this game, Ares."

"No, Domina. That is why they are sent to hurt him but not kill him. Just enough—"

"Such that he has to turn to stone to survive."

"Yes, Domina."

Excellent. Ares was a most loyal servant, and she appreciated that he kept track of her stonemen. But she still needed to appear to be furious with him. "You must be punished for this transgression. You should never act without my consent."

His head bowed, but she saw a strange smile curve his lips. "Yes, Domina."

Clearly he wanted this punishment. Curious. "I think you will play soccer. Do not allow the ball to enter the rope cage. If you do, it shall go worse for you."

She waved her hand and the bloody basketball court disappeared. In its place was a green field with a soccer goal in the back. Ares stood naked in front of the net. Tall, muscular, and glorious in his power as he bared his teeth.

But how to make this challenging? "The others shall be playing polo. With iron maces."

Twelve opponents appeared, each on a horse and carrying a long iron mace with which to hit one of a dozen soccer balls. Or Ares' head.

She watched as Ares recognized each of his stonemen opponents. Every one had a reason to despise him for he had betrayed or damaged them enough so that even she had heard about his misdeeds. Which meant he had been diabolical indeed.

How would he react to facing twelve of his most vicious enemies? To her delight, he made a rude gesture at them. She smiled, liking his arrogance, but not enough to help him. Though given his abilities, he might not need any.

"Begin."

CHAPTER 7

"**D**amn it! *Run!*"

Kane glared at Jacqueline. Why wouldn't she listen? Couldn't she feel the danger coming?

Of course not. It was only him with the itch between his shoulder blades that told him another of his kind was near. Or rather two others.

He whipped around, trying to feel for where the nearest stoneman was even if he couldn't see him. Yet.

There.

The sound was at the edge of his awareness. Someone was stomping up the hill with footfalls heavy enough to shake the hillock. Too heavy for a normal man. Rather heavy for a stoneman too. If he had to guess, it was a slave who used his fists more than weapons. Good. Kane was better than average at grappling.

He slid behind the cover of the oak tree and scanned the green.

Where was the other one?

"Kane, you're scaring me," Jacqueline came to his side.

In a battle between stonemen, split seconds made a difference. But even knowing that, he looked to Jacqueline. She was alone, and he quickly glared around them. Where the hell were the servants? Bloody hell, they'd run off without grabbing Jacqueline.

"You can't be here," he said, keeping his voice to a bare whisper. The less clues the other men had about their location, the better. They would sense him, just as he could feel them, but that was a general feeling. Sound gave a very specific clue. He leaned forward to whisper into her ear. "Go back to the house."

She tugged on his arm. "With you. I'm not abandoning you." At least she kept her voice equally quiet.

"They know where I am. Go."

"But—d"

"Hsss!" He slapped a hand over her mouth. The first stoneman was close enough that Kane could hear the snap of twigs beneath his feet as he climbed up the hillock.

He listened carefully. *Thud. Thud. Thud.*

Steady march. Maybe he was heading somewhere else. Somewhere that had nothing to do with Kane or Jacqueline.

Thunk.

Stopped. Probably because the man had sensed him.

Kane shoved Jacqueline against the tree trunk. "Climb up," he hissed. Then he bodily shoved her upward to the lowest branch. She scrambled onto it because he'd given her no choice. And when she turned to talk to him, he'd held up a finger against his mouth to tell her to be silent.

Then he waited, his senses attuned to everything everywhere just in case. Fortunately, this was something he was trained in. Zeva made sure her stonemen were experts at fighting against all sorts of odds in all kinds of terrain.

Same information as before. Two stonemen. One still approaching, the other stopped nearby.

Kane risked a glance around the tree trunk. There he was, an onyx-skinned warrior with tattoos on much of his body and a good four stone larger than Kane in size and weight.

Damn. If this man was well trained, then wrestling would not go Kane's way. Best try negotiation. The rules were relatively simple. The stonemen followed orders without hesitation or emotion. Which meant so long as he didn't interfere with the mission, then the stonemen would pass them by.

So he stepped out into the light. "Whom do you serve?" he asked.

"Zeva."

Bloody hell. The same goddess he served. Which meant the two of them were equally skilled in war.

"She is my mistress as well," he said. "Why are you here?"

"To face you in battle."

"Me?"

"You are Kane."

Not a question, so there was no point in trying deception. But this didn't make sense.

"Zeva is forbidden from interfering with me right now. I'm on holiday." That wasn't exactly the right word, but it was the best one he had.

Thump. Thump.

The warrior was closing the distance between them. Another twenty paces and he could attack. That meant he was bringing the battle here where Jacqueline was in danger.

"Just me?" Kane pressed.

"Just you," the stoneman answered.

Good. Jacqueline would be safe so long as she stayed out of the way. Which meant he had to move to the lower ground where he had less of an advantage. And where the other one was coming at a faster clip.

"I will meet you. Stay there."

"No."

Damnation. He had to engage now.

He moved sideways and down, away from Jacqueline. "What is your name?" he asked, playing for time. Zeva had countless numbers of warriors. Too many to keep track of. In Idola, they fought and died. Then they went back to their statue bodies. No conversation necessary.

"I am Tachus." Pause. "How did you get a holiday?"

"It's my escape clause. It involves three days every year."

Another pause. "What is an escape clause?"

Kane frowned. "Were you cursed?"

"Yes."

Poor bugger. "I'm sorry for you. I negotiated my service."

The man's brows rose. "You asked for this?"

"I was young and stupid."

The man nodded slowly. "So were we all at one time." He spread his arms as if to say, come at me, but Kane wasn't going to just jump in. That was the surest way to lose.

"I thought everyone had an escape clause," he said, by way of stalling. "A way out of their service. You don't know yours?"

Tachus shook his head. "We must battle now."

"Are there rules?"

"I am not to break off any of your body parts."

So this wasn't a lethal attack. Just a delaying tactic.

"And you'll stop when?"

Tachus shrugged. "When it is over."

"Which will be when what happens?"

No answer. Probably until his three days were up. Which was explicitly against the terms of his contract.

Damn damn damn.

But there was no help for it. He had to take this fight away from Jacqueline, so he gestured down the hillock. "I will fight you down there."

"No. You will fight me now."

And then Tachus charged.

It had been years since Jackie had climbed a tree, but it wasn't like Kane had given her any choice. He'd all but tossed her up in there, and she'd obliged him by climbing deeper into the foliage. The man obviously thought some kind of danger was coming, and though she wondered just what kind of bad guy could be in rural England, she'd decided to go with discretion.

Plus, she'd expected him to be up in the leaves with her.

Nope. He'd gone and had a bizarre discussion with the black-skinned scary guy with the tribal tats.

Goddess. Curse. Escape clauses.

It didn't take long for her to realize that this was part of the adventure Saturnalia. Frankly, she'd been quite happy with the sex kind of adventure, but she supposed they had to give other types of drama too. All part of the fun and games.

So she relaxed onto her perch and decided to enjoy the show. It would only endanger the actors if she tried to get involved.

She listened closely to the conversation, but there wasn't much more of it. Tachus was all Arnold Schwarzenegger: We must do battle now. She could tell Kane was trying to feel the guy out, find out what exactly was the plan, but he only got so far. Two minutes later, big guy attacked.

There was no subtlety in the movement. One minute Tachus was standing talking, the next he was barreling forward. Kane was quick on his feet though. He sidestepped but Tachus had been ready.

The black man swerved and nearly caught Kane, but her lover was really fast on his feet.

Lunge, swerve, twist.

Crack!

Kane got the big one with his fist. A lightning fast punch straight on that curving tat on the guy's forehead.

Jackie was so excited she nearly cheered.

Two more hits. *Pop pop!*

Lighter taps, but the big guy was reeling.

Until he wasn't. He feinted left, Kane followed, catching him on the right with another powerful blow. But this time Tachus grabbed him. Two big powerful arms gripped tight, pinning one of Kane's arms uselessly to his side.

Shit.

Kane fought. He still had one hand free, and he pummeled Tachus for all he was worth, but it was a losing battle.

Then there was twisting and pitching. Kicking too, but it was all arms and legs and grunts. Jackie couldn't make out what was going on, and though she'd crept down to the lowest branch to see better, she didn't dare jump to the earth. She'd land right on them.

"It's all pretend," she whispered to herself. "It's playacting."

Except it didn't look fake. It looked like Kane was losing his breath by the second, and that Tachus wasn't easing off no matter how many blows he took to the head.

And then suddenly there was another man. A big Viking of a guy complete with a horn helmet and thick fur pants. Odd enough, but he was also carrying a shotgun…and holy shit, what was that smell?

It didn't matter.

Shotgun Viking was running up the hill. She'd been so focused on Kane and Tachus that she didn't even see the hulking redhead until he was standing there, shot gun leveled straight at the two fighters.

"Stay. Down," he said, the two words grating like icebergs colliding.

Finally someone to stop the mayhem. She was busy breathing a sigh of relief when Kane got the upper hand. He got his other arm free and was doing something with his legs. Something that had the black man grunting as he was slowly rolled over. Tachus was still gripping tight, but he was no match for Kane, and Jackie was awed by the sheer power of the move.

Kane was now on top, and he abruptly lifted up Tachus' torso and slammed it straight down onto a tree root. Unstoppable force meeting immovable object. The vibrations up the tree nearly toppled her off her perch.

But at least it would knock Tachus out.

Bang.

The shotgun went off, catching Kane point blank in the back.

Blood splattered everywhere.

Jackie was deaf from the blast.

Then she saw Kane's eyes widen. He may or may not have caught sight of her. She didn't know.

She just saw him fall.

CHAPTER 8

Too stupid.

Too slow.

Kane felt the blast hit him and knew immediately that it had been a shotgun from the second stoneman. All that discussion with Tachus had been a delay. Not his delay, theirs. Even the fighting style had been to slow him down such that the other man could get here and shoot him.

But now it was too late. He was done for. Not dead. That bitch Zeva was going to make sure he survived for all ten thousand years. But he had to turn to stone now. His injuries were too complete.

Or he could just let himself die.

It wasn't a thought he was proud of. It wasn't even a rare thought for him. Ten thousand years of painful, soulless servitude or an end to it all? Such was his despair that he considered it an evenly weighted choice.

But then he saw her. Jacqueline. And hope lurched painfully in his chest. He had to survive for her. For a possibility with her.

He made the switch. Bleeding man to statue in the slow blink of an eye. He could heal the worst of his internal injuries this way and wait for Hugh to seal up the horror of his back.

He felt himself solidify, his view abruptly shifting from her shocked face to the ground as he fell face first into the dirt. He hated the stiffness, the sudden lack of any movement, and the muting of everything. Green became gray, sound was muffled, and even the hard impact of the ground against his body felt like the distant thud of a gong.

And then, lying immobile and vulnerable, he realized his mistake. *Another* mistake.

Jacqueline was completely vulnerable. Certainly Tachus' goal had been to delay Kane, but what about the other stoneman? What was his mission?

He had to heal fast. He had to—

"Is it enough?" Tachus asked.

The other stoneman answered without words. He released another shotgun blast into Kane's legs.

Damn. Damn. Damn.

"That'll be enough," the other answered. And then he turned and began stomping away.

Good. He was leaving. Jacqueline was safe. But what about Tachus? What was he–

"Next time," Tachus said, "you need to do as he says. You need to run."

Bloody hell. The stoneman knew where Jacqueline was. Did that mean he was going to kill her now? No!

Kane started the shift back to human, but knew within seconds that he would die before he could lift his head. The second blast had cut through vital arteries in his legs. The stone had to be fixed and the arteries healed before he could do anything to help Jacqueline.

Too stupid.

Too slow.

"What did you do to him?" Her voice was shaking. Terrified.

"We hurt him so he must waste time as stone to heal."

Three days a year was all he had. And now the thrice-damned goddess was taking that from him too.

"Wh-what are you?"

"Cursed." Tachus stepped forward, his large boots crushing the grass in Kane's peripheral vision. "Were you close?"

"Close?"

"To his escape clause."

Kane wondered the same thing. Certainly Zeva had never sent someone after him before. And not just one stoneman but two. Had he been close? Could he have freed himself this time?

Jacqueline's voice came out stronger, less terrified. Good. Though that didn't lessen the danger. Kane wouldn't relax until Tachus was miles away. "I—I don't know. I didn't think it was real."

Her words hurt him worse than any shotgun blast. All this time, everything they had done, she'd thought it was playacting. His entire life, a silly game to her.

Logically, he knew he shouldn't be surprised. What sane person thought stonemen and crazy goddesses were real? But pain still cut through his heart. He felt real. The feelings he had were definitely real. Fear, hope, lust and…and maybe something more. It was all desperately clear to him because everything else was a gray wash of violence and boredom.

Only three days out of a year. And in two hundred years, only she had touched him.

She hadn't believed a word of it.

If he could, he would have shut his eyes. He would have run to Idola and allowed himself to get cut to pieces in whatever sick game Zeva devised. Better the physical agony than this mental anguish.

He wasn't even real to her.

Meanwhile Tachus kept speaking. "It is truth, but you have false hope. The Goddess will never release him. She is too close to winning her game." And on those crushing words, the man turned and stomped away.

* * *

Jackie watched the huge man walk away. He could have killed her easily, but his conversation had been almost casual.

She waited a beat. Maybe two as she tried to wrap her mind around what had happened. Mostly she just wanted strength to return to her body. She was watching the man leave. He was ten steps away. Far enough, she rationalized, though she knew that if he attacked, she'd have zero chance of survival.

She half jumped, half collapsed out of the tree. She landed beside Kane's arm. Undamaged, she saw, though that was about all of him that was smooth stone. The rest was a pitted mess of abused marble and bloody clothing.

"Kane?" she whispered. "How can...How is..." She swallowed. "I don't know what to do."

He was lying face down, slightly lifted though because his arms had been in front of him. Mentally, she reviewed what had happened. He and Tachus had been fighting. She'd been so focused on their battle that she hadn't even seen the other man approach. Not until the deafening report of the shotgun.

Then she'd seen Kane arch in agony and start to fall. His eyes had been on her, his arms flung out as the impact had hit him. And then he'd simply converted to stone as he fell.

Dropping down onto the ground, she peered at his front. No harm there that she could see. Even his clothing was intact. She reached out for his face, wishing she understood.

Then she heard it. Pounding feet and the Earl's low moan.

"Oh no. No no no no."

She looked up and saw he was accompanied by at least six footmen and the butler, each carrying a gun. Not military-grade anything, of course. In fact, one of them had what looked like an ancient blunderbuss. All six fanned out and as ridiculous as they appeared, Jackie was both relieved and annoyed by their presence. Relieved because those stonemen weren't that far away. Annoyed because they were late. Too damn late.

Meanwhile, the earl dropped to the ground beside Kane, still moaning as he went. The sound even grew louder as he pulled away the torn fabric to expose the pitted mess to the sunlight.

"Oh no no no no."

"He…Is he going to be all right? What do we do?"

"Oh God. We need a stonemason. Oh, oh, this is bad. I'd never survive this."

She straightened up, looking at his ashen face and wondering what the hell she was missing. It's not like Kane was in pain. Unless he was? "Is he hurting?"

"What?"

Damn it, the man was useless. "Kane! Is he in pain?"

"Him? Oh…no. He's healing. But he can't manifest like this. Oh God, look at his legs."

"So if we fix him–er, the statue–he'll be all right?"

"What? Yes, I believe so. I don't know! He's never been damaged like this. I take good care of him! I do!"

What the hell was his problem? "So how do we fix him?" Her voice was getting tight and angry.

"I told you! With a stonemason."

"So have you called one?"

He blinked at her. Once. Twice. Then abruptly he pulled out his phone and scrolled through.

"Maybe you're right," he muttered. "Maybe if we get him fixed up quickly, she won't notice. Here it is!" He jabbed the call button and pressed the phone to his ear. "Come on. Come on. Where are you? Hello? Hello! Who is this?" Pause. "I don't care. I want Joseph." Another pause as his face when ashen. "No, no, I need him to come right away! I don't care what it costs."

Jackie looked down at Kane, unable to focus on his bloody clothing. Instead she shifted so she could better see the expression on his face. The angle was awful, and she wanted to turn him over but that wouldn't help his hurt side. And besides, she'd never be able to move him. He was too heavy. Instead, she lay flat on the ground so she could look into his eyes.

"I don't understand any of this," she told him. "Not one little bit. But I'm not leaving your side until I can talk to you again. Until you're whole and perfect. I promise."

She heard the earl put his phone away and she glanced up. "Is he coming? The stonemason?"

"Joseph is sick or busy or something. And too damned far away."

"What—"

"But his assistant is coming. A woman. She's just a couple miles away. Lucky that." He frowned as he looked back at the house. "I'll have to tell the staff that she should drive right here. Right up here." He started walking, but she called out.

"Can't you just call the house and tell them?"

He paused. "What? Oh. Of course." He pulled out his phone and dialed.

Jesus, the man was incompetent!

Which is when she saw James. The young man was running full tilt toward them. He was a fast runner and soon made it to the little hillock. His eyes widened as he saw the mess that used to be Kane. Then his gaze shot to his father.

Not a word was said between the two. Not even a sound. But there was something communicated there. Something between father and son that bolstered the father and weakened the son.

James was the one who looked away first. His voice was quiet, but he spoke clear enough for her to hear. "What happened?"

She shook her head. "Two men appeared. Kane—" She swallowed back her tears. "He threw me up in the tree. The others ran." She shot a venomous look at the butler's back. He was nearest to them but facing outward, a pistol in his grip.

Which is when the earl spoke, his voice more calm than he had been so far. "Sambridge came to me. He'd already ordered the guns. A stoneman attacked."

"Two," she corrected. "Tachus was first, then the other—a Viking-like guy—just shot him. In the back and then again in the legs." The only thing that kept her talking was the fury that started coursing through her at the memory. She was starting to come to grips with what she remembered, and that more than anything had her boiling mad. "Then they left. They just left."

James swallowed as he dropped to his knees beside Kane. Gingerly, he lifted up the ruined clothing and then paled to gray as he swayed right there on the ground. Swayed enough that she thought he might faint.

"What am I missing?" she demanded. She was still lying down so that she could see Kane, but even from this vantage point, she could sound authoritative. Or pissed off. Either way, she was getting answers now.

James looked at her then at his father. He was asking for permission and at the man's slow nod, James started speaking.

"Kane will be fine," James said.

His father spoke up. "The stonemason is on his way. Kane will be fixed up in no time." He sounded as if he was trying to reassure himself.

"But you see, there are rules for the curator," continued James.

Jackie frowned. "The curator?"

"The one in charge of the statue. My father."

"Rules? Like don't let your stoneman get shot?"

James paled again, but he nodded. "Rules like whatever happens to the stoneman can be done to you."

It took a moment for Jackie to process the words. It took even longer for her to realize that this was why the earl was losing it. Because Kane could turn to stone and heal. He could stop all the damage while the mason was called and then get fixed up right and tight.

The earl, on the other hand, would be killed. Wasn't that one of the first things he'd said? That there was no way he could survive shotgun blasts to the back and legs.

"I need to update my will," the earl said.

"Father!" James cried, pushing to his feet, but the earl held him off.

"It's all right. Get the mason working and then come to the house. We'll talk then."

"But—"

"Let me make sure your mum is taken care of. You and your brother will be fine, but let me do this."

"Of course, sir."

"Good lad." Then he walked calmly away.

"I didn't know," Jackie whispered.

"It's not for sure yet," James said, his eyes not leaving his father. "It doesn't always happen."

"But I don't understand. The first guy said he served Zeva, and Kane said he did too. Why would she send men to attack her own guy? That doesn't make sense."

James whipped his head around. "What? What did you say?"

She mentally reviewed every word that had been said between Kane and Tachus. And when she wasn't sure of the meaning, she closed her eyes and repeated everything exactly as she remembered it. At the end of her recitation she opened her eyes and looked at James. "It was—"

"Don't say her name. The last thing we want right now is her attention."

"Right. But why would War do this?"

A woman's voice answered. "To sabotage his three days."

Jackie jolted at the words, pushing up to better see the slender woman climbing the hillock. She was hauling a backpack with one hand and gripped a tool belt in the other.

James pushed to his feet. "Who are you?"

"I'm Allie, the stonemason. Your father called." She looked down at Kane. "For that mess, no doubt."

"Er, yeah." Then he frowned. "But what do you know about Kane's three days?"

"We all know, lad," she said with a wink, though honestly, the woman looked like she was barely out of high school. "You've been having the Saturnalia for two hundred years. You think you could keep that a secret from the locals?" She dropped the backpack and tools onto the ground. "Besides I'm not just any local. I'm Joseph's apprentice, and he's taught me lots."

"Fine," James huffed. "But can you fix him?"

She pulled out a couple pair of scissors and handed one to Jackie and the other to James. "Let's get his clothes off and have a look, shall we?"

It was a crime to destroy this beautiful clothing, but as it was already shredded there was little to be gained by being gingerly. With a terse nod, Jackie began cutting away on one side, James on the other.

Meanwhile, the woman tugged open the backpack and lifted out a...well, what could she call it but a small cauldron? Then Allie poured ingredients into it from any number of little sacs and vials that she pulled out of what must have been a Harry Potter bag of all holding. Good God, how large was that thing?

Jackie stretched to see, but Allie neatly blocked her view.

"Plaster does a bad job," James said, grunting as he tried to drag the sleeve of the jacket off Kane's arm. It wasn't budging without lifting up Kane who was too damned heavy.

"That's true if this was just plaster and that were just any old statue. But it's not and he's not. They're both magic and that's a fact."

Good lord, they were all talking like magic spells and evil goddesses were real. But then again, how could she doubt? Her lover had just turned into stone.

Jackie pulled off the jacket, shirt, and cravat from Kane's right side and crawled over to start work on his pants. It was going to be damned hard to get those boots off though.

"Leave the boots," Allie said. "He's not damaged down there."

At least not that she could see. "So you can fix him? How long will it take?"

"Well now, if this were Joseph, it'd be five days minimum."

"Five days! But he only has two more." Less if you counted the fact that today was half gone.

To the side, James nodded grimly as if he had expected as much. "You won't get to talk to him, Jackie," he said softly. "Not until next year."

She swallowed. Next year. Another whole year until she could speak to him again. Touch him. She had so much she wanted to say, and they'd barely begun.

She bit her lip to keep from crying. God, how had she fallen in less than a day? It was just really good sex, she told herself. Except she knew that it had been so much more. The connection between them felt so strong.

"You really like him, huh?" That was Allie, her eyes unnervingly intense. "A stoneman that you didn't even think was real."

"He was real. He *is* real." She gestured to the ruined statue in front of her. "It's just this part I'm struggling with."

She sighed. "It's the modern age. You've lost all belief in magic, and you mark my words, it'll come to bite ya in the arse." Her words sounded light, but there was a deadly intensity in her eyes. Worse, she took the time to glare at James too and emphasize her last words. "Bite ya hard right in the arse."

James stared her down. "My father's updating his will. I think I know about the dangers of magic."

"You don't know nothing, now step aside, lad."

He did as he was ordered, and he didn't even make an ugly face at the girl, which Jackie thought was admirable restraint. She was rude at best, freaky crazy at worst. But if she could fix up Kane, then Jackie would happily dedicate herself to learning everything there was to know about stone magic and evil goddesses. Absolutely everything.

Allie worked quickly, smoothing a grayish paste onto Kane's back and legs. She moved with a kind of hypnotic grace, first applying the mixture and then shaping it with hand and tools. It took forever or no time at all. Jackie couldn't tell.

Except that when the woman finally sat back with a satisfied grunt, the sun was a good deal lower in the sky and James seemed to shake himself as if he were coming out of a dream. Jackie too as she looked at the perfect white form of her lover.

Then Kane started to shiver. A tremble at the base of his spine, as if the stone hadn't set. But it had. She was sure of it because Allie had given it a good thump with her fist when she was done. A thump that had woken both her and James, but now Kane's skin was trembling and it wasn't white but a golden brown.

She watched with her jaw slack as that patch of golden skin expanded, slowly at first then with lightning speed. It zipped up his spine and flowed across his waist. She saw his muscles flex and the honey brown of his hair come to life. And then his whole body turned to flesh and he gasped. A single ragged deep breath.

"Kane?" she whispered.

His head lifted up and she heard the creak of stone, but he was moving. The statue was moving. "Jacqueline?" he mouthed. There was sound too, but it wasn't intelligible. Still, she understood and dropped to her knees before him.

"Are you all right?" she asked as she stroked his cheeks. He was alive. He was flesh and blood beneath her fingers.

"Yes. You?"

She blinked away her tears. When the hell had she started crying? "I'm so confused," she said, and yet she wasn't. He was here. He was alive. And she didn't care about the rest except that it never, ever happen again. "Don't go getting blown up again!" she ordered. "I can't take it."

"Never," he said. And then he kissed her. Deep and hard and so ardent that he nearly matched the desperation with which she kissed him.

He was alive.

He was whole.

And…and…

She broke away. She pulled back and glared at him. "What the hell are you doing? We've got to find my True Bliss. Like right now!"

His lips curved and his gaze turned frankly sexual. "I thought that's what we were doing."

"Idiot," she said as she rapped him on his bare shoulder. Not stone but solid, she thought. And warm with life. "We've been doing that. It's time for the next step."

"Which is?"

She took a breath because sometime between when Allie had started slapping on that mixture and now, Jackie had come up with an idea.

"Hurry up and get dressed. You're going to meet my mother."

CHAPTER 9

"**M**other of God, that's fast." Kane had faced and killed innumerable enemies, received every wound it was possible to get, and become proficient at over a dozen different weapons.

But he had never driven in a car.

Jacqueline frowned at him from behind a large wheel. "We're only going 100 kilometers per hour. That's barely over sixty."

He swallowed. "Sixty?"

"Miles per hour."

He blanched. "Nothing should go that fast."

She chuckled. "You said you understood cars and airplanes and the like."

"I do." He tried to keep his voice steady, but it didn't really work. "But…um…"

"It's different when you're sitting in the front seat?"

He nodded.

"Don't worry. I'm a very safe driver when I remember what side of the road I'm supposed to be on."

His head whipped around to hers. "What?"

"In America we drive on the other side of the road. You guys in England are just backwards."

He sniffed. "Or you colonists can never get anything right."

She chuckled. "Spoken like a true imperialist." She winked at him. "I've got news for you big guy. The United States has been leader of the free world for over a century."

The pang he felt at her words wasn't patriotism. It was the realization that he'd missed so much. His own country's place in the world had shifted over a century ago, and he'd barely noticed.

"Hey," she said as she reached over to touch his hand. "England's still pretty badass."

He gripped her fingers in his. "Is that good or bad?"

"Good."

She squeezed him back, and he held on for dear life. Because damn it, the land was flying by much too fast.

He took a moment to accept that something wasn't going to come hurtling through the window and impale him. He'd been in chariot battles, and that was the most common way to die. Crashes were the second most likely, but after a half hour of watching the cars whiz by, he was beginning to realize that there were rules to driving. And here was the real surprise: most people seemed to obey the rules.

So he started to breathe easier. His grip on her fingers relaxed, though he kept the connection of their hands. And while he was working on controlling his own panic, he distracted himself by asking about hers.

"You're taking this very well," he said. "The stoneman myth. I lived it, and it still took me weeks to accept. Years even."

"That probably had something to do with being turned into a statue."

"No," he said dryly, "that had more to do with being plucked from a life as a privileged aristocrat and dropped into battle. That's one of War's favorite games. Take her new stonemen and kill them in all sorts of gruesome ways. Gets them settled into the right frame of mind."

She took a deep breath. "Which is?"

"Fight or die. Fight well or be in pain. Fight really well and get a day away to rest."

She looked away from the road to stare at him. A long, slow look that had him wondering about the speed of this car and the other drivers. But then she looked back at the road and they didn't crash. He relaxed a bit more though he could tell that she was a quiet mass of shock.

"Jacqueline?"

"I'm just trying to process it all," she said softly. "I can't imagine what you've been going through. Two hundred years of war." She took a shuddering breath. "Were the three days off every year helpful? Or did it make everything worse?"

He wondered that every year. "Better, I think. But the first day back in Idola is always hard." Insane would be a better word. Usually he just threw himself into battle, accepting painful deaths over and over as his punishment for failing. And War was all too happy to allow him to eviscerate or be eviscerated on her whim.

Jacqueline pulled his hand to her lips, pressing a kiss to his roughened knuckles. "We'll figure this out. I swear, Kane, we'll find my bliss."

He smiled, feeling his heart swell with tenderness. She was his partner in this now. The first true partner in two hundred years, which was an odd thought because throughout it all, his family had been there for him. Year after year, they'd helped as best they could, trying to figure out the problem. But it was different with this woman. She was determined in a way that pleased him and loyal to him when she had no need to be. She'd sworn to stay by his side when he was a statue. And now she was taking him on a new avenue of exploration, one that he hadn't ever considered before.

No one had ever suggested that a woman's family would be part of her bliss. Which, of course, made them all colossally stupid. The women of his day never said a word without their mother's permission. Naturally, finding bliss would include her mum.

"Tell me about your mother. Tell me how to please her."

"Relax," Jacqueline said with a smile. "She's a simple woman who just wants to see her daughter happy."

"Not enough information. I need to know how to please her."

"That's the problem. You're thinking about pleasing her to gain an end. Please someone sexually to gain your freedom." She sighed. "I know it's hard to understand, but try to just be yourself. She'll like the real you. I do."

He grew silent. After two hundred years of war, he didn't know if he could find who he was again. "What does she like?"

"Men who are nice to her daughter." She released a breath. "Okay. Here's the run-down. We came over here on vacation together. I told her I had a job at your Saturnalia, and so I left her in London to explore the sights while I was gone."

"I cannot tell her about the stonemen. We cannot tell outsiders—"

"I know. And by the way, your whole yearly Saturnalia stretches that rule nearly to breaking. You know that right?"

Yes, he did, but so far, they had gotten away with it.

"We won't tell Mom anything more than that we met at my job. Believe me, she doesn't want to hear about her daughter having wild, monkey sex with strangers."

He frowned. "We have not used monkeys ever."

She chuckled. "Figure of speech. Mom used to be a nurse, so she takes care of people. Dad died a few years back, so she's gone on a campaign to find out what she likes and dislikes in a world without the man she loves."

As sad as living two hundred years without love had been for him, perhaps it was worse to have it and then lose it. "I am sorry your father is gone."

"Me, too. He would have loved talking to you. He was quite the amateur historian."

"But your mother now—"

"Just ask her about the London sights. About her painting. She's started doing that and is surprisingly talented. And then just listen. That's what she wants most of all. Someone to talk to, someone who will listen." She turned to look at him, her expression steady. "I've gotten really good at that over the years."

"What?"

"Listening and not judging." She flashed him a quick smile. "You can tell me anything."

He looked at her, startled to see that she meant it. She would listen to his tales of violence and horror. Not because she liked the blood, but because he might want to talk of it.

But he shook his head. "I do not want to think of it ever."

She took a deep breath. "I get that. I never wanted to talk about the number Alan did on me. And I'm not comparing your experience and mine. Far from it. Yours is obviously exponentially worse. But at some point, I did want to talk. If you do, I'm here."

She had to look back at the road. They were nearing London, and the traffic was increasing. So while she focused ahead, he studied her. Why would she say something like that? Why would she offer her time and her compassion to him? Even for the few more hours that he had left?

In two hundred years, the women he had pleasured had only wanted one thing: more pleasure. And he had done everything he could to give it to them. But not Jacqueline. She was talking to him as a person, not a sexual servant. And in two hundred years, no one had given him that gift: listening. And waiting. She was waiting until he was ready. The gift of time was the most precious of all.

"Are all American girls like you?"

She smiled. "Like what? Bossy and stubborn?"

He didn't even know this word—bossy—but that's not what he meant. "Giving. Kind."

"Surely you have met kind people before."

He had, but it was rare. Among stonemen in service to War? It was the rarest of them all.

"Is your mother like you?"

"She was a nurse, remember? Kindness was her middle name."

He smiled, genuinely looking forward to the meal ahead. He even managed to calm his anxiety throughout the laborious task of finding parking and walking through the maze of bright lights and people that was modern London. It was bewildering, and he'd never felt more alone. If it weren't for Jacqueline's steady presence—and the warmth of her hand in his—he might have turned craven and run. But he didn't, and soon they were walking into a restaurant that boasted an elegance reminiscent of his youth.

He saw her mum immediately. A plump woman with crinkles around her eyes and gray blonde hair cut in close waves about her head. She smiled as they entered, and Kane recognized the quirk of the lips, the fullness of the expression, and the warmth in her eyes. All things she shared with her daughter, and so he stepped forward and bowed as he had years ago.

"Good evening, Madame Myles," he said. Then he remembered that gentlemen didn't bow anymore, though the lady flushed prettily.

"Oh my," she said as she tried to drop into an awkward curtsey.

"Hi, Mom," Jacqueline said as she gave the woman a kiss. "I'd like to introduce you to Kane Addison, a close relation to the Earl of Winsley. He's, um, kind of old school."

"Yes, I can see that. It's very nice to meet you."

He smiled and discovered that he had absolutely no idea what to say or do next. Fortunately, Jacqueline did. She walked over to a stiff-necked man behind a podium and said something about a reservation. It was embarrassing to him for her to take the lead. He was a gentleman or he used to be. He should take control. But there hadn't been restaurants in his day, or at least none that he had ever visited. Pubs, certainly, but not this cavernous place of tables, footmen called waiters, and women baring more of their bodies than was decent in public.

At least Mrs. Myles wasn't in a short skirt. She wore pants and a jacket like a man, which he understood was the style. But that didn't make it normal in his vision, and he was hard-pressed to not stare even as they were escorted to a small table. He stood awkwardly, waiting for a footman to help with his chair. None appeared. In fact, no one helped the ladies either, which he found deuced odd.

So he began fumbling to sit down, and when that was awkwardly accomplished the woman asked him the most impertinent question he'd ever heard.

"Tell me about yourself, Mr. Addison. What do you do for a living?"

It took him a moment to realize that she was asking how he made money. Crass didn't begin to cover what he thought of the question. In his day, it was insulting to suggest a gentleman had to work for his bread. But before he could begin to form an answer, Jacqueline was answering for him, also a most lowering thing for her to do.

"He's in the military, Mom. He can't talk about it because it's top secret."

"Ooh! A real life James Bond," her mother said with a giggle. Then she looked at him, a sparkle in her eye because, obviously, she'd just said some sort of joke. "Do you work for MI-6?"

MI what?

"Mom, really. He can't talk about it."

"Oh, of course." Then the lady flushed and looked down.

He started cudgeling his brain for something else to say. He remembered being suave with women once, but that was two hundred years ago, and apparently he had lost the knack. And while he was still squirming, a footman brought menus. Bloody hell, the prices were exorbitant. Mrs. Myles noticed when he nearly choked on his tongue. Of course she did.

"Is something the matter?"

"Oh, no. Thank you. Just surprised is all." He looked to Jacqueline. "Are these prices typical?" By his reckoning, one dinner could buy a family two hogs and set them up for life.

Jacqueline looked up from her menu with a sympathetic smile. "Inflation is a killer," she said, and he had absolutely no idea what that meant. Which brought up another problem. He had no ability to pay. He had no coin and no cheques.

Bloody hell, why hadn't he thought of that before being shoved into these bizarre clothes and pushed into a car?

He glanced at Jacqueline, at a loss as to what to do. There was no way to express it without her mother finding out, but he had to say something before they ordered.

"I have no coin," he said in an undertone. "I cannot—"

"I know," she said gently. "Don't you remember? This is my treat. It's a celebration of your leave from the military." She turned to his mother. "He's got to go back tomorrow, but he's trying to get out."

"Really?" answered her mother. "Is it difficult? I have no idea how the military works in England. Do you have to sign a contract for so many years and then do tours of duty?"

He had not the bloody least idea, though if there had been coin when he was young, he would have bought himself a commission. But he couldn't say that, so he struggled with the lie. "Something like that," he said. And there the conversation floundered again.

Then in the most humiliating moment of his entire adult life, Mrs. Myles leaned over and patted his hand. Two soft presses that left him speechless with rioting emotions. Humiliation was first and foremost, but there was also an unmanly need to cry. Tears burning hot and clogging his throat. No one had touched him in such a way since he was a boy. Not even his mother had done such a thing, but his nanny had been prone to pats. Gentle touches, soft taps, and only the occasional hard swat. All Mrs. Myles had done was touch his hand twice, and emotions rushed at him. The loneliness, the loss of everyone and everything he'd ever loved. Two hundred years of violence interspersed with seventy-two hours of frenzied coupling. No maternal touch. No simple human connection. Nothing until now, and he could barely breathe through the agony of loss.

And all the while, the woman had no idea that she'd just unmanned him at the one time he'd most wanted to be strong. "Top secret again," Mrs. Myles said. "But if you get your wish, what will you do?"

"Not kill anyone ever again." The words were out before he could stop them. It was his fondest wish. That and to eat good food and have a dog. So simple and yet so unattainable. And perhaps, he'd like it if she patted his hand again. In private. Somewhere where he could howl out his devastation or sob like a child.

"Oh," Mrs. Myles said. "Oh yes, I suppose that would be important." And then the hand pat again.

Bloody hell. "I seem to have lost the ability to appear in public," he said. Unable to take more, he slid his hands into his lap where they immediately fisted against his slacks.

"That's understandable, Kane," Jacqueline said. "And you're doing fine." She glanced at her mother. "He's been what they call 'in country' for a long time. It's hard to transition out."

"Oh my yes, I imagine it would be."

In country? He'd been in Idola, but her euphemism would work just as well.

The waiter appeared and listed off a half dozen chef specials. The women ordered first, thank God, because whatever Jacqueline did, he echoed. He felt like a child in small clothes waiting for a cue from his nanny.

That was bad enough, but the larger picture was even more grim. The whole idea had been to give Jacqueline a moment of True Bliss by pleasing her mother. But he was so far from being pleasant that he couldn't help but fail. It was a misery, but he couldn't do anything other than soldier on as if this had a prayer of working.

"Tell me how you two met," her mother said. "Surely that's not top secret."

"Hardly," Jacqueline said with a laugh. "His family puts on that event that I'm covering."

Good God, she couldn't be suggesting to her mother that she'd just gone to a three day sexual escapade, could she?

"The Saturnalia? But that's a…it looks like…"

Jacqueline laughed while Kane's ears burned red hot. "It's not as depraved as the marketing makes it sound."

No, it's worse. Did she have any idea the things he'd done in the name of finding someone's True Bliss?

Meanwhile her mother frowned. "So you two just met?"

"Yup," Jacqueline said with a salacious wiggle of her eyebrows. "But it's been a memorable meeting."

"In what way?" Mrs. Myles pressed.

"Yes, my dear," Kane said, as he found some composure in teasing Jacqueline. "In what way?"

He thought she'd be embarrassed. He thought she'd spit out some cleverly constructed lie, but he'd underestimated her. She gripped his hand on one side and touched her mother's arm on the other.

"Mama, he's made me believe in magic again."

If Kane had been drinking, he'd have choked on it. As it was, every part of his body seized up tight. She couldn't talk about that. He'd told her she couldn't talk about the stonemen or anything like that. But again, he'd underestimated her.

"I can't explain it, Mama, but when we're together, such amazing things happen. We go on a picnic and I see…" She shrugged. "Magic."

Mrs. Myles' eyes shimmered with delight. But then she looked at him, and he had to confess the truth. "It's not like it sounds. I just…" What? "I just talked with her and…and…"

Jacqueline squeezed his hand. "And you don't talk to many people, do you?"

No, he didn't. "My, uh, job makes it hard."

"And when you get out, it'll be even more magical. It'll be—"

Freedom. Safety.

"Peace," he rasped. "It'll be peaceful." And she didn't know how beautiful that word was to him. Except maybe she did because suddenly both women were patting his hands, one on each side.

Then there was little for him to do or say except eat his food. It was wonderful, this meal of tastes such as he'd never before experienced. Cooking seemed to have come a far way in two hundred years. Mother and daughter chatted easily, bringing him into the conversation here and there. They didn't seem too upset that he had little to contribute, but by the end he had to make his bid for bliss. He had to try, and he'd spent the dessert course working out his exact words. Then he needed the entire walk to Mrs. Myles hotel to gather the courage. Damn it, he'd never needed courage before, but somehow facing a girl's mother was miles different from facing down cannon fire or a rifle barrage.

At her hotel room door, she took his hand and this time he didn't flinch. She began first, and like a crass idiot, he interrupted her.

"It was lovely meet–"

"Please let me explain something," he said. Then he flushed. "My apology."

"Go ahead, dear."

He nodded slowly. "I know I'm not what mothers dream of for their daughters. I…I didn't turn out how I dreamed either." That was said with a glance at Jacqueline. This statement was as much for her as it was for her mother. "But I've been waiting countless years for a woman like your daughter. She's given me hope again, and I will do everything in my power to honor that gift."

"Oh my," said her mother.

"And the aristocrat comes through," murmured the daughter.

Then both women were misty-eyed though, damn it, he didn't know what that meant.

He was about to ask. He was foundering for words when something else triggered in his brain. Something dark and slumbering but no less menacing.

There was a stoneman nearby, he realized. And this one was as pure an evil as he'd ever felt.

CHAPTER 10

"Domina, I have news."

Zeva was bored with modern sports. There was nothing like a good, old-fashioned bloodbath. So inspired by the last Hobbit movie, she'd put five armies facing each other at the edges of a bowl shaped terrain. Then she stood in the center valley and lounged against a flag pole. Whichever army got the flag won the battle. And the winners got something they all seemed to want: a week of freedom.

Of course, that was why she was at the center. No one ever won the flag, but that didn't stop them from trying. She'd started the battle twenty minutes ago, and there was large scale fighting all around her. But it was Ares who made it most quickly to her side.

"Domina. News."

She had to give it to the man, he certainly knew how to catch her attention. Despite being cut to pieces—literally—a day ago, he was still fighting his way to her through the armies. He was making slow progress, probably because he was still weak from his injuries. She'd reattached all his parts to where they were supposed to be, but the rest of the damage she'd left to heal slowly. And yet he was impressive as he fought his way through the warriors to her side.

"Domina—" he repeated as he stood before her, his arms raised in supplication. "It's interesting."

And that's how he caught her attention. Because if there was anything she liked more than the fury of battle, it was interesting news.

With a wave of her hand, she froze everyone in place. Then she smiled at Ares who was just turning to face a foe. It gave her pleasure to watch his face because with everyone frozen, he had time to realize he was about to die in three different ways—hand grenade, battle axe, and a fire-breathing dragon. That last was her nod to Smaug.

"I have slowed time," she said. "I did not stop it, so speak quickly."

"Kane," he said, and she admired the steadiness of his complexion. He hadn't blanched at all, which meant he knew no fear. Or at least never the outward expression of it. "He is well and very near my statue. And he was laughing with his woman."

She frowned. Her stonemen did not laugh outside of battle. She thought it was bad form. "Didn't you dispatch two stonemen to stop him?"

"They delayed him."

"Not enough."

"Obviously."

"But you think you can do better."

He lifted his chin, daring to look her in the eye. "Domina, it was my mistake to attack him. The better choice is to dispatch her. There is no prohibition against—"

"Killing her." She frowned at him. "You have failed me in this matter."

"Which is why I offer myself to remedy the situation."

"And when you are done?" she prompted. He had best know what was coming when he returned to her.

"I will submit myself to your punishment, of course."

She grinned. She did like punishing him. Almost as much as he seemed to enjoy it.

"Very well. Do what you must." Then she flashed him a grin. "But only after you have escaped here. Or died."

She waved a hand. Time resumed, and she got the pleasure of seeing him kick aside the grenade such that it blew off the face of the brute with the battle ax. He might have survived the explosion. He was diving to the side, but then the dragon caught them all.

One long blast of fire. It was a special slow burning fire that clung so that her men would not forget—even in the heat of battle—to watch the skies. Plus, she got to watch them die in long moments of screaming agony.

It wasn't that she enjoyed their suffering. Far from it. These were her own warriors after all, and they held a special place in her plans if not her heart. But every man's reaction to repeated suffering was different. The stoic ones were fascinating to her. Any man, woman, or child could scream and flop about. But a certain few had learned to endure, and that was what interested her. At least for today.

Ares endured.

But when his flesh had melted away, she allowed him to die. Which would then put him in his statue body in order to animate and take care of Kane's woman.

Then, after this battle, she would turn her attention to Kane's curator. It wasn't his fault that Kane had become damaged from the stonemen attack, but that didn't matter. The cause never mattered, just that she was within her rights to exact the same damage upon him. Which is when the curator usually began bargaining for his life.

And that was fun indeed.

CHAPTER 11

Jackie was just about to kiss Kane full on the mouth—right in front of her mother—when she saw his eyes blaze. He'd been turned toward her, so hopefully her mother didn't see. But the woman couldn't fail to notice the sudden tension in his entire body.

"We must go, Jacqueline," he said in a low undertone. "Now."

"Go?" her mother said. "But I thought we could talk some more."

"Sorry, Mom," Jackie said quickly. "We've got to get him back. This was just an impromptu visit to see you."

Then Kane gripped her hand. "You should stay with your mother. Inside." He started to push her into her mother's room, but Jackie dug in her heels.

"Not happening. You can't drive, remember? And cars are the fastest way out of London."

"What?" her mother inserted. "Why can't he drive?"

"It's a medical safety thing 'cause he's a terrible driver." Jackie tried to keep her tone light because it was supposed to be a joke, but his tension—and therefore hers—was ratcheting up by the second. "We'll get it fixed in no time." Then she pressed a kiss to her mother's cheek. "Good night, Mom. I'll see you in a couple days."

"Okay but—"

"Bye! Lock the door behind us." Then she pushed her mom inside while simultaneously hauling the hotel door closed. "Will she be all right?"

Kane nodded. "If I get away from her." He touched her cheek. "You should—"

"Stay with you." She grabbed his hand. "Elevator or stairs?"

He frowned. "Stairs. Definitely stairs."

She smiled grimly as they headed off. Elevators were another modern marvel that he liked in theory but was uncomfortable with in experience. She couldn't blame him. Small box, no control, no sight of where they were going. For all that he was on holiday, as he put it, he was still a warrior at heart, and he saw things as a fighter would. Elevators were not defensible positions.

They started down the stairs as quickly as possible. Thank God she'd chosen low heels. She couldn't imagine doing this in stilettos. Unfortunately, her mother had been on the twelfth floor which meant that it took them a bit to sprint down the stairs.

He led the way, she scrambled after him. For all that he was big, he was quick and not even winded, whereas she was gasping for breath by the time they hit the third floor.

He slowed to give her a chance to recover, his gaze searching the floor as if he could see through the cement. "It has awoken. You must run. As soon as we get to the main floor, you must run for your car and never look back."

"Bull *gasp* Puppies." Damn, she was out of shape.

"Bulls do not have puppies."

"I'm not *gasp* abandoning you."

"You cannot help me."

She saved her breath. He was right. She was useless when it came to kick-ass karate moves and the like. And she only knew how guns worked in theory. But she had lungs. She could scream and as far as she could tell, there were rules about these stonemen revealing themselves to the general population. The touristy side of London was about as public as you could get.

They made it to the main floor, slamming open the lobby door, only to come face to face with the stoneman. They both reared back, and Jackie's brain kicked into fact mode. Short, stocky man with thick muscles and scars everywhere. Still, he was handsome in a menacing, Roman soldier kind of way.

"Do all you guys wear togas?" His outfit was a metal skirt, naked chest, and red plummy helmet, but toga was the word that came to her mouth. Especially since her mind was completely absorbed in staring at the sword in his hand. "Is that real?"

"Run," said Kane to her as he squared off with the Roman guy. "What is your mission?"

The man smiled, and she completely revised her estimate of his handsomeness. He was creepy. As in crazy light in his eyes, gleefully enjoying anything involving blood spatter. Ew. Then he spoke, his voice like glass grinding against stone.

"Why do you fight, Kane? Succumb and join in Zeva's glorious win."

Jackie looked around, desperate for an escape. They were at the edge of the lobby in a tiny alcove that hid them from most people's view. Unfortunately, the only way out was back into the stairwell or through creepy Roman guy.

"There is more to life than fighting," said Kane. "Why do you help her?"

"Because when she wins, this will end."

"It can end differently," Kane pressed. "What is your escape clause?"

The crazy man laughed, the sound increasing the ick factor exponentially. "When all of my descendants are dead."

Jackie frowned. Wait. He was a Roman soldier. "Just how many kids did you have?"

He snorted. "Too many to count."

Okay, so that officially sucked. His only chance at escape was to see his family wiped out.

"Look, we can help you," she said. She wasn't exactly sure how, but they could figure something out.

"Oh you will," he said with another one of those really creepy smiles. "You'll die."

Then he attacked. Not Kane, which is what they'd been braced for. He lunged past Kane to grab at her. Fortunately Kane was ready, and he shoved her out of the way. She slammed backwards into the stairwell, letting out a good "eep!" Some screamer, she was.

Didn't matter because the fight now was fully engaged. Kane was rapid fire punching, keeping Roman guy from wielding his sword. They were also wedged in the doorway which kept the bad guy from getting to her. And now she had the breath to let out a really good scream. She let fly, pleased when the sound echoed up and down the stairwell.

Deal with the publicity of that, psycho-Claudius.

It worked. Or the sounds of crashing and grunting drew attention. In a moment there were shouts from hotel staff and suddenly people were grabbing onto Roman guy and trying to haul him backwards.

They tried. The man was strong. He shoved them off easily, throwing them against the wall before coming back for her. Kane blocked him though she had real sympathy for the hotel staff. She heard one guy land with a sickening thump before dropping limply to the ground. Oh, this was bad. They had to get out of here.

Then she heard something on the lower level. A door opening and closing. The basement. Right!

"This way," she screamed.

Two more guys had jumped on the Roman. They weren't bringing him down, but they were unwieldy enough that the man dropped his sword and had to throw them off. That gave them time to run.

Kane spun on his heel and together they bolted down the stairs and out that door.

Ugly tile, undecorated halls, and machine noise from down the hall. Probably the laundry. Where was the parking garage?

Down there!

A woman looked like she was leaving work as she hoisted her purse and keys. Jackie took off toward her and Kane followed. The woman squeaked when she heard the noise, pressing her hands to her chest as she cried, "Blimey!"

"Parking garage?" Jackie gasped. "Where are the cars?"

The woman pointed with shaking hands, and they took off again. A moment later they were through the door and into the lowest level of the garage. But their car was parked on the fourth floor. Damn.

"Up!"

Jesus, she needed to work out more. They took off running. The garage stairs were on the opposite side, of course. She found them quickly, and then it was screaming pain in her side as she tried to climb. Kane didn't even pause as he slammed past her, scooping her up as he went. He had her flipped over his shoulder as he kept moving impossibly fast. Impossibly strong.

"Fourth floor!" she cried. Good thing she still had the keys which she awkwardly fished out of her purse. Oh shit, the bouncing on her ribs was killing her, not to mention being half upside down trying to give directions. "To the left. I mean right! Right! Blue Prius." Oh wait. That was her car at home. They'd driven the family car. "Black Mercedes." Like Kane could tell the difference.

He slowed down and set her on gently on her feet. "Quickly."

Well goodness. He did know one car from the other because they were right in front of the car. She hit the unlock and scrambled forward, still working to get her bearings now that she was right side up.

She got in and slammed the keys in the ignition. Kane was a step behind her, having fumbled a bit with the door opening. But then he was inside and she was jamming the car into reverse when she heard the noise.

An inhuman roar that sounded like glass and gravel. It grated on her spine and made her hunch in the seat. Obviously Roman dude had found them. Too bad for him that she was out of the parking spot and shifting into forward. She'd have just slammed on the gas with her car, but this was a fricking manual transmission and she was out of practice.

Then they were in trouble as pyscho-Roman stepped into the center of their path. Oh shit. He had his sword out, and it was covered in blood.

Oh shit. Oh shit.

"Now what?"

The man raised the weapon.

"Go," said Kane his voice low but no less urgent. "Go forward, Jacqueline. Go forward! Now!"

Psycho Roman had lifted his sword. Not just lifted it but flicked it over his head as he prepared to throw it dagger style.

Jackie slammed on the gas. The car lurched but then caught and roared forward like the fine machine it was. And then a sword slammed through the windshield. Right through it. Right in front of her eyes.

Oh shit. Oh shit. Oh shit.

She should be dead right now. She should have her brain matter splattered across the back seat except right where it would have impaled her eyes, the sword had landed *chunk* into Kane's statue arm.

Then the car lurched. She'd been so freaked, she hadn't even realized that she'd still been slamming the car forward until she hit him. Pyscho Roman flew up the bumper and over.

And Kane's arm fell off. *Thud.* Right into her lap. The sword had gone so deep into the marble that it now broke off.

She would have screamed if she had the breath. She didn't. She was still trying to drive the car around the tight turn in the parking garage.

She failed at it, slamming into a column. And the damn sword clattered through the splintering windshield to fall onto the dash.

She cursed, slammed the car into reverse, while behind her she saw the Roman guy stand back up. He was bloody and his nose and half his face were clearly smashed, but he was standing and stomping right toward them.

Well too fucking bad, sucker. You're in my rearview mirror now.

And she was moving forward. In a Mercedes.

Even with a smashed windshield, she could maneuver the tight turns. It took all her concentration, but she still kept Kane in her peripheral vision. He was straining. Half statue, half human still.

She didn't have the breath to ask. Jesus, his arm was in her lap!

Except it wasn't. He reached forward and grabbed it with his good arm. Then he shoved it back where it ought to be.

Oh shit. She'd have to get him back to the stonemason. At least they still had all the parts.

"How long can you hold the half statue?" she cried as she roared through the garage gate. The wood thing splintered and she had to duck around the pieces.

"Can't," he rasped.

Shitshitshitshit. He couldn't go fully human. He'd bleed out. His arm was broken off.

"Dump me," he said with a groan. "Hide. Harder to find you. Away from me."

"I'm not dumping you!"

Wind blew hard in her face. Damn it, she couldn't go fast without a windshield, but she had to get away from the hotel.

"Just hold on," she said to Kane. When he didn't answer, she glanced over and released a quiet whimper. He was fully statue again. And weirdly, the arm seemed to have reattached somehow. Or he was holding it in place. She didn't know and she couldn't spare the focus to find out. And she couldn't fracking drive liked she wanted without a windshield. Not with a damned statue sitting in the front seat.

Damn!

There was only one choice. So while still maneuvering the London streets, she fumbled in her purse to find her phone. She had to find someplace with lots of people. Someplace she could take a breath and maybe get another car.

"Siri!" she ordered her smart phone. "Get me directions to Buckingham Palace. We're going to meet the freaking Queen!"

CHAPTER 12

Jackie didn't have a deep plan when she guided the car to Buckingham Palace. She knew the Queen wasn't in residence, but there were always tourists, lights, and—best of all—guards with their big black hats. So she drove there, her face whipped raw by the wind, then parked in the most brilliantly lit place and started making phone calls. She got Allie's phone number from Hugh and prayed that the woman made palace calls.

She did, but the woman wasn't happy about it.

Worse, the palace guards weren't too keen about having an American in a broken down Mercedes sitting right between the Palace and St. James Park. Fortunately, she managed hysterical woman just fine, especially with the freaking sword in the car and police reports about a crazy attack at her mother's hotel. It helped that this was the Earl of Winsley's car, and he went all aristocrat on the head guard through her phone.

He wasn't threatening or anything, which surprised her. No, it was more, "What's your name? How can I express my gratitude for you helping out the dotty American? Just placate her. We all have one of those people in our family tree, I'm afraid. You know how it is."

In short, he bribed the guy, and so she was able to sit there until Allie showed and fixed up Kane. At least that was the plan until the woman pulled up in her truck all bristling annoyance as she stomped over. Even the guards backed away from her glare, but Jackie didn't have such luxury.

"Good God, I've never seen a woman get in more trouble so fast. What the hell were you thinking coming straight to the Queen? You know she doesn't even live here."

"I know, I know. Can you fix him?"

"You shouldn't have put a bloody sword through his arm."

"I didn't!"

Allie rolled her eyes and stomped over to the driver's side door. Climbing in, she got a really good look at the mess that had been done to Kane. "If you'd just figure out what you want, then he can give it to you and this'll be all over." She glared at Allie through the windshield space. "You're running out of time, you know."

Didn't she know it. "I thought I'd be happy when my mother liked him."

"Well? Does she?"

"Yeah, she does. You should have seen her face when he said…" Her voice trailed away. As beautiful as that moment was in her memory—and it was a shining star of a moment—the very next second had been the beginnings of the attack by psycho Roman. But it had been bliss—or so she thought—no matter how brief.

Except he was still a stoneman.

"What the hell do I want?" she muttered to herself. Start with the obvious. "I don't want to be attacked by freaking psychotic stonemen—Roman or otherwise."

"Ares is over there," Allie said with a jerk of her chin. "Even he can't attack in the middle of all this."

"Which is why I drove here in the first place." Pretty smart though now what was she going to do? One glance over into the shadows, and she was shuddering in horror. There he was, Mr. Psycho. Except she had light and police and a growing number of lookie-loos all around her. Lord, she hated playing a hysterical woman, but sometimes that's what the situation called for.

"Oh my god!" she screamed, pointing at their stalker while yelling at the police. "There he is! There he is! The guy in the skirt!" Take that moron. First lesson in fitting in was to not walk around in red helmet and metal skirt.

She saw the plume of the helmet suddenly jerk as palace guards started calling out. Then psycho guy—what was his name?—Ares started running and was followed by palace guards in big black hats plus Bobbies in their shorter, rounder helmets. It was straight out of a comic movie, and if she weren't in the middle of it all, she would be laughing uproariously.

As it was, all she could do was stare at Kane's arm and pray that Allie got it cemented on somehow. The woman was working amazingly fast. And given all the bright lights around them, Jackie ought to be able to see what she was doing better. No such luck. The woman was contorted in the car, working her magic and blocking all the good views. But then she sat back with a grunt of satisfaction.

"Is he…?" Her words cut off. She didn't need to ask because she was looking right at him.

He was healing. Stone to flesh. She'd seen it before but it was no less magical now. And within a few moments, he was fully human.

The first thing he did when he could move was look for her. And when he found her he gasped out a word.

"Hurt?"

"I'm fine. Thanks to you, I'm fine."

"Roman?"

"On the run. His name's Ares." And how the hell did Allie know that?

"He won't stop coming," Kane said.

Which is when Allie thumped him on the head. "So figure it out already!"

They both turned to look at her. With her square jaw and work roughened hands, she was the least gentle person on the planet. But something in her eyes softened. On a sigh, she fished into her pocket and pulled out her keys and a hotel keycard.

"I'll take care of yer car. Go on. Ares will be on the run for a while. Them Bobbies got radios and cars. He's fast but he can't outrun a coordinated search, and they'll be looking all night." She shook her head. "Idiot sister sending an idiot Roman to expose us all."

"What?" That was Kane, his eyes narrowing as he looked at Allie. "What did you say?"

She huffed. "That you've only got a few hours to figure this out. Now go!" She tossed the keys at Jackie, who fumbled to catch them. And when she finally got them in her hands, the woman gripped her wrist. "It's up to you, girl. Figure it out!"

Then she shoved Jackie back far enough that she stumbled. Kane moved quickly, catching her before she fell, which was a pretty neat trick seeing as he had to leap out of the car first. But when they were both on firm ground, they turned back to Allie. Somehow in the time they'd taken to stand up, she'd whipped out her phone and dialed. With a shooing motion of her hand, she turned her back on them.

Jackie wanted to talk more to the woman. She seemed to know way more than what she was letting on, but this wasn't the time or the place. So she chose instead to be grateful and skedaddle. Grabbing Kane's hand, she hustled to the truck. Twenty minutes later, they were stepping into the honeymoon suite of the London Ritz.

Jackie dropped her purse with a thud that the thick carpet muffled to nearly inaudible. "Just how much does stone masonry pay?"

Kane grabbed her and wrapped her in his arms, pressing his face to her shoulder. "I haven't the foggiest idea."

"And you don't really care, do you?"

He shook his head, but didn't lift it from where he was pressed tight against her.

"Kane?"

"I surrender, Jackie. I'm finished."

"What?" Alarm shot through her. She wanted to pull back to look in his face, but he wasn't releasing her.

"I'm going to call Zeva. She'll let you be if I give up trying."

"But you can't!" Damn it, why wouldn't he look at her? "Ka—"

He silenced her with a kiss. A deep, powerful, penetrating kiss…good bye.

"No," she murmured into his mouth, but he didn't give her the chance to object. His mind was made up and inside his soul felt quiet. For the first time in his entire two hundred plus years of life, there was a silence in his heart that was almost peaceful. Perhaps the better word was numb, but either way it was better than pain. Better than the anguish of constant killing. Better than knowing if he didn't surrender, she would be killed. Likely in front of his very eyes.

He couldn't bear that.

So he kissed her and prepared to end this—

"One last try," she gasped as she ripped her mouth from his. "We have the time, Kane. Your three days aren't up until tomorrow evening. We can try again."

He touched her cheek. "I've been trying for two hundred years."

"But not with me." She stroked her hands over his shoulders, her gaze intense on his face. "Damn it, we have so little time, don't shorten it even further."

He released a slow sigh. It was so hard to keep hoping. So hard to believe. "Jacqueline—"

"I'm falling in love, Kane. With you. Don't give up on that yet. Not when we're just starting."

He looked at her, his mind shocked into silence. He wasn't numb. This was the opposite of numb. It was more like he felt everything at once. Shock. Adoration. Agony. But over it all was a gratitude that knew no bounds. Simple awe mixed with such thankfulness that he couldn't contain it.

Someone loved him. After all his friends and family had died. After two centuries of killing mixed with three nights of frantic coupling—someone had the audacity, the sheer stupidity to love him. Or nearly love him. Or whatever it was that she said.

"Kane? Say something."

"I…" What did he say? What words would match the completeness of his joy at that one moment? The hope she inspired in him was gone, but in its place was happiness. After everything, someone cared for him. "Jacqueline, if I could, I would spend every day of my life worshiping you."

She touched his cheek, but her gaze was still on his eyes. "I don't want adoration. I just want you whole and happy. With me."

He shook his head. Didn't she understand? He wasn't ever going to be whole. Maybe if they'd met two hundred years ago, back when he wasn't so ruined. Maybe then, they'd have had a chance. But the world had pushed too far ahead of him. He would never fit in now. Never be the kind of man she deserved.

"I only have now."

"Then don't run away."

"I couldn't," he whispered. "I couldn't if I tried. I wouldn't get two steps before turning back to you."

She stroked his lips, her fingertips light as they traced him. He sucked her fingers inside, licking them and nipping at the pads when she smiled. He watched as her gaze grew sensual. Felt it when her body became pliant against him. And without a real thought, he scooped her up in his arms and carried her to the bed.

He would show her now. He would touch her in such a way as she would know all the things he couldn't say. And for her, he would believe again. Or at least not doubt so very much.

So he kissed her as he set her gently on the bed. He applied his considerable skill, honed over two hundred years, to giving pleasure to her. He knew when her breath began to catch that he could undress her now, making every reveal of flesh, every lift and stroke of fabric against her skin, part of her seduction. His gift to her.

She was more than willing, but he stopped her from helping.

"Let me pleasure you," he said.

"Let me share with you," she answered.

He agreed because he would do anything she asked. So he eased off her clothes, and she helped him with his. And soon they were both naked, but he was still in control.

He began first with her belly—soft and flat. He liked the way it quivered under his lips. He could feel her breath shiver and her hips shift impatiently though all he did was press tiny kisses to her skin.

The breasts came next. He molded them with his hands, he teased the nipples with his fingers, and he spent long moments in the kissing of them. Here she liked strong suction, sharp nips, and then the soothing caress of his hands. He knew this because he'd only paid attention to one breast, but the scent of her arousal was heavy in the air.

"Kane," she gasped. God, he loved it when she said his name like that. "Kane!" she repeated. "Let me…Let…Me!"

She abruptly surged upward, pushing on his shoulders. He allowed her to angle herself over him. He let her push him down into the mattress and kiss him however she wanted. And he reveled in it. Not just the way she licked his nipples to hard nubs. Not just the way her breasts dangled so perfectly for one hand or that the wetness between her thighs was available to the other. He pleasured her from this position on his back, and he let his cock throb with hunger and his body ache with need.

This too was part of the dance, but he had so seldom experienced it. And in this way, he saw the difference between giving a woman pleasure and sharing in the act of love. They were sharing this moment. And while he stroked between her thighs, she engulfed his cock in the wet heat of her mouth.

Heaven. Sweet, delectable heaven as she sucked him up and down. He reached over and lifted her hip. The leverage was hard, but his stoneman strength made it easy to set her legs on either side of his face.

Sixty-nine, and he gave himself to the taste of her.

He knew what to do. He'd learned her likes before, but there was always the difference between moments. This time she arched down against his mouth. This time, she gasped when he sucked her clit. This time, she quivered when he thrust his tongue inside her.

He delighted in the way she timed her movements with his. Swirling her tongue along the underside of his cock just when he was circling her clit. Stroking her hand hard down to his base just when he was spreading her wide to feast up and down her slit.

And when she arched in her first orgasm, he held her against his mouth and kept it going for as long as he could.

Until she collapsed and he flipped her over onto her back.

She looked at him, her eyes dazed, her body still pulsing, but she managed to say the one thing he had been missing.

"I love you."

There wasn't even breath behind the words, but he saw the shape of her mouth and he lost all control.

He thrust himself into her. He buried himself as deeply as he could and he pounded even harder against her.

Her orgasm had slowed, but his aggressiveness had her convulsing again. Such pleasure as he had never known consumed him. She wanted him. Her body pulled at him and her lips kept forming his name.

She loved him.

And he wanted every dram of her.

So he took her, again and again.

And when he released, he poured himself fully into her.

He thought he was marking her with himself, but he was the one who felt taken. Or given. Or merged. Or simply dissolved into all that was her.

"Jacqueline," he cried.

She took everything, and she smiled as she spread her arms.

His. She was his.

He collapsed into her. Satiated. Complete.

One.

And in this way, he found his first moment of true rest in two hundred years.

But when he woke, he was still a stoneman.

CHAPTER 13

Jackie opened her eyes a few hours later to see him sitting in the hotel chair, his leg outstretched, his face in shadow, but his entire air one of brooding despair. She didn't even have to ask. His body was slumped, his eyes hooded, and he watched her the way a king surveyed the devastation of a ruined kingdom.

She bit her lip, her own despair washing through her. It didn't work. She thought back to their lovemaking. It had been the best physical experience of her life, but there had also been a desperation in their coupling. A need and a hope that had nothing to do with love. Had it tainted the experience? She hadn't thought so, but they were looking at degrees of bliss here. Which meant it hadn't been Total Bliss. Those were the words. Or was it True Bliss? Didn't matter because as satisfying as their lovemaking had been, it hadn't been one hundred percent pure bliss.

"I had a dream," she said, the words flowing easily from her lips. "It was a wonderful dream about our future."

He didn't speak, but she knew she had his attention.

"You were a history professor. I was a novelist writing about our experiences saving the stonemen one at a time. And we had children, Kane. Such happy children as would make you smile. Do you know what they were doing?"

"No."

"They were laying out sheets of those air bubble things that come in packages. Like big pillows of plastic air. And they were jumping up and landing on their bottom on the plastic to pop them."

He tilted his head. "I don't understand."

Of course not. Bubble sheets hadn't been invented in his time. "I'll show you. First thing after you're human again, we'll go to a packing store, buy a roll of them, and jump up and down on them."

He remained silent for a while. She wanted to get up and go to him. She wanted to climb into his lap and kiss him again as they talked about the future. But his mood was infecting her. It was hard to stay positive for just three days. How had he managed it for two hundred years?

"Kane—"

"You should have children. Beautiful ones that pop bubbles and eat treacle until they're sick."

"We will—"

"You should have your mother singing with you by the yule log and a husband who can drive a fast car and buy you beautiful jewelry."

"You will—"

"And you should live a long and happy life surrounded by people who love you."

She didn't have an answer to that. They'd known each other for such a short time. Yes, she loved him. There was no other word for this deep well of yearning she had for his happiness. Not her own, but his.

But did he have it in him to love her? Did he have only war and despair left?

No, she didn't believe that. She'd seen his humor during their picnic. She'd felt his kindness when he tried to talk with her mother. And he'd been fiercely protective of herself and the servants when the other stonemen had attacked. He was a good man, but his problem was nearly overwhelming. And it was up to her to solve it because it was her bliss they were searching for.

She rolled closer to him on the bed, but she didn't touch him. Instead, she stretched and was pleased to see his eyes follow the curve of her body, the arch of her spine. So he wasn't inured to her yet.

"What is your dream, Kane?"

"To see you safe and happy."

She smiled. She liked that he thought of her, but she couldn't let him stay with that. "For yourself. What do you want for you?"

"An end, Jacqueline. Just an end."

She plopped her chin on her hand. "Not good enough. I need you to have dreams for yourself." Then she thought over the things he had wanted for her. One of them was a husband who would drive a fast car. "Do you want to learn to drive? To race?" Wasn't that the dream of every little boy?

He sighed. "I did race. Curricles and phaetons, carriages and even once dray horses." He shook his head. "How young I was."

"You need to remember being young."

"I need to accept that my time is past. That I have been holding onto dreams that will never be."

She sighed. "What dreams? Tell them to me."

His gaze grew abstract. "A wife and children. An estate with green grass and maybe a seat in the House of Commons." Then he shook his head. "A boy's dreams, Jacqueline. They no longer fit me."

She frowned. So it wasn't that he'd given up on dreaming. Just that those boyhood dreams were past. "So what do you want now?"

He sighed. "I told you—"

"And I said not good enough. Look deep, Kane. What do you wish?"

"That there be no more stonemen. No more fighting. No more of this parody of life for me or any of the other souls trapped by those insane goddesses." He dropped his head back and looked out toward the night sky. "I have only myself to blame for my predicament. So many of the others were cursed. So many were tricked or manipulated or simply taken."

"Taken?"

"Some. I don't know the full rules."

"But you could find them out, right? We could piece them together. Save more stonemen?"

"I cannot even save myself, Jacqueline."

Now she did get up from the bed. She got up and walked over to him. She was completely naked as she straddled his lap. He wasn't erect, but as she settled against him, she felt him grow. She felt him shift to hold her and soon there was a heat between them where they connected.

"Listen to me Kane. I know you've been doing this for a long time, but I've just started. You have no idea what I can do once I put my mind to it."

He pressed a kiss to her lip. "She will not let you live."

"Why? Because I'm close to freeing you? That's it, right? Because we're—"

"It doesn't matter. I cannot protect you as a statue. And my sanity will not survive if she kills you."

She sighed. "I'll hire a bodyguard."

"You do not know what we are capable of. Especially *her* stonemen."

"You're right," she said softly. "I'm completely out of my depth here, but that's what love is. I've fallen for a two-hundred-year-old guy who's a statue most of the time. Big deal. Every couple has their problems."

"Jacqueline."

"Do you love me, Kane? If you do, then you'll fight for us." She dropped her forehead against his. "And that means fighting for yourself because there is no *us* without *you*."

"Or you."

She stretched up onto her knees. His cock was big and hot between them, and she easily slid down over it. She was wet, he was slick, and together they fit perfectly.

"This is great," she said as she squeezed him. "But it's just sex." She pressed a hand to his heart. "This is what I care about."

He held her gaze. He looked at her and said nothing, but his eyes seemed to burn her from the inside out. He wanted to believe. He wanted to hope. He wanted so much, but was afraid to say it aloud.

"Two hundred years," she said softly. "Did you never talk with any of those women? Did you never tell anyone what you were feeling?"

"Just you," he said. Then he began to move. His buttocks flexed, pushing him deeper into her. She rode him. She arched into his movements, she pushed down when he thrust up, and she kissed him gently.

"You have to believe."

"I believe in your belief. Is that enough?"

She rewarded him with a kiss. "For now," she said against his lips.

She rode him slowly. Though he controlled his thrusts, she made sure that he kept the pace leisurely. She wanted him to enjoy this. She wanted him to think that they had all the time in the world. And when he reached between them to thumb her clit, when her own tension coiled to near breaking, she leaned forward and whispered her feelings into his ear.

"I believe in you," she said. "Because I love you."

The words triggered a frenzy in him. A gasping need that translated into slamming thrust. He had no words, but she saw them in the tears in his eyes. So she said it again.

"I love you."

"Jacqueline!"

CHAPTER 14

A res found them mid-morning. She and Kane were entwined together on the bed when he burst through the door. Jackie awoke with a gasp and scrambled to react, but she didn't have near the reflexes of her lover. Kane was on his feet in a flash, naked and bristling though he had no weapons against a stoneman brandishing a gun and wearing Kevlar.

Kevlar? Psycho Roman had adapted quick.

"Ares stop!" Kane said as he stepped protectively in front of her. "Can't you see she's no threat? We've tried and tried, and I am still stone. Leave her alone."

Damn. It hadn't worked even though they'd talked the night away in between bouts of intense lovemaking. They had done everything right, and she still hadn't had her moment of True Bliss. And now they'd run out of time.

Ares' lips peeled back into a semblance of a grin. "As long as she lives, you will still hope."

Good, thought Jackie. Though a second later she realized that meant she was about to die. Which really sucked.

She scrambled off the bed looking for a weapon of any sort. But they didn't have one except for her lungs. So she started to scream. "Help! Help! There's a madman here!"

Which is when the shooting started. She noticed the noise first. Loud and frightening. Nothing at all like on TV. And then she realized she'd stopped screaming, and though she thought she ought to be at the door by now, she found herself flattened against the wall.

She was terrified for Kane. He'd flung himself at Ares, and she saw blood on his beautiful body. God, Kane! She had to get up and go to him, but nothing worked right. She must have been stunned by the…

By the…

Oh shit. She'd been shot.

She looked down, surprised that she didn't hurt so much. One hit to the belly. That was bad. Another to her thigh. Not so good, but to the side. No pumping blood, so the artery wasn't cut. Very good.

Then her sense of sound came back. Or rather, she was able to distinguish individual sounds like grunts and punches and the crashing of furniture. The two men were grappling, the gun…she didn't know where. And Kane bellowing.

"Zeva! Zeva, I call you! Zeva!"

No. No, he couldn't give up trying. She wanted to say that, but her breath must have been knocked out of her when she landed against the wall. Only tiny breaths were coming and they…

Oh shit. That hurt.

She hurt a lot.

Damn, she was completely useless in a fight.

Which is when Allie walked in. Just sauntered in as if she hadn't a care in the world. Kane and Ares were rolling on the floor, slamming fists into each other, grappling and…hell, Jackie couldn't make sense of it. And worse, she couldn't get up to see or help or anything.

Then Allie stood in front of her, shaking her head in disgust. "Good lord, how hard can a moment of True Bliss be?"

Jackie blinked. "Pretty hard, apparently." That's what she wanted to say. Nothing really came out except a gasp. She didn't have the breath.

"You've got less than two minutes left before you die. The belly shot was bad. Knicked the renal artery and cut into your spine."

Oh shit. That was really bad.

"I can fix it."

She blinked and thought, what? Then a second later she thought, not me. Don't bother with me. Help Kane.

Allie crouched down and shook her head. "Can't help him. He's not my stoneman. But you could be."

What?

"I'm Alethia. One of the sisters. I can make you my stoneman. It'll fix you up now and give you greater strength in the future. Your first task will be to find Zeva's stonemen and free them. As many as you can, as quickly as you can. You won't be a statue. Decide quickly now before Zeva—"

"This is a messy situation here, isn't it?" another woman interrupted. Jackie couldn't move very well, but her gaze cut over to another figure stepping into the room. She was onyx black, shimmering cold and dark in the sunlight. Not stone exactly. More like metal that flowed some and crinkled some as she walked.

Zeva, she presumed.

"Making a stoneman, sister? Right in the middle of a fight? How intriguing."

Allie straightened. No. Her name was Alethia. She faced off with her sister and Jackie wondered where the family resemblance was. The onyx one with the sword was classically Greek with high cheekbones and lithe, muscular features. Alethia was just...Allie. Youngish, muscular, with rough features and nimble hands. Except that there was this aura of light around her. As if her very cells gave off a kind of iridescence.

"Pause them, will you?" Alethia said as she gestured at the men. "They're making it hard to hear."

The warrior sister looked at the men who were still crashing about the floor. Jackie couldn't see anything, but a chair was toppled, an end table broken, and the grunts were rather loud.

"I rather like the sound."

Of course she did. Bitch.

"Now, now," the woman said as she stepped over the fighting men to look down at Jackie. "Is that any way for a lady to think?"

Hell. They could hear her.

"Of course we can hear you, though I'm not sure why I bother." She squatted down right in front of Jackie. "I don't understand what he sees in you."

Maybe because you don't see people at all. You just see weapons.

Jackie had meant it as a sarcastic dig, but the goddess seemed to take her words at face value. She tilted her head and seemed to think about it. "Is there a difference?"

Yes.

"Well, I'm afraid you're not going to live long enough to explain the difference."

Oh shit. The bitch was right. She was cold and weak and getting fuzzier by the second. Decision time.

She looked at Alethia/Allie and dipped her chin in a nod. *I accept*, she thought as loud as she could.

But the warrior bitch lifted a finger. "Tut tut. Not so fast. There is the matter of the escape clause." Then she straightened and touched her finger to her chin. "Hmmm, what should it be?"

Obviously this was just a delay tactic. Wait until the human died from blood loss and then there wouldn't be any negotiation at all. Except Alethia hadn't been idle during her sister's conversation. She'd pulled out her backpack and lifted up some paste.

"Not yet," her sister called.

"Just to give us time to negotiate. That's within the rules. In fact, I believe you did that with at least three dozen of your stonemen."

The warrior bitch sniffed. "That was different."

"It was not." Then Alethia looked at Jackie. "Exhale as best you can."

Jackie didn't really have a choice. Time—and her blood—were slipping away too fast. So she exhaled, and as she blew out what air she had, Alethia threw the wad of goo straight at her belly.

It was like getting hit with a cannonball. If there had been any air left in her lungs, it went out in a whoosh while the paste hit her stomach and seemed to burrow through her entire body.

Then things began to stiffen up. Her belly. Her back. She tried to straighten away from it. A natural reaction to the horror of what was happening, but nothing moved. Nothing even rippled. It was hard and painful, and if she had the breath, she would have screamed. But she didn't. She couldn't.

And bit by bit she turned to stone.

Her mind was screaming. Every part of her was horrified. And the pain just went on and on. Oh God, oh God, she was stone!

Alethia watched, her expression bored, but Zeva rolled her eyes. "They always say the same thing: Oh God, the pain. The pain. Yawn." She turned to her sister. "They are so weak. I spend years training the sniveling out of them."

Alethia crouched down until she was eye to eye with Jackie. "Do you accept?"

Zeva put a hand on her sister's shoulder. "I haven't given the escape clause."

Her sister didn't even look. "So create one. Or have you gotten so indecisive that this is beyond you?"

"Ha. Fine. Here it is: Go a year without freeing a single one of my stonemen." She sniffed. "Shouldn't be too hard."

Jackie knew she ought to think deeper about this. She knew it wasn't a good idea to negotiate like this, but she'd caught a flash of Kane and Ares. They both looked horrible. Bloody, wounded, staggering and gasping for breath. She might have held out if Kane had the upper hand, but it didn't look that way. Kane was naked. Ares had that Kevlar. And the bastard had just thrown Kane against the television which shattered beneath him.

Yes! Yes, I agree!

She felt the magic take hold. Damn, she felt it expand like an oil slick through her body. Every cell was coated in it and suffocating beneath the stuff. It was worse than dying and she screamed through every hideous second. But in the end, she felt her body heal.

Her leg stopped throbbing. Her belly seemed to solidify in a good way, as if knitting the pieces together. And a moment later…breath.

Whole breath.

She was not stone anymore, but healthy and strong.

She shot up to her feet and threw herself forward. She didn't know how to fight. She'd never thrown a punch in her entire life. But she knew how to jump onto a bad guy's back and wrench him away from Kane.

Ares batted at her, but she'd caught him by surprise. She had hold of his head and was wrenching it backwards as hard as she could. If she was lucky, she'd snap his neck.

But at that moment, Kane got his breath back. She saw his eyes widen in horror—nothing but horror would have him make that face—and then he screamed.

"Zeva! I wish to negotiate! Zeva, now!"

The metal warrior released a sigh. "Oh, very well. For the moment." With a wave of her hand, Ares stopped fighting. Kane too stilled. Oh shit, they were both hardening into stone. The only one who could still move, except for the goddesses, was Jackie. And though she suddenly felt stronger than an ox, she still wasn't going to haul off this guy's head. Not when he'd turned to marble.

"Shit," she said as she slid off the thing's back. Then she looked around. There had to be a weapon somewhere. A piece of furniture. Something to knock his head off. After all, he was vulnerable as a statue, right?

"Come on, come on," Zeva said. "This is getting tedious."

Strangely enough, the statue of Kane could still speak and he did so with a rasping grind of sound. "I will stop using my three days. I will stop trying to free myself. I will do this if you leave Jacqueline alone."

Jackie's head snapped up from where she'd grabbed a piece of the busted end table. "No! No, you can't!"

"Hush!" Alethia snapped and suddenly the breath froze in Jackie's chest. She couldn't speak. She couldn't make a sound. And the shock of that robbed her sense for a moment as she realized she had no true control over her body. None at all!

Meanwhile, Alethia was stepping toward Kane. "Why would you do that? Why would you give up your salvation for her?"

Zeva huffed. "Because these mortals are idiots. Besides," she said as she waved to Jackie. "She's a stoneman now. She's fair game. I can kill her whenever I want."

Alethia shot her sister a glare. "You can try."

Kane's face crumpled. Jackie would have sobbed if she could. She never wanted to cause him pain, but here it was. A huge cluster fuck, and all she'd ever wanted to do was make it easier on him.

"Why?" Alethia pressed. "Why do you offer your salvation for her?"

Kane looked at Jackie, his entire posture defeated. "Because I love you. Because you gave me hope and brought laughter back into my life. You reminded me what it was like to see the sunlight and eat a fine meal. Because when I am with you, I believe in such wonderful things. But mostly, I believe in you. In your strength and your goodness when there has been none around me for so long. Because I like the way you smile and the mole on your right hip. Because of a thousand different little things that tell me you are the most special woman in the world. And I would do anything to keep your light alive in this world. If not for me, then for someone else. For anyone. Because I love you."

Then there was a sound. A noise that was inaudible, but felt nonetheless. A bell perhaps. A crystal clear vibration that began quiet but then built stronger, clearer, and so pristine it brought tears to her eyes even as it rattled her teeth.

They all heard it.

They all felt it.

And then Zeva began to curse.

But that was nothing compared to the shock and elation that shimmered through Kane's entire body. He was still beautifully naked, so Jackie saw the entire thing. Flesh became golden with light. What had been pale marble before now grew flushed with color.

He gasped.

He dropped to his knees.

And then he looked at her.

"Thank you," he whispered.

What? What had just happened?

Alethia answered. "You had your moment of True Bliss. He is free."

"But she is not," Zeva spat. Then she glared at Ares. "Kill her."

Which is when the shit hit the fan. Or more accurately, security showed up at the door brandishing weapons and barking orders.

Alethia grimaced and looked at Jackie. "Take his hand."

Jackie hadn't even processed the command, but her hand shot out anyway and gripped Kane's. Then the goddess waved her hand at her sister.

"Ta ta!"

And they faded out.

The last thing Jackie saw was Ares leaping at her. He could likely have snapped her neck in a second, but the world—including him—disappeared only to reform in...

In...

Another hotel room?

WTF?

"We're just down the street," Alethia answered. "I couldn't take you far. We've already risked too much, and you're going to have to control your screaming. What were you thinking getting humans involved?"

Jackie glared at the goddess. "That a madman was attacking the love of my life."

"Well that's my first command. Learn how to fight and not scream for help." She looked at Kane. "Are you willing to be her curator?"

His hand tightened on hers. "Goddess please, you cannot—"

Alethia waved him to silence. "Cease prattling. I will not release her."

Kane bit his lip, his head dipping. "Yes," he said softly. "Yes, I will devote my life to keeping her safe."

"Good. Because there isn't much time left. You heard Ares, did you not? Zeva is close to winning."

"Wait," Jackie said. "Winning what? Winning how?"

Alethia huffed out a breath. "Second command: Get smarter. The one with the most interesting and capable stonemen at the end of the Earth wins."

Beside her Kane sucked in a breath. "She has many stonemen."

"Yes. I believe she thinks she can win inside of a year."

Jackie frowned. "That's why she made my escape clause only a year."

Alethia nodded. "I believe so, yes."

"But the Earth isn't about to end. It's…Oh." It wasn't about to end. Unless some stoneman decided to blow it up.

Holy shit.

"So this is all a big game to you? Earth is just a playing field?"

Alethia shot her an annoyed look. "I said get smarter, not state the obvious."

Jackie had no response to that. She was still coming to grips with all of this. She was a stoneman now. A pawn in a mystical fight for Earth? Or rather to destroy Earth? Oh hell.

Kane stepped forward, moving protectively in front Jackie. It was a ridiculous move. He was human now with all the human weaknesses, right? And besides he was facing off with a goddess. But he didn't back down and when he spoke, his words were strong and hard.

"What do you wish of her?"

"I already told her. She's to unmake Zeva's stonemen."

Jackie frowned. "Unmake?"

"Find their escape clause. Get them free. Lower her numbers."

Obviously this confused Kane. He paused and his head tilted slightly as he looked at Alethia. "That is how she is to serve you?"

"Yes!" Alethia was becoming more Allie by the second. Whereas before she'd seemed suffused with light, now her skin was duller. Quieter. More human. Made it a little easier to talk to her.

Jackie felt her shoulders ease down as she began to process that the danger was gone. "So, I'm not going to be stuck on a pedestal or anything? Turned into a statue?"

"Do you want a pedestal? It would make it easier for Zeva's stonemen to find you. And make it harder for you to free them."

"Um, no thanks. I'm happy as…" Well, not really quite as she was, but then again, being able to heal at will had its advantages. "So you want me to free the others."

Allie rolled her eyes. "I've turned an idiot."

"No, no, I've got it. I just…I thought this was a bad thing. Being a stoneman and all. I thought…" She looked at Kane. She thought she'd given up everything to help him, but it turned out that…"I can stay with him?"

"You will not survive without him."

That was probably true. She looked at Kane who was smiling at her. "We can be together," she said.

"Yes," he answered.

She stepped forward. They hadn't let go of their hands, but now she moved into the crook of his arm. "I love you, Kane. I have from almost the very beginning."

"And I have waited over two hundred years for you, Jacqueline. I love you with everything I have and more. I will keep you safe. I will teach you how to fight. We will save the Earth from Zeva—"

She kissed him, hard and deep. She pressed her mouth to his and held on to every part of him. He was warm and alive and so very human it made her want to laugh and cry at once. Instead she just kissed him for a very long time.

And when they separated she touched his cheek. "Just keep saying we."

"We."

"I love you."

"I love you."

It was some time before they realized the goddess was gone. That they were alone in another hotel room. And that they had quite a lot to do in the hunt for Zeva's stonemen.

Which they would start soon.

After a little time in bed.

And in the shower.

And in every way that was pleasurable for a very long time.

EPILOGUE

James looked up from his computer to see his father finishing yet another glass of brandy as he stared at Kane's empty pedestal. He was doing what the men in his family always did: they brooded. It was rather irritating.

Fortunately, James had inherited his mother's more fiery temperament. He laughed easily, was prone to unreserved fits of temper, and could charm even the most stoic family member into a smile. Except for his father this morning.

The man had spent the night drinking and staring at the pedestal. The women from the Saturnalia had been sent home. Fortunately, thanks to the "footmen" hired for the three day event, they had all left in good, if not quite sober, humor. All that was left was for Kane to return to his statue form for another year.

It was almost routine, though in all James' life, Kane had never left the grounds before, much less gone to London. He'd never singled out an individual woman before. And most important, he'd never smiled as James had seen him do that morning of the picnic.

That morning before it had all gone to shit and his father had gone to the bottle. James, of course, had gone to the internet to research all he could find out about curators and what happened to them when the statues were harmed.

He was halfway down another internet rabbit hole when he heard his father gasp. He looked up and didn't at first understand what had happened. Everything looked the same to him. But his father was staring at the floor...

No, not the floor. The empty space where the pedestal usually sat. Except the thing was gone. Gone? But that meant...

"He's done it," his father whispered. Then the man leaped to his feet. "He's done it! He's given that dodgy American woman her bliss!"

James pushed to his feet, walking with his father to where the pedestal should have been. "Are you sure?" he asked, though it was a stupid question. His father was no more sure than James was. But that was pretty sure.

In all the centuries, there were only a few recorded stories of a stoneman regaining freedom. And in one of those stories was the mention that the pedestal disappeared. Gone. Because it wasn't needed anymore.

His father grinned and started dancing around in a circle, weaving and waving about more from the brandy than any glee. Still, James couldn't resist joining the man.

Kane free at last. The family, free of the thrice-cursed Saturnalias. The unending pile of gold in the basement likely ended now as well, but that didn't matter. They had enough assets. Two centuries of accumulation from an unending source will do that for a family.

And now they were finally, absolutely, wonderfully free!

"How dare you dance, mortal?" A woman's acid voice cut through the room.

James spun to a stop. His father was less graceful, but he managed to grab the back of a chair before toppling over completely.

"My lady Zeva," his father whispered. Then he awkward dropped into a bow. "Goddess, we greet you."

James lifted his chin. Immortal or insanely powerful made no difference. He would not cower before this bitch who imprisoned men as statues. He had talked with Kane over the years. He knew what she did to her men, and he would not bow to her. However, he was not so bold as to stare into her eyes. He kept his head up, but his gaze down. And what he saw was a woman made of shimmering black metal and garbed as an Amazon.

Also, she was impossibly beautiful. Appropriate to a goddess, but he had not expected a warrior queen to be so…feminine.

"You greet me?" she hissed. "You greet me when my stoneman was injured in your care?"

His father's chin shot up. "It was not my fault!" he cried. "Kane was attacked." He took a wobbly step forward. "He was attacked by your order."

"You think that makes any difference?"

It should. It would in a sane world. But they had left the realm of sane two hundred years ago.

"Goddess," his father said, dropping to his knees. James wasn't sure if that was deference, drunkenness, or simple terror. "Kane is released. No harm has come from the attack. All is well!"

James winced. That was not the thing to say to a goddess who had just lost a warrior. From her perspective, all was not well.

"Insolent! Ignorant! Idiot!" the woman screamed. And in her hand grew fireballs glowing white hot. The heat was blistering from across the room. His father was a bare three feet away, and his pate gleamed wet with sweat.

"Forgiveness, Goddess! Have mercy! I did my best!"

She raised her arms—two fireballs burning white hot— and James knew a moment of true panic. His father was about to be incinerated right in front of his eyes.

"No!" he cried. "No, you're not allowed!"

The goddess turned, her eyes black pools that trained on him. "You dare question me?"

"The rules," he said. After all, he'd spent most of the last twenty-four hours pouring over the rules of the stonemen and their keepers. "They say you can't harm the curator."

Well, not exactly. They said that she could visit exactly the same punishment on the curator as happened to the stoneman. He was hoping that...what? That she wouldn't know the rules to her own game? That was a faint hope, but it was all he had.

Her eyes narrowed and her lip curled in disgust. "At least you're not a sniveler." She collapsed her fingers into fists. The fireballs disappeared in a puff of acrid smoke. "What was it then? Shotgun?"

In her hand appeared a shotgun. The exact same make and model as had been used against Kane. He knew because he'd asked Kane for details. She lifted the gun, inspected it from all sides, and then aimed it directly at his father.

"Once in the back, once in the leg, correct?"

James swallowed. What could he say except for lies? "I'm not sure that's the right weapon."

Her lips curled. "It is."

"And maybe it was only one shot. In the leg."

"Two. Do you think I cannot see what happened right now?" She looked to the side, her gaze going abstract. Apparently she was replaying the attack somehow in her mind. "Two shots."

"What if I offered a bargain instead?" He couldn't believe he said the words. Certainly he had thought of it. He had known it might come to it. But he hadn't thought he'd have the courage.

Except he did.

And now the goddess was dropping her weapon and turning to look at him.

"What bargain?"

"You have lost Kane, yes?"

Her answer was a low feral growl. No wait, that wasn't from her. Suddenly on the other side of him was the largest, meanest, most magnificent wolfhound he'd ever seen. Black fur, red eyes, and dripping fangs as it stalked around him. Bloody hell that was unnerving.

"I'll...um...I'll take that as a yes." His voice wasn't as strong as he wanted. In truth, he was shaking like a leaf, but he locked his knees and concentrated. He needed to make the best bargain possible or they were both dead.

"Bargain quickly mortal," Zeva said, though the words could have come from the wolfhound. It was hard to tell when spoken so low and threatening.

"Um, I could take his place. Spare my father. I'll serve you for…um…twenty years?" The number make him wince. Twenty years would put him in his fifties when he was done.

"Kane owes me nearly ten thousand."

Right. "You've already lost him. This is my bargain."

Her lips curled. "There is fire in you."

Felt more like bile. "I'll make an excellent warrior."

"Perhaps," she said with a slow curve of her lips. "What other skills do you have?"

"Computer skills. I'm a programmer, actually. Make video games and the like." Probably not useful for a warrior.

"Are you good at it? Are you unique?"

Ah. That was part of the game. The goddesses were trying to get as many unique stonemen as possible.

"I'm very good. I've already sold a dozen apps, one of which just sold for a million pounds." Give or take a few hundred.

Her head shifted and to see the metal crinkle like that made him think he was dreaming. Or watching a computerized fantasy. Either way, the shift in reality unsettled him. Or perhaps it was because the wolfhound was so close he could feel the heat from the beast's foul breath as it scorched through his jeans. Hellhound? he wondered.

"A thousand years." She arched her brow. "A bargain."

He swallowed. "A month off each year."

"No."

He swallowed. "A week then. An insane warrior is of no use to you."

She and the beast laughed at the same time. Hyena-like snorts on the one side, nails on the chalkboard on the other. Both sounds made his spine tighten in horror.

"I have hundreds of insane warriors. I assure you, they are very useful."

"A week," he repeated. "Every year."

She snapped her fingers and spoke to the air. "Lalia, we are making stonemen today. Care to play?"

A woman in a tight business suit appeared. Her hair was in a bun and her eyes were luminous behind the glasses. She had a book in her hand. A paperback with…A romance novel? She looked up in irritation.

"I am busy."

"I have an offer." Zeva gestured to James. "A thousand years and a day off each year."

"Two weeks," James corrected.

She laughed and ignored him. "What escape clause do you give?"

The new goddess looked at him, her expression bored. Then her gaze narrowed in on his father, still crouched there, but trembling now as the wolfhound had gone to inspect him.

"What has he to do with it?" she asked.

"He is the doomed father. The son offers to serve so I do not put holes in his worthless father."

"Really?" The new goddess stomped over to his father and jerked him to his feet with a rough grab to his arm. "You would sacrifice your son?"

"N-no," his father said, his gaze rolling about in his head. But eventually, he landed on James. "No. Don't."

James didn't look away. It was a son's duty to protect his father.

Lalia dropped his arm and stepped with clicking high heels over to James. "You would do this? Sacrifice to prevent an old man's death. Is that love?"

Love. Duty. Words scrolled through his thoughts, and they included things like adventure and nobility.

"Yes," he finally said. "It is love."

"Hmmm." She turned to her sister. "How did you find a man of honor?"

Zeva shrugged. "This family has always been interesting."

"Very well. Here is the out clause." She looked back to James. "You must break another one's spirit." She smiled.

"For a man of honor, that will be hard. Unless, of course, you are not so honorable after all."

James swallowed. He hadn't thought he would be given such a choice. To break a soul? That was repulsive!

"There you go," Zeva said as she threw the shotgun up in the air. It went up, up, and disappeared. Then she slapped her hands together. "One gone, one gotten. All in all a disappointing day."

She pointed at James.

"A thousand years. Three days off a year. And in that time, you may try to break someone's soul. Do you agree?" Her smile was chilling. "Or do I bring the shotgun back?"

"I agree." God, he'd said it. He'd made the bargain.

To the side, a pedestal appeared. Large and dark, this one made of onyx black metal.

So fast. It was happening so fast. Had he really just promised a thousand years?

"I am broken!" his father cried. "Don't take my son. I am broken."

Both goddesses turned to him, but it was Lalia who spoke. "You are a coward and no fit father." Then she snapped her fingers and winked out.

Then it was James' turn. He felt the cold begin. His toes and fingers first. Stiffening, chilling, growing numb in expanding waves toward his torso and spine. He cried out. It was the pain of cold so horrifying it seized everything.

He would have screamed if he had breath, but there was nothing. No air. No sound. Just pain.

And then he was walking. Step after step, each more grating than the last. Like stone rolling inevitably toward his pedestal.

No!

The goddess pronounced his doom.

"Training first," she ordered. "If you are still sane after that, we will study together how to break a person's soul."

The End

MADE FLESH

The Stone Men Series

Anna Argent

CHAPTER 1

A fter tonight's date, Sue Sullivan was certain that bad boys, like wild animals, were best viewed at a distance. Preferably from behind bars.

She stripped out of her wrinkled dress where her date Eddie's questing hands had left their mark. It was bad enough that he'd pawed at her. It was even worse that he'd been sure she'd enjoyed it, all the way to the point where she'd nearly run from his car to get behind the solid wood of her front door.

Sue shuddered and washed away the remains of her bad date in her deep clawfoot tub. It was the only saving grace of this rundown farmhouse she'd inherited. Well, that, and the seven-and-a-half foot tall stone sculpture of a naked man that stood proudly in her living room.

Despite how out of place the monument was amongst the peeling paint and creaky floorboards, she had to admit Mr. Dalton Thatcher was a tasty bit of eye candy.

The rest of the farmhouse had a mile-long list of serious repairs needed—a list she'd unfortunately also inherited. Still, there was something comforting about knowing that this home had stood for over a hundred years, sheltering generation after generation. Just because the roof leaked now didn't mean it always would. And as creaky and sagging as the floors were, she was so used to the sounds the house made, she often had trouble sleeping anywhere else.

There was charm and history here, somewhere behind the crooked walls, faulty plumbing and ancient wiring. When she was done renovating, the previous beauty of the old farmhouse would once again be restored.

Sue forced herself out of the warm water and into a bathrobe. Cold drafts licked around her bare ankles, hurrying her steps as she went to settle in front of the fire downstairs with a glass of wine and her laptop.

The computer wasn't nearly the kind of company she'd hoped for tonight, but at least it kept her lap warm, if nothing else.

She logged into the chat room she frequented, and immediately, a video image of Charlotte Tanni popped up on her screen requesting a chat.

Charlotte's hair was cobalt blue with blazing orange streaks. She wore enough jewelry to strain the tendons in her slender neck, but Sue guessed that was a professional hazard. As a jewelry artist specializing in mixed-media creations, Charlotte was always trying out her wares to make sure they stood up to the test of daily use before she sold each new line.

Tonight, every one of her fourteen ear piercings sported a different style of earring. Her neck was draped with enough chain, cord and leather to be considered an homage to Mr. T. Her wrists were adorned with at least a dozen bracelets, and each of her fingers sparkled with no fewer than two rings. It was a wonder the woman could still type.

Sue accepted the video chat and braced herself.

"You're home early," said Charlotte. "Bad date, huh? I told you he wasn't good enough for you, but did you listen? No. Of course, not. You never listen. Here I am, your assigned mentor and guardian in your new life as a curator, and you don't even have the sense to listen to a word I say."

"Perhaps because there are so many of them to choose from," said Sue.

"Ha ha. Very funny. You're like some kind of freakin' comedian or something. So go ahead, make me laugh. Tell me just how bad it was. Go ahead, tell me."

"Horrible," Sue admitted. "Eddie was all over me, pawing at me. Which was bad enough, but since he's a mechanic, the grease imbedded in his fingerprints left stains on my black dress."

"Which black dress? You have three."

"I *had* four. Now I have three."

"You need to stop it with the bad boys. I keep telling you this, but you never listen. What part of *mentor* don't you get?"

"You're not even old enough to drink legally. Why in the world would they have assigned you as my mentor?"

"For your information, I'm twenty-three. And when it comes to curator years, I'm way older than you. Accept it. I'm your Yoda."

"My uncle's will gave me no choice but to accept your interference in my life. But you're only my mentor when it comes to…that." Sue's gaze slipped past her screen to the statue watching her.

It really was a beautiful piece of art. Dense, sinewy muscles hugged tight to a large, sturdy frame of bones, all covered by smooth, taut skin. She swore she could even see each individual hair along his forearms, as if the sculptor had chiseled them one at a time.

His face was a study of masculine angles, but his expression perplexed her. The statues she'd seen before always seemed stoic, relaxed.

Mr. Thatcher's expression was anything but.

He seemed fierce. Perhaps frustrated. Maybe a little sad. There was no peace in his face anywhere, and Sue had often stroked his cheek as if she could magically help him find some.

Of course it never made the statue feel better, but it certainly gave her fingers a little tactile thrill every time she touched him.

She could have had an even bigger thrill if she'd let her fingers stray lower. As it was, she'd had to cover his...endowments so as not to be constantly distracted by them. A trip to the craft store had earned her the largest leaf they had. Between that and a sturdy strip of tape, she'd covered Mr. Thatcher enough to give her no improper reason to stare.

Charlotte's chrome-colored fingernail tapped on her desk. "He's a man, Sue. Not a thing. You need to stop pretending otherwise."

"*It* is a chunk of stone, carved by a skilled hand. Nothing more. And no set of children's tales are going to change my mind or the laws of physics."

"You're going to hurt his feelings."

"Stone has no feelings."

Charlotte sighed in frustration. "Have you read the manual I sent you yet?"

"The one telling me all the rules about how to behave when the statue comes to life? No, sorry. I've been too busy trying to find a life out here in the Middle of Nowhere, Nebraska."

"It's important, Sue. You need to know the rules. What if your stoneman were to come to life right now? What would you do?"

"Assume Eddie drugged my wine so he could get under my skirt."

"You have to take this seriously. It's part of the job."

"My only job is at the law firm."

"What would your uncle say?" asked Charlotte.

A streak of sadness wove through Sue. "Uncle Herman is gone. He was a sweet man to leave me his entire estate, but just because he believed some crazy story doesn't mean I should, too."

"You promised. When you signed the papers, you promised to take care of his house and take over his duties as curator. Part of that is reading the damn file I sent you. I really don't think it's too much to ask. And even if it is, so what? It's not like you have anything better to do tonight."

"Ouch," said Sue. "That was a low blow."

"So was what you said about Dalton not having feelings. You may not care about these men, but I do. I bet you haven't even looked him up in the archives to see why he's standing in your living room, have you? Well, I have, and he was a good man. Noble, even. He was from humble beginnings, but he worked hard and built that farmhouse you're living in with his own two hands, and he did it so his wife-to-be would have a place to call home. He had to fight and work for everything he had—the way real men did back in the day. I can't believe you won't even find the time to learn about the man who put a roof over your head."

"I've been a little busy trying to keep said roof from caving in on my head. Did you know that everyone around here thinks this place is haunted? No one wants to come do the repairs I need done."

"They must all sense Dalton's spirit."

Sue couldn't help but snort. "Please."

"I'm serious. You may not have seen Dalton turn to flesh, but I'm sure the folks around there remember him making an appearance. Even if, like you, they're too skeptical to consider something beyond what they can see. At least their heads aren't so far up their asses that they can't look around."

"I believe in logic. I believe in art so beautiful it defies description. I do not, however, believe that a block of stone can animate. That is why I never should have been chosen for this job. It's ridiculous."

"You'll believe everything when it happens. Let's just hope that by then you've read the rules and it's not too late."

"I'm fairly certain I'll be fine. As long as I don't accept dates from any more bad boys."

Charlotte let out a sad sigh. "I hope so. I'd hate to lose you the way we did Theresa."

A little tremor of unease shook just beneath Sue's skin. "Who's Theresa?"

"She was a skeptic, too. Didn't believe her stoneman would animate. One night he did. She freaked. Got in his way and tried to stop him from leaving. I think she was more worried about what the neighbors would think about a strange naked man strolling out of her house than she was about her own safety. Sadly, she hadn't read the rules, either. She didn't know that standing between a stoneman and the objective he's ordered to accomplish could kill her."

"What happened?"

"Her neck was crushed. Best guess was he picked her up and flung her aside so he could pass."

"So, what you're saying is that some murderer is walking around free because this poor woman's death was blamed on a statue? That's insane."

"Anthony has big hands. There was no mistaking what happened. The cops could find no leads, so the case is still considered unsolved. We curators know the truth, though."

"Oh, for heaven's sake. This is silly. I'm going to bed."

Charlotte leaned toward the camera, making the pendants around her neck jingle like a giant ring of keys. "Read the manual, Sue. I mean it. Don't be an idiot."

"The only idiotic thing I've done recently is to think I could cure my boredom in this town by dating a bad boy. Lesson learned."

"You have my number, right? I'm only a few hours' drive away. If you need me, call, okay?"

"I'm not going to need you, but thank you for the offer."

Charlotte's slender shoulders lifted on a heavy sigh. "I worry about you. Your whole life has been uprooted. You had to find a new job, move across the country. I know you loved your uncle, but the transition can't be easy. You need to let me help you."

Sue's heart warmed, and she let it come through in her smile. "You're sweet. It's why I put up with your nonsense. Now go play with your blowtorch or whatever it is you do for fun."

"Night, Sue. RTFM." *Read the fucking manual*.

"Fine. I will. It'll be worth it just to get you off my back."

Sue disconnected the chat and printed out the stupid file Charlotte had sent her weeks ago, right after Sue had moved in. She refilled her glass and curled up under a heavy blanket on the couch.

From here she had a fantastic view of the fire, as well as the statue flanking it. The golden glow flickered across his glossy contours, making him even more beautiful than he was in daylight.

She wasn't sure how that was possible, but the proof—all seven-and-a-half feet of it—was right there.

She stared at him for a long time, wondering who he'd been. The carving at the base stated his name. Dalton Thatcher, 1832-1856. Below that was a single name scrawled in curling script. She assumed it was the sculptor, Pyrenia.

There were no visible tool marks. If not for the fact that the statue obviously had to be cut from stone, Sue would have thought it had been molded from clay and smoothed to perfection by skilled hands.

Talk about a labor of love. She could just imagine how much fun it would be to run her hands over a form like that, shaping each intriguing detail to match her deepest fantasies.

Another draft blew through the room, making the leaf over Mr. Thatcher's impressive endowments lift for a second. That second was long enough for her to get a glimpse of his masculine glory and make her wish she could find a good man nearby.

Sue really missed sex.

She could try to pretend that her social life had taken a turn for the worse since moving to a town one-tenth the size she was used to, but the sad truth was, she had no more dates before than she did now. She wasn't flashy enough to catch the eye of most men, and the ones who did look were often married men suffering from a midlife crisis.

No, thanks.

The farmhouse lights flickered. Another draft swept through, making the fire spark and flare brighter. A moment later, there was a hard knock at her front door.

Sue cinched the tie on her robe tighter and peered through the front window.

Eddie stood there, head bowed apologetically. His black leather jacket gleamed under her porch light, showing off a pair of wide shoulders that had sucked her into her bad decision to accept a date with him in the first place.

Sue put on her stern face and opened the door just enough to let him see her glare. "What do you want?"

The smell of booze wafted through the opening. "I want to apologize. I shouldn't have groped you like that."

"No, you shouldn't have."

"I feel really bad about it. Can I come in so we can talk?"

"I'm not dressed. You should just go. Apology accepted."

"I'm the only mechanic around. A fancy girl like you isn't going to change her own oil. It's a small town. We're bound to run into each other. I don't want it to be awkward. Please, it'll only take a second."

It was the earnest look of contrition on his face that won her over. "Okay, but just for a second."

She opened the door wider to let him in. He passed her, and she shut the cold air out behind him. Not that it made much difference as drafty as the house was.

Eddie scrubbed a hand over his head and gave her a sheepish grin. "This isn't at all the kind of place I expected you to live in."

"It's not my usual taste, but I'm learning to love it. I don't suppose you know any handymen who aren't afraid of ghosts, do you?"

He frowned. "Ghosts?"

"Yes. Apparently no one wants to work on the house because they think it's haunted."

"Not haunted," he said, nodding his head toward the statue. "It's that guy. People around here swear they've seen him over the years, walking around town."

"That's ridiculous."

"Yeah, well those are the kinds of stories we grow up with around here. Dalton's like our own headless horseman."

"Isn't there anyone who isn't afraid of him?"

Eddie stepped closer. "I'm not. Maybe I can help you fix the place up."

"You'd do that?" she asked.

"Sure. For a girl like you, I'd do just about anything."

Maybe Eddie wasn't as bad a boy as she'd first thought.

She couldn't help the smile of relief that touched her mouth. "I can pay, of course."

He put his hands on her shoulders and closed the distance between them. "Baby, I'd never take your cash. But there are things you do have that I want."

Sue's instincts kicked in. She tried to shrug him off, but his hold on her was too tight. "You should go."

He backed her up until the drafty wall hit her butt. "I think I should stay. Tomorrow we can talk about repairs. Tonight we're not going to do much talking at all."

He lowered his head to kiss her.

"No!" Sue shoved against him as hard as she could. She turned her face away, straining her neck to get out of the path of his mouth.

In an instant, he turned feral. His grip tightened until it was painful, and he shook her hard enough her head bounced against the wall. Dust rained down on them, along with small chunks of plaster.

His eyes lit with a kind of dark excitement, and she knew she was in trouble—the kind she wasn't equipped to handle alone and unarmed.

There were no neighbors within screaming distance. Her phone was on the other side of the room. It might as well have been miles away. In the last few seconds of him manhandling her, it was clear that she was physically outmatched.

The only chance she had was to outsmart him.

"A friend of mine is on the way over," she lied.

"Bullshit. You're not dressed for company. It's just you and me, baby."

"I don't want this. I want you to go. Now."

"No, you want me. I saw it in your eyes all night." His flammable breath hit her dead on, making her gag.

Sue clawed at his arms, but his leather protected him. "Leave. Now. Or I call the police."

He laughed. "Baby, by the time the cops get all the way out here, we'll be done. You know you want this. Besides, who do you think the cops in this town will believe? A man they've known all their life or some prissy city girl who just wandered in?"

"No!" she screamed. "The answer is no!"

He looked down at her, his eyes empty. "I didn't ask."

Fear coalesced in her gut like an icy tornado. Her lungs seized. Her blood froze solid.

He shoved her face to the side and started kissing her neck while he groped her breasts. Sue pushed as hard as she could, working to put just enough room between them so that she could kick him in the balls.

Nothing worked. He was too strong, too determined. She had no weapons, no way to call for help. Screaming would only sap her strength, and likely excite him further.

She knew what was going to happen. She could see it play out through the cracks in the denial hardening over her.

Eddie was going to rape her.

Sue's head was pinned in place. Dalton's statue filled her vision. She saw him waver within her tears. The firelight shifted across his body, giving him the illusion of motion.

She reached behind her on the wall, searching for some kind of weapon. All she could find was a single framed black-and-white photo of the farmhouse when it had been new and shiny.

Without remorse, Sue pulled the historic photo from the nail and smashed it over Eddie's head.

Glass spilled down over both of them, slicing shallow cuts wherever it passed. He lifted his head and gave her a look that promised revenge.

"Nice try, but a few little scratches are all part of the fun," he said. "You should use your fingernails next. I dig that."

His knee shoved between her thighs. Terror gripped her in its frigid, bony hands, stealing the last wisp of her breath. Her vision started to sparkle as she struggled to get enough oxygen.

She must have passed out or something, because the next thing she knew, she was dreaming. Dalton's body started to move. He stepped down off the stone platform and, with a bellow of rage, charged.

CHAPTER 2

Frustration coursed through Dalton as he stood frozen, forced to watch the lovely Miss Sullivan try desperately to fend off her attacker. His curse held him immobile unless and until her safety was at risk. It didn't matter that he could see her fate coming for her. It didn't matter that he knew exactly how disastrous a decision it had been for her to let that good-for-nothing horse's ass in the door.

All that mattered were the rules. His contract forbade him from interfering unless his curator was in immediate danger.

As she was now.

Energy raced over his body, trickling in like warm rain. He willed the process to hurry the hell up, before it was too late. The chilly stiffness that was his constant companion melted away, and his limbs became fluid and mobile once again. Every time it happened—every time his stone form was made flesh—he could hardly believe he'd ever felt so good. So alive.

The instant he was free from his stone prison, able to move, he did.

He grabbed her attacker by the back of his neck and squeezed hard enough to gain the man's attention. Once he had that, the man tried to take a swing.

Dalton let him.

The man's fist hit Dalton's jaw, and the sound of finger bones cracking was unmistakable. Before the leather-clad no-good had finished squealing in pain like a piglet, Dalton picked him up and flung him out through the front door, onto his car.

The hood of the car crumpled under the man's impact. He lay still, unmoving.

Dalton turned toward his curator.

Fear and tears stained her pretty face. He'd spent hours staring at her, watching her move through the room that served as his permanent home. With her arrival, some of the boredom he faced had lifted for the first time in decades, leaving him feeling almost lucky.

What man got to view such a beautiful sight each day? What man got to watch a woman like her move and smell her skin? What man was blessed with the sound of her voice as she sang a tune while she worked in the kitchen?

He knew such luxury wouldn't last. Miss Sullivan wasn't cut out for the job of curator—she didn't even believe he was a real man—but he was determined to enjoy her presence in his life for as long as it lasted.

There were no guarantees that his next curator would be as kind and lovely as she was. Not all stonemen were so lucky.

Miss Sullivan's hair had been pinned up for her bath. He'd been able to smell the scent of vanilla and lavender clinging to her as she'd come down the stairs. It was a scent he'd learned to love within days of her arrival.

Her skin had been pink and dewy from the bath, and the fine, dark hairs at the nape of her neck had curled into damp ringlets. All he'd been able to think about at the time was how much he wanted to nuzzle that skin and find out just how sweet she would taste.

The fight had pulled her hair free of its moorings, letting it cascade over her shoulders in a tangled brown wave. Dalton wanted to touch it so badly he had to curl his fingers into a fist to keep from doing just that.

In his stone form he could see, hear, smell and feel, but his sense of touch was so rarely stimulated.

Except when she stroked his cheek.

He ached for those moments when her fingertips would trail across his flesh and give him the heat of her body. It reminded him of a glimpse of sunlight in the middle of winter, precious for its fleeting nature. As that warmth lingered along the surface of his stone form, he could almost remember what it was like to be a real man. The feeling was both glorious and sad because he knew it would end all too soon.

She stared up at him now, disbelief plain in her warm brown eyes. Her robe tie had come loose enough that he could see a pale line of smooth skin running down between her breasts. Curled up on the floor like she was, all it would take was one stout draft for him to see just how pretty she was below the tie of her robe.

Dalton's mouth watered.

He'd been subjected to so much naked flesh and hedonism he thought nothing could arouse him anymore.

He'd been wrong.

Disbelief strained her tone. "You're…real."

"Of course I am. Aren't you my curator?"

"Um. Yes. But…"

"Then why do you sound so surprised? Your friend told you I was alive. Your life was at risk. It was my duty to act." He crouched in front of her, moving slowly so he wouldn't give her more of a fright.

A fake green leaf fell to the floor between his feet—the one she'd taped over him to protect his modesty. She didn't know that after all these decades, nudity was so common for him he hardly thought about it.

Miss Sullivan, however, did. Her eyes widened and her face flushed.

"Are you hurt?" he asked, reaching to help her up. "Do I need to call a doctor?"

She blinked a few times, staring at his outstretched hand like she didn't know what to do with it.

Maybe her skull had gotten rattled harder than he thought. Maybe that's why he hadn't yet turned back to stone the way he would once the danger had passed.

Fearing the worst, Dalton lifted her onto the couch, being careful not to untie her robe the rest of the way. No telling what he'd do if that happened.

Lose his head. Settle it between her thighs for a long, slow feast.

He could imagine how much she'd hate that on the heels of her jackass date's advances.

Time to lock his desires away, where they wouldn't cause her any distress.

Once she was safely on the couch, he searched for injury. His fingers moved carefully, like they would over the wounded leg of a skittish colt. His search moved on slowly, but all he found were a few shallow scratches on her limbs and a tender spot on the back of her head.

"I think I have a concussion," she said.

He hid the spike of worry her words gave him and forced his tone to come out slow and casual. "That *is* serious. I should get you to a doctor."

"You can't take me anywhere. You're only in my head. Proof Eddie scrambled my brains."

"Your brains are fine, miss. So is the rest of you." Very fine, he noticed as he tucked a blanket over her bare legs in an effort to be an honorable man and stop leering.

Her lips parted as if she were about to say something. No words came out, but Dalton's entire focus narrowed down to those two plump lips. With her head angled up toward him as it was, he could almost imagine that she was silently begging for a kiss.

His blood heated and thrummed through his limbs. The hot proof of life beating through him was a precious thing to be savored. With Miss Sullivan here to make his blood burn a little hotter, the sheer joy of being flesh was even sweeter.

How long would he have in his human form? Long enough to remember what it felt like to be a real man?

She reached up and touched his cheek, just as she had so many times before. The impact of her skin on his hit him like a speeding train, knocking the wind from his lungs.

He could feel the faint tremor running through her fingertips. They were chilled from her fright, and all he could think about was giving her his warmth the way she had given hers to him so many times.

Dalton covered her hand so she wouldn't pull away too soon.

"I'm imagining this, aren't I?" she asked. "Dreaming?"

"You're awake and this is all real," he assured her.

"You really are alive?"

"I am. Sorry if I scared you."

She shook her head slightly, making one of her hairpins slide down on the silky strands. "Thanks for getting rid of Eddie."

"Protection is one of the few benefits you curators have. And it was my pleasure." He gave her a single nod, his fingers automatically going to the brim of a hat he now never wore.

She shivered and tugged her hand away. "How can I repay you?"

Touch me. "No need. It's part of my contract."

"Contract?"

From outside came the noise of a loud car revving to life. Eddie was leaving.

That familiar cold tingling formed at the base of Dalton's spine, warning him that it was time to return to his base. The compulsion was hard to fight, and he didn't want to solidify wherever he stood, making it hard for Miss Sullivan to explain his presence to company. Not to mention the fact that he'd be nearly impossible for her to move. The danger had passed. It was better if he did what he knew was demanded of him and left her in peace.

"I have to go now," he said. "But if you need me, I'll be right here for you."

As that tingling turned to pressure, Dalton pressed a kiss against her forehead just to see what it would feel like to have his lips graze her skin.

Smooth. Warm. Silky. Oh, so sweet.

He took that feeling with him as he stepped onto the stone base. A moment later, his world turned cold.

He could still see Miss Sullivan lying on the couch, but she was once again out of reach.

Dalton was alone again, inside his stone prison.

Sue sat on her couch in stunned silence for a good ten minutes, trying to make sense of what had just happened. The whole thing seemed so unreal.

The broken picture and bits of plaster on the floor were proof that she hadn't imagined all of it. The shallow cuts on her forearm and the stinging pain were more proof.

Slowly, she turned her head enough to look at Dalton's statue.

He'd changed positions. Not a lot, but enough that she noticed the difference. The fierce expression on his face was softer now, and instead of staring straight ahead, he was looking right at her.

Sue's stomach did a slow, lazy roll that made her head spin.

She hadn't imagined it. This wasn't a concussion talking. She hadn't hit her head that hard.

Dalton Thatcher was real. Alive.

On shaking legs, she walked over to him and looked up. "Charlotte wasn't lying. You really are in there, aren't you?"

Of course he didn't answer, even though she almost expected him to do so.

"I have no idea why you helped me, but thank you." She stroked his cheek as she had dozens of times before, but this time it felt different. More personal. "I don't know what to do to repay you, but I'm going to figure out something."

With that promise made, Sue went back to her laptop and contacted Charlotte.

The laptop's screen filled with the image of the other woman as she accepted the video chat. A new piece of jewelry dangled from her pierced nose, just grazing her top lip. It was made out of dozens of tiny, flat metal disks hammered to a primitive-looking texture.

"Did you read the manual like I told you to?" asked Charlotte. "It doesn't seem like you had time to read the whole thing. Unless you're some kind of genius freak or something. Are you? I mean, I know you're smart with all that law stuff, and that you probably read pretty fast, but there was a lot there to—"

"He animated," said Sue, interrupting the other woman.

Charlotte's cobalt eyes—the exact same shade as her hair—widened. "You got in his way, didn't you? He hurt you, didn't he? Damn it, Sue, I told you to read the freakin' manual."

"No, he didn't hurt me. Just the opposite. He saved me."

The dangling nose ring jingled with the breath from her low whistle. "Then you must have been in serious danger. What happened? Are you okay now? Should I get in the car?"

"Eddie came over, drunk. Decided not to take no for an answer. Then *he* was there, tossing Eddie out on his ass. It happened so fast I wasn't sure it really happened at all. Except for the proof." She eyed the broken glass and plaster that she hadn't yet cleaned up.

"If you'd read the manual, you'd know that your stoneman will animate to protect you if you're in danger. It happened to me once, too, when I was a little girl. Vincent saved my life from a werewolf."

Sue held up her hand. "Stop right there. I'm still having trouble believing what I just saw. Don't you dare go throwing werewolves into the mix, or I'll strangle you with your own necklaces."

"Fine. No one else believes me about the werewolf, either. No skin off my nose. I'm just glad you're on board now."

"Whoa. On board with what?"

"Being a curator."

"I never said that."

"Your stoneman just saved you from an Eddie-sasterous fate. Are you telling me that you're going to shirk your duties to him—the man who so gallantly came to your rescue?"

"No."

"Then open your damn eyes, Sue. Do your damn job. *Read the fucking manual.*"

"I will. I swear. I just needed to talk to someone about this so I wouldn't feel so crazy."

"You're not crazy. You're lucky. Some curators go their entire lives without ever seeing their stoneman animate. There are dozens of men and women who would love to be in your shoes."

"I'll try to remember that when the nightmares start."

Charlotte smiled like a woman with a secret. "You could have good dreams about him. I know I've had my fair share of them about Vincent. There's this one where he—"

Sue was so not going along on that mental porn ride. "Nope. This is where I stop you so I can go read."

"You do that. But first, tell me what you think of my newest design." She moved her nose and the dangling, jingling jewelry piercing it, closer to the camera. "I call it the personal wind chime."

"It's unique. Pretty."

"But you'd never wear it, right?"

"Sorry, hon. Not my thing."

Charlotte sighed. "Maybe if I added more crystal…"

"Good night, Char. For real this time."

"Night. Pleasant dreams." She said that last part with a smirk.

Sue ended the chat and picked up the pages she'd printed earlier. The scratches on her arm had stopped bleeding, and most of the adrenaline from her attack and rescue had worn off. Her hands were shaking only a little when she started reading.

Rule 1: Don't get in a stoneman's way. When sent to do the bidding of his sculptor, the stoneman must obey. If you try to stop him, he might hurt you.

Rule 2: Protect your stoneman from theft, damage and destruction at all times. They are helpless in their stone form. Any damage that comes to a stoneman in your care may be inflicted on you by his sculptor if she so chooses. This punishment may extend all the way to the curator's death.

Rule 3: Never reveal the secret of the stonemaen to anyone. You must protect his true nature from outsiders.

Rule 4: Never trade, sell, or abandon your stoneman. He is an inheritance. If your direct family line is at an end, you may gift your stoneman to a trusted friend or relative so long as they agree to follow the rules.

Rule 5 (Charlotte's addition): Stonemen are tools. Weapons. Don't get emotionally attached to them any more than you would to your favorite hammer or vibrator. You'll only get hurt.

The manual went on from there, talking about decorum, expectations and other things Sue probably should know, but she was too fidgety to keep reading. The words kept swimming on the page, making understanding them impossible.

She found herself standing in front of the statue again. Dalton continued to stare at her couch.

She could still remember what that fine body felt like for the few seconds she'd been pressed against it. Her shock had dulled some of the ride from the floor to the couch, but she could still feel the hard contours of his chest and the easy strength of his arms. He'd had a kind of earthy scent to him, somewhere between rain soaked soil and new sawdust. Beneath that was something else, something richer and darker, but she couldn't place it.

Whatever it was, the scent had gone straight to her head, making it spin as her lungs worked overtime to breathe in as much of him as she could.

Unless that had been the hyperventilation talking.

Sue stared at him for a long time. She could hear the old clock on the mantle marking the seconds as they passed, but time meant nothing to her right now. Her entire focus was filled with giant, stone manly man.

"Are you in there?" she asked.

Of course he didn't answer, making her wonder once again if she'd dreamed the whole thing.

She pressed her hand over his heart, wondering if she could feel it beat.

She felt nothing but ridiculous. It was a silly idea, but she found her hand liked the way it fit along the contours of his chest. Even though he was hard and cool to the touch now, the memory of his living heat and the firm cushion of his flesh was still vivid.

All she could think about was running her fingers over him, looking for proof of what had just happened. There was so much of him, she hardly knew where to move her hands next.

She knew where she wasn't putting her hands. Statue or not, she was too much of a lady to molest him. Though the temptation to do just that was growing by the second.

Not going to happen.

His missing leaf distracted her enough that she went in search of where it had fallen. She found it near the front door, its tape stuck to the ancient floorboards. She got a fresh piece of tape and went back to put the leaf in place again. When she bent down, the altered position of his feet showed her a small opening in the stone base she hadn't seen before.

The hole was less than an inch across, inlaid with an intricate twisting pattern that looked almost snakelike. In fact, it appeared to be the exact inversion of the pattern on the gold ring her uncle had given her with his estate.

She went to her desk and found the small ring box tucked in the back of a drawer. Sure enough, the flashing gold surface was the same as the one in the base. Just to be sure, she fitted the ring in the hole.

An instant later a whooshing sensation swept over her, spinning her head. The room grew brighter. The texture of the floor under her feet softened. The air grew warmer and more humid.

When Sue opened her eyes, she was no longer in her rundown little farmhouse. She was somewhere…else, standing in front of a beautiful woman wearing only a live snake.

The woman's voice reached out to her, stroking her senses like a velvet glove. "I hope your reason for disturbing me is good enough I don't simply slay you where you stand."

CHAPTER 3

Dalton's essence stood mute at the side of Pyrenia, his sculptor, holding a cluster of grapes for her enjoyment.

He'd been summoned to Idola, the home of the sculptors, immediately following the incident with Miss Sullivan and her over-eager suitor. Pyrenia's greed for his attention was too strong to allow him to stay away from her after having touched another woman. She would re-stake her claim on him before letting him return to his stone shell.

Dalton was sure the process would be both long and unpleasant.

Every second he was away from Miss Sullivan he worried about her. If Eddie came back, Dalton didn't know if he'd be aware of the danger in time to protect her. After giving her his promise to do so, he felt honor-bound to be back by her side.

Maybe now that she knew he was real, she'd touch him more often. Even the thought was enough to make him shift in impatience.

Pyrenia shot him a dark glare. Her fiery red hair seemed to grow larger, standing away from her head in fury.

Dalton settled himself before he could anger her further. He'd be trapped here in Idola for as long as it pleased her, and no amount of fidgeting would change that.

It had taken him years to figure out what this place was. Growing up the son of a farmer in Nebraska had done nothing to prepare him for his life as a stoneman. He was used to homes being fixed in space and time, and Idola—which seemed to float about wherever and whenever its inhabitants pleased—had left him confused.

Tonight, Idola was a lush, tropical garden filled with sunlight, hovering at the base of a small waterfall. Fragrant flowers bloomed everywhere, and butterflies with crystalline wings fluttered nearby, making a tinkling sound as they passed.

Pyrenia lounged on a throne formed from half a dozen of her male slaves. Their skin had been oiled to a dark brown sheen that reminded the men of what they truly were—stonemen, just like him.

She crossed her naked legs, propping her ankles on the back of a young man kneeling on all fours. The snake Pyrenia wore shifted, wrapping itself around her curvy frame in search of more warmth.

Dalton was almost certain it wasn't going to find any.

Miss Sullivan appeared standing in front of Pyrenia. The look of shock on her pretty face was enough to tell Dalton that she'd never been here before.

"I hope your reason for disturbing me is good enough I don't simply slay you where you stand," Pyrenia said.

Miss Sullivan opened her mouth, then closed it again.

"Speak, curator. You delay my pleasure."

"Uh. I don't know what to say. I don't even know where I am."

"Idola, home of the sculptors. You requested this audience with your ring, did you not?"

"I didn't mean to." Miss Sullivan's eyes slid across the gathering of men and women here to serve Pyrenia. As soon as she saw Dalton, her eyes widened, and the slightest smile touched her mouth.

He shook his head as much as he dared, trying to warn her to silence.

She didn't heed his warning. "You," she said, looking right at him. "You saved me tonight. Thank you so much. Is this where you live?"

Pyrenia stood from her throne of naked flesh. Two of her slaves rushed forward, tossing petals of fragrant flowers in her path. As she closed the distance to Miss Sullivan, the scent of roses and jasmine rose up from the crushed petals under Pyrenia's bare feet.

The snake slithered from her shoulders to wind its way down her body and onto the thick grass. As her bare breasts were exposed, a flurry of sparkling butterflies came to perch upon her to cover her nudity. Her long hair curled over the juncture of her thighs, shielding her sex from sight.

The snake slid closer to Miss Sullivan, its forked tongue leading the way.

She took a long step back. Her skin blanched, and her hands fisted in her robe, holding it tightly closed. "I've obviously come at a bad time," she said. "I'll just be going now."

She looked around as if searching for an exit. Of course, there was none.

"Nonsense," said Pyrenia. "You've only just arrived. I'm certain your trip was of vital importance."

"Honestly, I didn't know I was taking a trip at all. You can tell by the way I'm dressed—or not dressed as the case may be. And I certainly didn't know I'd be interrupting your…" she waved her hand at the array of naked slaves holding trays of food, "…snack."

"Did you not put your ring in the stoneman's base?" asked Pyrenia with deceptive sweetness.

"I did, but I didn't know it would bring me here."

Pyrenia tilted her head to the side. "You're new to your duties?"

"Yes, ma'am. Very new."

The smile that curled Pyrenia's lips was one of sheer cunning. "Lovely. We should chat. Dalton, dear?"

The grapes he held disappeared. He was compelled forward, certain of what his mistress demanded from him. Within seconds, he had one knee on the soft ground, the other forming a seat for Miss Sullivan.

"Sit," ordered Pyrenia. "We have so much to discuss."

Once again, the need to warn Miss Sullivan screamed in his mind. This time, he couldn't shake his head. He couldn't even blink. All he could do was relax against the welcoming smile that he was forced to wear as he held his hand out for Miss Sullivan to take a seat atop his naked thigh.

She balked at his nudity and flushed with embarrassment. "I shouldn't. I'm not even dressed for such…lavish company. I'll just go."

"Sit," said Pyrenia, more forcefully. The false sweetness in her tone disappeared, replaced by caustic bile to reveal the true personality beneath.

Miss Sullivan scurried forward. As she did, her robe melted into a crimson gown so short, Dalton could see the soft curves of her backside from his low vantage point. Her breasts barely held the tissue-thin creation up, and every fiber of Dalton's body wished for a heavy wind to blow it right from her.

Wanting to see her body made him a weaker man, but he couldn't seem to help it. He hadn't been this drawn to a woman since he had walked the earth of his own free will.

"Oh my," she said as she saw what she was now wearing. "It certainly is…festive."

"So glad you like it."

Before Miss Sullivan could rile Pyrenia more, he took his curator's hand and guided her to sit on his knee.

She kept her eyes above his waist and sat so that her leg would not graze any part of his manhood.

As soon as he felt the smooth heat of her bottom against his thigh, he knew she wore nothing beneath the short gown.

Pyrenia's idea of a joke, no doubt.

It didn't matter that none of this was real. They didn't truly exist here—only the essence of who they were. Illusions. Their bodies were still back in the farmhouse, frozen and helpless. Even though he knew that it wasn't Miss Sullivan's soft backside gracing his thigh, it still felt real. It still made his body perk up in interest.

He tried hard to control his manhood's reaction to Miss Sullivan, but some things were simply impossible. He'd long ago learned that it was easier to accept those things than it was to fight them and lose.

Pyrenia missed nothing, and she stared at him for a second, a knowing smile on her full lips. "Lovely. So glad everyone is comfortable." Her gaze moved to Miss Sullivan. "Now, something must have compelled you to seek an audience with me. Tell me what it was."

"I swear, I didn't intentionally do anything."

"So there's nothing you want?"

"Want?"

"Why else would you come here if not to seek a boon from me?"

A boon. Much like the one that had enslaved him over a century ago.

Dalton couldn't even tense his muscles to warn her, despite the anxiety strumming through him. He was a puppet here, incapable of doing anything Pyrenia didn't want him to do.

"I'd never impose like that," Miss Sullivan said.

"Nonsense. It's no imposition at all. I'm always happy to meet a new curator and welcome her into the fold."

"You didn't sound happy when I arrived."

Pyrenia's glower was warning enough that Dalton had no need to issue one of his own.

"I'm sorry," Miss Sullivan hurried to say. "What I meant was that you didn't know who I was then. It's no wonder you reacted the way you did."

"Tell me what you want or be gone."

She shifted nervously against his thigh. The move caused her womanly heat graze against his skin in a way that made his pulse spike. It also unbalanced her enough that she grabbed his shoulder to steady herself.

Her gaze caught his and held on tight. In this light, her warm brown eyes showed bright rays of deep russet and bronze. The black fringe of lashes lowered as her gaze drifted down his body and back up again. A blush stained her cheeks, reminding him that she wasn't used to nudity. He'd bet his last dime she'd taped that fake leaf over his groin again.

The leaf wouldn't have been large enough to cover him now, not with her sweet fragrance in his head and her living heat radiating into him wherever they touched. It had been over a century since he'd been with a woman, and until this moment, he hadn't realized just how long a time that truly was.

Pyrenia let out a throaty laugh. "So human of you, Dalton. So delightful. Perhaps she came here for you. I have to admit I like the idea of having you take her while I watch." She settled back on her human throne as if preparing for a show.

"I think I'll be going now," said Miss Sullivan as she scrambled from his lap. "I have to go to work early in the morning. It's been a long night. I'll just be on my way." She turned and started walking.

Before she got more than a few yards, another form shimmered to existence. She wore jeans and a plain white shirt. Her straight, mousy brown hair was pulled back in a ponytail at the nape of her neck, and unlike Pyrenia, there wasn't anything about her that sparkled.

"Alethia," said Pyrenia with a pout. "You're here to spoil my fun, again, aren't you?"

"Let the woman go," said Alethia. "You've had enough fun at her expense." As she spoke, Miss Sullivan's robe winked back in place, securely tied, hiding all of her intriguing curves.

Dalton wasn't sure if he was more disappointed or relieved.

"She came here of her own free will. She must have wanted for me to play with her."

"I did not," Miss Sullivan said. "I told you I didn't even know what the ring would do. All I want is to go home. Or wake up—whatever will get me out of this place fastest."

Alethia laid a hand on the curator's robe. "You should have known better."

"I see that now. I promise that as soon as I get home, I'll read the manual."

"See that you do." Alethia looked at her sister. "Are you ready to let her go now?"

"Not yet. I sense she wants something. She can go when she tells me what it is."

"I don't want anything but to go home. I was just trying to learn more about *him* when I was zapped here." She waved at Dalton as she spoke.

Pyrenia beamed. "Excellent. I will allow you to get to know your stoneman."

"Pyrenia," said Alethia in a warning tone. "What are you up to?"

"Nothing that concerns you. There is, however, this delicious little trinket I've had my eye on for a while. I propose a quest."

Dalton tried to open his mouth, grunt, blink, anything. Nothing worked. He had no control over his actions, leaving poor Miss Sullivan to walk right in to Pyrenia's trap.

"What kind of quest?" she asked, taking the bait.

"The kind where you find an item I seek, and in return, I give you a few days with your stoneman. Nothing could be simpler."

"You're trying to trick her," said Alethia. "She doesn't know our ways. She can't protect herself."

"Fine. Then she shall have a champion to speak for her. Dalton?"

Suddenly, Dalton's body became his own again. He stood and went to Miss Sullivan's side. He didn't dare turn his back on his mistress, but he did pitch his voice low so that she wouldn't easily overhear.

He took Miss Sullivan's hands in his. "Please let me handle this. I know exactly what this woman is capable of doing."

"I don't know you. Who's to say you aren't the one trying to trick me? Walking around naked like you are, saving me from Eddie, coming to my aid now…that's exactly what I'd do if I was trying to trick some unsuspecting woman into trusting me."

"You don't know anything about me, do you?" he asked. "You didn't even bother reading the archives to see why I was here, did you?"

She flushed with embarrassment, and he knew it was true. She hadn't even cared about her duties enough to find out the kind of man he was.

Frustration tightened his throat, but he ignored it. Every second that passed was only going to make Pyrenia more impatient.

"I accept the role as her champion," he said to his mistress.

"Hey. I didn't agree to that," said Miss Sullivan.

Alethia pointed a finger at her. "Hush. He's doing you a favor."

Pyrenia grinned. "Excellent. I offer you, Dalton Thatcher, a week of freedom from my rule. A week to spend as you choose, with whom you choose."

He nearly staggered at the offer. He'd never had more than a few hours of freedom here and there, and each of those hours had been hard won. To have an entire week to be a real man again was far too tempting.

And Pyrenia knew it.

All he had to do was hold firm. In a moment, she'd spout some horrible task he had to perform—one not worth a week of freedom. She'd demand that he steal a newborn for her to raise as her own, trick some unsuspecting person into handing over his free will to Pyrenia, or destroy the life of an entire family serving one of her sisters.

Dalton had never once given in to her disgusting lures, so all he had to do now was stay true to the man he used to be and say no.

"I want you to find a puzzle box for me."

He waited, sure the rest of her request would be coming any second. When it didn't, he asked, "That's it? Only find a box?"

"It's a rare and ancient box. Only one exists. And you won't have much time in which to find it."

"But there's nothing more we have to do?" he asked, again, certain there had to be some kind of catch.

Alethia stepped forward, the only voice of sanity the clan of sister sculptors had to offer. "What are the terms?" she asked.

"I give the woman three human days. Dalton may travel with her for protection, but if he displeases me in any way, she will be on her own."

"What does the box look like?" asked Miss Sullivan from behind him. "Where would I look?"

Dalton took her wrist in his grip and gave her a gentle squeeze, praying she'd be quiet. "What happens if she doesn't find it?"

Pyrenia dangled her leg over the arm of a burly slave who formed part of her throne, baring the flesh between her thighs completely. A swarm of colorful beetles skittered over the throne, up her leg and shielded her sex from sight. Their iridescent wings shimmered under the sunlit canopy of trees.

Dalton barely suppressed a shudder of revulsion. Miss Sullivan made a choking sound.

"You didn't answer his question," Alethia said.

Pyrenia shrugged. "Nothing drastic will happen."

"Name it," insisted Dalton.

"I'll simply remove her from her position as curator as she'll have proven herself unfit for the duty."

"That's it?" asked Miss Sullivan. "You're not going to torture me or kill me or make me wear a beetle bikini?"

"Nothing of the sort. Though you should try the beetles before you dismiss them. They're delightful. You'd love the way they tickle."

Miss Sullivan's throat worked as she choked down her disgust. "Thanks, but I'll pass."

"How will you remove her from her position?" asked Dalton.

Pyrenia pouted and swung her long leg over the arm of one of her slaves. "I'd simply unmake her existence. She'll never have been born."

CHAPTER 4

Now Sue was starting to realize just why she needed a champion to speak for her. She'd been about to agree to Pyrenia's seemingly innocuous demands.

Thank goodness Dalton knew what questions to ask.

"Yeah," said Sue. "That doesn't work for me. Sorry."

Pyrenia let out a huffy snort. "Fine. I'll settle for altering the past so that you never agreed to the terms in your uncle's will. Your life will flow on after that point as it would have if you'd turned him down."

"You can do that?" asked Sue. "How in the world can you do that?"

"You really should read the manual, dear," said the woman in jeans and a T-shirt.

Never again would Sue shirk her duties. She was going straight home, brewing a big pot of coffee and pulling an all-nighter.

If she got out of this situation alive.

"So, do we have a deal?" asked Pyrenia.

"State the terms again," said Dalton, his tone one of hard demand.

Pyrenia sighed. "The ignorant curator will find my beloved puzzle box within three human days. Dalton may help her in his flesh form—or he may leave her to enjoy other…pursuits. If she finds it and brings it to me, she wins him a week of freedom from my rule. If she doesn't, her past will be unraveled to the time of her uncle's death, after which point, she'll refuse the terms of his will and another will take her place as curator."

That week of freedom burned in his mind like a beacon. The lure of it made him ache. It had been so long since he'd been his own man and made his own choices. Even the thought of it was enough to make him want to force her to comply.

He couldn't do that. There was no way for Miss Sullivan to know what a precious gift his freedom was, but there was also no way for her to know how ruthless Pyrenia and her sisters could be. They lived to toy with human lives. And while she wasn't as twisted and ruthless as her sister Obelia was, Pyrenia ruled with her own brand of torment.

Could he really put Miss Sullivan in a situation where she could alter the very course of her life as she knew it?

Then again, how could he turn down such a tempting prize as a week of free will?

Dalton turned to her and spoke in a low voice. Each word had to be ripped from his throat. "You don't have to do this. Say no and you'll go home."

"And what about you?"

Dalton swallowed twice to shove down his initial greedy response. Instead, he did what he would have done decades ago, before his enslavement, when he'd still been a good and decent man. It took a couple of tries, but he finally managed to say, "I'll be fine."

Dalton was lying. Sue was sure of it. She didn't know how, but she could tell that his casual acceptance of her decision had cost him. Big time.

Still, as much as she owed him for saving her, and as much as she really did want to help him, this was a big decision.

If she agreed to Pyrenia's bargain and didn't find the box, she'd never meet Charlotte. She'd never meet Dalton. Her uncle's house and the statue would be passed on to some unknown party who may or may not be worthy of the job.

Not that she'd been employee of the year so far, herself. But still, she was resolved to do the job right from here on out. And giving up her new life—despite its many flaws— was a big thing to risk. There was no way of knowing where she might be now if she wasn't living in the farmhouse.

"What about your vacation?" she asked. "Being frozen in stone all the time can't be much fun."

"Don't worry about me." The words rang true, but the look of longing on his face was easy to see.

He wanted this. Badly.

"When was the last time you had a week off?" she asked.

"Never," said the plain looking woman standing nearby. "It would take him centuries to earn so much time."

Centuries? Okay. She was definitely working on a bigger scale of time than she was used to. "So a week off is a pretty big prize," said Sue.

"Huge," he agreed. "But not vital."

"I'm waiting," said Pyrenia, her tone one of impatience tinged with menace. "I don't like waiting."

"I'm going to do it," she whispered to Dalton. "It's only three days of my life."

"What if your alternate life is horrible?" he asked.

"What if it's not? What if I meet some handsome gentleman who makes me happy for the rest of my life?"

"What if the rest of your life is only a few days long after you turn down your uncle's inheritance? You could be hit by a truck."

She couldn't think like that. She could die in a car crash tomorrow. Her mother had warned her of that often enough after she got her driver's license that she believed it. She didn't want to live her life in fear. Besides, Dalton had saved her ass tonight and she owed him.

Sue stepped out from behind her chiseled champion and gave Pyrenia her toughest bad girl glare. "You're on."

* * *

The human woman disappeared with her champion.

Alethia studied her sister, trying to figure out what was going on inside her twisted mind. "What game are you playing?"

Pyrenia put on her innocent face, which was such a strain it was almost laughable. "Me? No games. I'm simply sending some playthings on an errand for me."

"What's in the box?"

"A toy."

"What kind of toy?"

"The kind that wouldn't interest a woman as boring as you."

"You're going to hurt them, aren't you?" asked Alethia.

"I'm not Obelia. I have no interest in their pain. I will, however, enjoy watching them scurry to do my bidding."

"And if the human is victorious?"

Pyrenia shrugged one beautiful shoulder. "What is a week in one slave's life to me when there are so many who seek to please me?" As she spoke, one large, magnificently built man stepped forward and fell to his knees between her spread thighs.

Beetles scurried away and a look of relaxed enjoyment covered her face as her slave went to work pleasuring her with his mouth. Two more joined in, massaging her arms as they suckled her nipples.

"Leave us," said Pyrenia, opening one eye. "Unless you want to join in?"

Alethia refused to be lured into her sister's games. "Not today, thank you. Perhaps another time."

"Enjoy your meddling, dear sister. I hope it keeps you warm at night."

Alethia willed herself away and descended to Earth, donning one of her usual disguises. There was more to this agreement than there appeared. If Sue was to have even a slim chance at surviving her bargain with Pyrenia, Alethia had much work to do.

* * *

Dalton couldn't force his eyes open. He was lying on the softest pillow he'd ever felt. The gentle sway of it kept lulling him back to sleep.

Something wasn't right, but he couldn't figure out exactly what it was.

It couldn't have been that important. A few more minutes of sleep wouldn't hurt anything. Would it?

Worry nibbled away at the back of his mind, gnawing on his sense of peace. Even the scent of vanilla and lavender couldn't soothe him anymore as it always had.

He pried his weary eyes open and realized that his head was cradled on Miss Sullivan's lovely bosom. The tie on her robe had loosened enough to give him a shadowy glimpse of what lay beneath. Tempting, womanly curves and the mysterious shadow of one perfect, stiff little nipple.

She was lying on her couch. He was lying on top of her, stretched out between her legs, his body completely content to stay put as her living blanket. His arms were wrapped around her tight enough that for a second he worried that he might have suffocated her.

Stonemen were strong. When he'd been new to his power, he'd underestimated his strength and done accidental damage.

Realizing the threat, he pushed himself up, taking his weight from her body. She sighed and shifted deeper into the cushions. Her arms slid over her head to dangle off the end of the couch. The move pulled her robe tight again, but also pressed the fabric against her taut nipples.

Lust prowled in his gut, glad to be free of his stone prison. She was laid out for him like an offering, sweet and warm and so very soft.

Dalton bent down to cover the delicious peak of her nipple with his mouth, but stopped as he realized what he was about to do.

He didn't know this woman. More important, she didn't know him. After her attack by the handsy jackass earlier, there was no way he could give in to his baser urges. For all he knew, Pyrenia was watching, just waiting for him to give her the kind of lascivious show she loved.

Still he couldn't move away, either. After decades of being unable to exert his will, it was rusty from lack of use. In his life as a stoneman, there was no such thing as doing what he wanted. He did as he was compelled to do. Even now, he could feel the tendrils of Pyrenia's power digging into him, binding him to her will.

This desire he felt, was it real or all part of his mistress's game? She often forced others to perform blatantly sexual acts for her amusement. What if this was more of the same?

There was no way for Dalton to know. He was simply glad that he retained enough control over himself to make the choice not to part the edges of Sue's robe and take her.

Perhaps watching him squirm was what Pyrenia really wanted. She could gain as much pleasure from watching him deny himself as she could from forcing him to overindulge. When it came to logic, he'd learned long ago that the creature who controlled him had none.

Miss Sullivan opened her eyes and caught him staring at her with blatant lust tightening his expression. Not that his face was the only part of his body giving him away. His cock was swollen and pressed too tightly against her thigh for her not to notice his interest.

He tried to open his mouth and apologize, but no words came out. His arms were locked in place, keeping him pinned right where he was.

Definitely Pyrenia's doing.

Instead of screaming or shoving him off of her, Miss Sullivan simply stared back at him. "Is this part of the dream?"

"What dream?"

"The one with snake lady in the bug bikini."

"That wasn't a dream."

"And this?"

"Not a dream."

"Oh." She swallowed and shifted beneath him.

The sinuous moved slid his erection along the inside of her bare thigh. He couldn't help the trail of wet heat he left behind or the way it slickened her skin.

He was only inches from heaven. It had been so long since he'd been with a woman. The demands of his human body were thrashing inside of him, coaxing him to obey.

Just a small shift of his hips. That's all it would take to be at heaven's gate.

The cords in his neck tightened as he fought his urges. He would not be like the man who'd attacked her earlier tonight. He would be the kind of man she deserved—the one who would pay her back for her kindness by getting up off the couch and putting some trousers on.

"You're not wearing the leaf now," she said, her voice wavering with nerves.

"It wouldn't exactly fit now."

She swallowed again, and a lovely pink flush crept up from under her robe to cover her chest. "No, it sure wouldn't."

"I should get up," he said, more to himself than to her.

"Probably so. This isn't going to help us find any puzzle boxes."

That was the slap in the face he needed to cool his lust and grant him back the control he had to find in order to move away.

He stood and picked up the small blanket she used to keep warm against the house's drafts. When he looked at her again, she was staring and wetting her lips with the pink tip of her tongue. Her eyes were huge and dark in the dying light of the fire, and everything in him ached to pin her down again and take her hard and fast. While he still could.

Dalton turned his back, and wrapped the blanket around his hips.

"We should find you some clothes," she said.

"Your uncle kept some here for me. I don't know where they were stored."

The noise of fabric rustling sounded loud in his ears as she rose from the couch. "There was a suitcase with your name on it. It had clothes inside. I think I put it in the attic."

"Thank you, Miss Sullivan. I'll go get it."

"Sue," she said.

He turned and looked at her. The instant he did, he knew it had been a mistake. Her hair was mussed in a way that made him think of wild nights filled with passion. He didn't know if he wanted to smooth it with his fingers or grab her by it and drag her down to the couch so he could tangle it further.

He uttered a distracted, "What?"

"Call me Sue."

"I don't know you that well."

"You can't call me Miss Sullivan. No one does that anymore. You'll draw too much attention."

He tried her name out, liking the way it felt on his tongue. Then again, there were a lot of things of hers he figured he'd enjoy on his tongue. "Sue."

She clutched at the edges of her robe, hiding the dark flush staining her chest. "That's better." The way she said it made him wonder if she was lying, but he didn't think it would be polite to ask.

"I'll be quick fetching the suitcase."

Sue nodded. "I'll throw some clothes on, too, and call in to work and let them know I'm taking a couple of days off. Then we'll figure out our next move."

They had three days to find the puzzle box. Dalton could easily imagine spending them in her bed, drawing as much pleasure from each other as they possibly could.

From the way she was looking at him with those dark eyes, his curator seemed to be imagining the same thing. Then again, that couldn't just be wishful thinking on his part.

It had been so long since he'd last had a woman. If she was willing, what harm could there be in indulging himself now?

He took a step toward her. Her fist tightened on the fabric of her robe.

"If you touch me again, things are going to get…complicated between us," she said.

"Complicated isn't necessarily bad."

"But losing your chance at a week of freedom from that horrible woman would be."

Her reminder hardened his resolve not to touch. "You're right. No sense in getting heated up."

She closed her eyes. "Don't say it like that."

"Like what?"

"All deep and sexy."

"I'm sorry. I can't change my voice."

"I know. That's the problem." She shook her head and took a long step away from him. "I'm going to stop talking now. There's really no safe topic of conversation available to us until I'm wearing panties."

Alethia had been on Earth for less than five minutes when she ran into her sister Thyra. Literally.

The airbag in Alethia's car exploded in a puff of confetti, covering every inch of the car's interior with glitter. It clung to her skin, and she knew she'd be finding little bits of the sparkly stuff for years to come.

The bitch.

The front bumper of the car was caved in where it had hit Thyra. She lay on the side of the road in a crumpled heap of broken limbs and bloody skin.

"Get up, Thyra," Alethia snapped. "Someone's going to drive by and see you."

Thrya pushed up from the ground, flipping twice in the air before she came to land on her feet once again. By the time she had, her body was whole, and her clothes pristine. "Did you like the sparkle bomb?"

Alethia shook glitter from her hair but said nothing.

"How did you know it was me?" Thyra asked.

"Pyrenia wants something. I knew that once you caught wind of that you wouldn't be far behind."

Thyra smoothed her long white skirt. As she did, her hair changed from raven wing black to a pale, moonlight blond. She shook the long tresses and crossed her arms in a huff. "She always finds the best toys. It's not fair."

"I'm sure there are other things to occupy your time besides getting in that poor human woman's way."

"I want that box," said Thyra with a full-lipped pout.

"I would have thought you'd be first in line to help the human find it. It's the only way you'll be able to deprive Pyrenia one of her plaything for a whole week."

Thyra's bangs grew until she could blow them out with puff of frustration. "A week is nothing. I have bigger plans."

"You're going to help free him?" asked Alethia.

"No, silly. I'm going to steal him from her. He's pretty. I want him."

"We've been through this before. Just because you want something doesn't mean you should have it."

Thyra's lips darkened from a petal pink to a deep, glossy wine color as she propped one hand on a curvy hip. "You were a lot more fun last century. You never want to play with me anymore."

"That's because your idea of play usually has a body count."

"They're just humans. They'll make more. In fact, I consider my acts a kind of recycling. Very green. You know how trendy that is these days." A lollypop zapped into existence in Thyra's hand. She sucked on it once with enthusiasm before tossing it to the ground and crushing it under her spiked heel.

"You can't go running around killing people anymore. Humans are all connected now. When something happens in one part of the world, the rest of the world knows it. If you don't stop, we're going to be discovered."

Those dark lips stretched into a smile that was all sharp teeth and malice. "I can hardly wait. I just love it when they start to scurry. Like giant bugs."

"We're supposed to stay hidden. What will Father say?"

Thyra's hair shifted until she was wearing two pigtails and a short, plaid skirt. "Nothing. I'm his favorite."

Alethia ran her hand over her car, straightening out enough of the damage her sister had done so the engine would function. "Just go home and leave the humans alone. Whatever Pyrenia wants, it can't be all that fantastic."

"How do you know?"

"Because Pyrenia wants it. Have you ever known her to want anything good?"

"Do you remember those shoes last year?" Thyra sighed and her appearance changed again. This time, she had green hair and was wearing a pair of shimmering emerald platform stiletto heels that would make even the most tricked-out stripper envious.

"She wore them for two minutes before tossing them aside."

"Forcing me to wear *used* shoes," said Thyra as if it were some kind of horrible disease.

Alethia's head was growing weary of running into the brick wall that was her chaotic sister. The only hope Alethia had of getting her job done was to send some sparkly bait in another direction to distract Thyra.

Alethia gathered her monumental powers of deception and let them fly. She lowered her voice to a conspiratorial tone. "I wasn't supposed to tell you this, but I don't see what harm could possibly come of it."

"What?" asked Thyra, licking her lips. They appeared to be covered in glittering reptilian scales now.

"Pyrenia told me that if I were to see you, I wasn't supposed to stop you from going after the box."

"But you are trying to stop me."

"I know. She irritated me earlier, and I was only getting back at her. It had nothing to do with you."

Thyra's clothes melted into a black leather bodysuit, complete with spikes and an array of weapons strapped to her body. Her hair was brown now, styled in an aggressive series of short, sharp points. "But if she wants me to go after the box, then she must have some other, bigger prize she's trying to keep me from finding."

Alethia managed to look surprised and perplexed. "You think? But this box is so mysterious. It must contain something glorious."

Thyra stomped her boot. "She sends me after sand while she goes after diamonds."

"What are you going to do?" asked Alethia.

Her sister bared her teeth. "I'm going to beat her at her own game."

Before there was time to blink, Thyra was gone.

Alethia slumped against the bumper of her car. She was on human time now, and already behind schedule. If she didn't get back on the road soon, all her efforts to distract her sister would be in vain.

CHAPTER 5

Sue had never wanted a man as much as she wanted Dalton. She didn't know if it was that blow to her head, the stress of this unbelievable night, or the fact that he was built for sin that did it to her. Whatever it was, the effects were potent, singing through her in a tempting refrain to toss him on her bed and ride him into the sunset. About three days from now.

This was all way too fast. She had to get a grip. No way was she going to be able to think, much less function with this raging case of hormonal poisoning she had.

Her vibrator Randy sat waiting for her in her dresser drawer. She didn't think she'd need more than ten seconds with him to get where she needed to go.

She eyed the drawer, but passed it by. The last thing she wanted was for Dalton to come strolling in while she was right in the middle of dealing with her cootchie crisis.

Instead, she grabbed her ugliest pair of panties to help her remember to keep her pants on, and got dressed. She tossed a few things in an overnight bag and was back out, facing the man who made her overheat.

He'd found his clothes. The tight jeans and flannel shirt were not exactly GQ, but on him, they were sexy as hell. And they were a long step above all that delicious nudity he'd been sporting a few minutes ago. At least as far as her peace of mind went.

"Do we know where we're going?" she asked him.

He shook his head. "I was hoping you'd know."

Her doorbell rang, jangling her already taxed nerves. Dalton laid a steadying hand on her shoulder and moved past her to answer it.

"That had better not be Eddie," she said as he swung the door open.

It wasn't.

Standing on her front porch was a tiny, frail man. He was bent with age, nearly bald, wearing a stained T-shirt that looked like it hadn't been changed in days.

"Special delivery," he said in a voice that had her thinking of cracked paint and splintered wooden fences.

Dalton took the envelope. The man held out his hand for a tip.

Dalton patted his pockets. "I'm sorry. I don't have anything to give you."

"Hold on," said Sue. "Let me get my purse."

All she had was a twenty, which he snapped from her hand before scurrying off toward his car. The thing looked like it had been recently wrapped around a telephone pole, but it started on the first try.

Dalton glanced at the contents of the envelope before handing it to her. On the first page was a large photo of a box about the size of a shoebox. It looked like it had been put together with small, interlocking pieces of wood. There were no latches or inscriptions that she could see, but the entire surface was covered with scratches and gouges that said someone had tried to pry it open more than once.

The second page listed a name and an address—the last known owner of the puzzle box.

She used her phone to do an Internet search for the woman, but she didn't find any phone listings or email addresses. The only thing she found was a picture of the woman holding the box in a newspaper article from a few years ago. There was a reward being offered for anyone who knew how to open it. As of the article's publication, years had gone by with no one claiming the reward.

"I can't find any way to contact her," said Sue. "Looks like we're going to Iowa."

"We only have three days."

"Good thing she's only a three-hour drive away."

Dalton's hopeful smile distracted her from what he was saying for a second. He was just too damn good looking for her to think straight when he smiled at her like that. "…and I'll have you to thank for it."

She didn't know what he was thanking her for, but if it got her another one of those smiles, she was all over it. "No problem. Glad to help."

He picked up her overnight bag and his suitcase, shifting everything so he could still open the door for her to pass.

His old-fashioned manners were so casual, she barely noticed he was urging her to hurry. By the time she'd locked the house, he had her car door opened for her and stood beside it, waiting for her to get in.

"Have you been in a car before?" she asked.

"I have, but it looked a fair bit different than the one you own."

"Are you going to freak out when we start going fast?"

"Hardly. Your uncle used to leave the TV on for me sometimes. It helped me keep up on the language and what's changing in the world as time passes."

"That's good. I'd hate for you to be one of those nut balls who thought we'd die if we broke the sound barrier."

"Mach Five was my favorite horse's name."

She paused by her car door and stared at him long enough to see he was joking. The little twinkle in his blue eyes gave him away. "You think you're funny, don't you?"

"I'll admit I'm a bit rusty." He waited until she was settled behind the wheel before he closed the door and walked around the car to get in.

The beam of her headlights hit him. Sue followed his long-legged stride, enjoying the simple sight of watching him move. Each step made his thighs and butt flex, forcing that denim to stretch tight. It was the kind of show women all over the world would pay good money to see, and here she was with a front row seat.

He eased into the seat beside her. She could smell the clean scent of winter clinging to him. It made her want to snuggle close and give him her warmth.

When he didn't move to put on his seatbelt, she pointed toward it. "Buckle up."

He didn't seem to know what she meant, so she leaned across his body and grabbed the buckle. Her breast brushed his arm, and a shower of fireworks exploded out from her nipple and cascaded down into her belly.

"Did you hurt yourself?" he asked.

Sue didn't dare look him in the eye as she latched him into the seat. "Just a static shock."

Before he could ask more questions, she pulled out of her driveway and headed east. "I didn't realize you liked to watch TV or I would have left it on while I was at work."

"It's okay. I've learned not to mind the quiet."

"Do you ever sleep?"

"Not the way you mean it. Unless my essence is summoned to Idola, I'm always aware of my surroundings."

"You mean you've been watching me for the past few months?" Her mind flew over the recent past, searching for anything embarrassing she might have done.

She glanced at him in time to see his smile turn hot. "I have. Even that time you got out of the tub to answer the phone."

Sue felt her face heat. "You could have at least averted your eyes. I gave you a leaf, after all."

"There is no power on this earth strong enough to make me look away from a sight as tempting as you all warm and wet, struggling to hold that thin towel over your dripping, naked body." He said it with a smile in his voice, as if it were one of his fondest memories.

"A gentleman would have averted his eyes."

"You're probably right, but I haven't been a gentleman for a long time. After a few decades of boredom, a man becomes so hungry for stimulation that he forgets the kind of person he used to be."

She hadn't thought of it that way. Just the idea of being frozen in that farmhouse, trapped and unable to leave was enough to make her want to scream. "In that case, I forgive you. At least now I know better than to walk around the house naked."

"Don't worry about modesty on my account. I'm man enough to take it."

"I just bet you are."

She merged onto the highway and they drove in silence for a while. As her mind spun through his words, she became more curious with each passing mile.

"What's it like?" she asked. "Being trapped in that statue?"

He was silent for so long, she almost thought he wasn't going to answer. "I try not to think about it too much. It's easier to simply let time flow around me without dwelling on the way it feels. I've seen what happens to men who fight their curse. It…darkens them."

"What do you mean?"

"Anger is toxic. It can eat at a man's soul until there's nothing left but poison and rot. It makes them bitter. Dangerous to the people around them. I saw it happen early in my sentence and have tried hard not to follow the bad example of others."

"Your sentence?"

"That's how I think of my service—it's a kind of imprisonment."

"For how long?"

"Counting the years is a good way for a man to lose his mind. Let's just say that your great, great grandchildren will be long dead before my sentence can be measured in years rather than decades."

"Wow. That sucks."

She saw him shrug from the corner of her eye. "I'm free now. Living in the moment." He glanced at her. "And this moment is sweet."

Her resolve hardened. "We're going to find that puzzle box. And when we do, I'm going to use some of the money my uncle left me to send you on the best vacation ever."

"You're a kind woman, Sue. Your uncle was right to leave me in your care."

"I haven't exactly been taking great care of you so far. But that's going to change. I'll make sure you have plenty of TV to watch and music to listen to. I'll even get you some audio books." She paused, considering the logistics of keeping him entertained. "You'll have to tell me what you like so I don't make you want to claw your eyes out the way I do when I'm forced to watch golfing."

"Anything is better than years of unbroken silence."

Sue gripped the wheel tighter, trying not to let her heart crack and give him an opening. She didn't mind caring for him enough to do her job, but she absolutely could not have feelings for him. He'd be a statue again in a few days, and she couldn't let herself pine for a man she could never truly reach. The last thing she wanted was to waste her life wishing for him to turn to flesh again while her chance to have happiness with a real man passed her by.

She cleared her throat to dislodge the effects of her chaotic emotions. "I'll mix it up for you. At least that way if you hate something, you won't have to be subjected to it for long."

"You are an excellent curator, Miss Sullivan."

"Sue. You go calling me Miss Sullivan in public and people are going to look twice. I really don't want to have to explain your mysterious disappearance or why I have a statue resembling you in my living room. Total serial killer vibe."

"I understand. I'll try not to draw any attention."

Yeah, right. With a body like that, there was no way he could win that battle.

"Are you hungry?"

"Always."

"Why didn't you say something?"

"I don't want you to make a fuss. You're already doing so much for me."

"Oh, for heaven's sake. If you want something, you should have it. You spend enough time cooped up in that statue, unable to have what you want. You're out now and shouldn't deny yourself just because you think I'll mind. I won't." She took the next exit where a 24-hour diner awaited.

"Are you sure about that?" he asked. There was an odd quality to his tone she couldn't translate. Something about it stroked over her senses, making her spine loosen and her shoulders relax.

"I'm sure."

She parked and turned off the engine. Before she'd had time to open her door, Dalton had lifted her over the console and into his lap. She gasped in surprise, and it opened her mouth just in time for him to kiss her. Not that what he was doing could technically be considered a kiss. It was more like he was staking a claim.

His arms held her cradled against him, caging her tight. Her legs dangled over the console into her seat. One of her shoes had fallen off, but she couldn't bring herself to care.

Waves of heat radiated out from him, and each one made her shiver with delight. His fingers wove their way through her hair, where he angled her head so they fit together perfectly.

His mouth feasted on hers like he was starving. His tongue thrust past her lips, staying long enough to tease her before retreating again. There was no slow buildup, no gentle slope toward desire. His lust was obvious in his hold, in his demanding kiss. He was like a blast furnace, forcing her to withstand the hot need that was rolling out of him.

She had no idea how long she was caught inside his world, but by the time he lifted his head enough to let her take a full breath that wasn't from his lungs, she was shaking from the delightful force of his efforts.

His mouth was wet and red. His blue eyes had gone dark as twilight and were filled with unsatisfied need. His cheeks had the same flush she could feel heating her own skin.

The fingers he had fisted around her hair loosened enough she could move her head again. Her whole body was humming now, vibrating with the kind of energy that could only be effectively burned off with a few hours of enthusiastic sex.

She was all for it.

He stared at her for a long moment before speaking. "That was what I wanted most. I hope you can forgive me."

Forgive him? For rocking her world and renewing her faith that bone-melting kisses were real? It had been so long since she'd felt this kind of demanding desire, she'd almost thought she'd outgrown it. Then again, maybe she'd never felt anything quite like this before. She couldn't think of a single man who'd ever turned her into a quivering pool of hormones with only a single kiss.

She struggled to find her voice. "That was definitely forgivable. No worries."

"People are beginning to stare."

Sue hadn't noticed. Nothing outside the confines of her car mattered to her right now. Her entire focus was on how she was going to get him to kiss her again.

Of course, if he kissed her like that again, the only way she could end up was naked. And it was best not to do that at a family restaurant on a busy interstate, even if it was late.

She forced herself to shift away from him. As soon as she did, he helped her slide back into her own seat.

One glance in the mirror told her that her hair was a wreck and her mouth was puffy and red from what he'd done to her.

Looking at herself made her want him to kiss him all over again.

He disappeared only to reappear at her side to open her car door. With her legs shaking as hard as they were, she gladly took his offered hand to steady herself.

"I've upset you, haven't I?" he asked.

"Upset isn't the word I'd use."

"You're trembling."

"Yeah, well, that certainly was…unexpected."

"I guess you haven't spent as much time thinking about what that would be like as I have."

"For the record, I've only recently learned you can kiss." Boy, could he kiss. "But now that I know, I don't think I'll be forgetting it any time soon."

He gave her a look so hot it nearly singed her eyelashes. "Neither will I."

CHAPTER 6

Thyra wanted to kill something. Perhaps a lot of somethings.

Alethia had been lying. This whole time Thyra could have been following the humans who were searching for the puzzle box. Instead, she'd wasted fleeting human hours investigating the false lead Alethia had thrown out.

Apparently not everything about her baby sister had changed. She still lied better than any creature alive.

At least there was still time to get Pyrenia's precious box before it became as used and worthless as those emerald shoes.

Thyra summoned her most ruthless stoneman, Tristan. Blood seeped from a hundred tiny wounds that age had inflicted on his stone form. With no curator protecting him, he was alone in the world, vulnerable and victim to the elements.

Served him right for refusing to kneel before her.

Until he learned to revere her as was proper, he could continue to suffer from the lack of a curator. Maybe in a few more centuries, he'd learn his proper station.

He stood before her, blood dripping into his eyes. He didn't blink or wipe it away. Neither did he bow to her as was her due. This warrior had been her slave for centuries and yet he still hadn't learned his place.

It was that refusal to give into defeat that she was counting on now to win the day.

She gifted her stoneman's essence with the knowledge he needed to do his job. "Find them. Stop them. Search for the box. If they find the box first, take it from them. Use force. Lots of force."

The stoneman nodded once. It was as much of a concession to her authority as she was ever going to get from that one.

Good thing she liked a challenge, or she would have slain him decades ago. At least she knew that if she lost him on this mission, she would shed no tears.

Dalton was sure that kissing Sue had been a mistake, but he couldn't bring himself to regret it. Not when it had been the highlight of his century.

He ate his food, but the taste of her mouth was still too fresh in his mind for him to think of anything else. He couldn't imagine anything being half as sweet or intoxicating as her lips.

It was a bad idea to kiss her again, but he was already wondering how long it would be until they were out of this place and back in the privacy of her car where he could taste her again.

Of course, if he did that, they'd never make it to Iowa before his time to earn his vacation ran out.

He had to remember the greater goal here. A few stolen minutes with Sue were wonderful, but they were nothing compared to an entire week of freedom from Pyrenia's rule.

Especially if Dalton spent that week with Sue.

As compelling as that idea was, he knew it was the wrong decision to make. He needed to be smart with his free time and use it wisely. If he spent it all at once, then where would he be? Trapped in enslavement again, watching Sue with no way to ever reach her or anyone else?

He couldn't do that to himself. He'd seen too many stonemen fall to madness because of mistakes like that.

No matter how much he wanted to use every free second he could with her, it was smarter to tuck some time away to save him when the strain of his imprisonment became too much to bear.

"Those are some seriously deep thoughts you're having," said Sue.

He only now realized how closely she'd been watching him. "Sorry. I should have been paying you more attention."

"That's okay. Your attention has a way of making me forget our plans. And as much as I want you to have your vacation, I'm also pretty keen on not having the last few months of my life stripped away and replaced with a random roll of the dice."

"What do you think your life would be like if you turned down your uncle's inheritance?"

"Boring. Lonely. Probably a lot like yours, I imagine."

"I have a feeling I'm not going to be nearly so bored in the future." As much as he appreciated her offer to keep him entertained, what he really wondered was if he'd ever get to see her wet, naked body again now that she knew he was watching. He would have gladly traded every TV show he'd ever seen for one more glimpse of her pretty backside and the full curve of her breasts.

Just the memory of it so soon on the heels of her kiss was enough to make his cock swell with arousal.

Fortunately, Sue was spared the sight as she stared out the restaurant window. "I don't have a bad life, but I'd definitely miss Charlotte."

"She's the colorful woman curator who's mentoring you, right?"

Sue nodded. "I've never met anyone so vibrant before. She drives me crazy, but I kinda love her."

For some reason, hearing Sue express her feeling so openly made Dalton envious. No one ever spoke about him like that, not even her uncle Herman, who'd gone out of his way to make Dalton's life a better place.

The only woman who'd ever loved him was long gone. Her family line had ended years ago. After that Herman Sullivan had been chosen as Dalton's curator.

He felt a telltale wave of pressure against his back. It had been so long since he'd felt that, it took him a second to realize what it meant.

Someone was coming. Another stoneman.

He stood and braced himself just as a wavering form solidified in the middle of the restaurant.

He recognized one of his own instantly. The stoneman standing before him was completely naked, wearing only the blood from hundreds of tiny cuts and gouges. His powerful body straightened, and those black eyes fixed on Dalton.

There was no humanity left in this creature. No mercy. He was brutal force walking.

Tristan.

He wouldn't have been here if he hadn't been ordered to come. With Thyra as his mistress, Dalton knew that this wasn't a social call. That sculptor was completely insane as evidenced by her willingness to drop Tristan into the middle of a crowded restaurant filled with innocent humans.

Dalton wasted no time. "Sue, get out. Get everyone out."

"What's going on?"

"Violence" he warned just as Tristan charged.

Sue barely dodged the mass of flying muscles that toppled the chair she'd just been using.

Dalton went down under the brutal attack from the bloody man who hadn't been there a second ago. They slid across the floor, leaving a sickening smear of blood behind. Tables and chairs fell like dominoes and people started screaming and running for the exits.

This late at night the restaurant wasn't crowded, but a few idiots pulled out cell phones and started recording. Sue had read enough of the curator manual to know that this was a bad thing. She wasn't supposed to let anyone find out about the stonemen. Having hers show up on YouTube was probably not going to win her any points with Pyrenia.

Sue ran up to the closest person—a teen who didn't look old enough to drive. She swiped the boy's phone and shoved it into her bra where he wasn't likely to go uninvited.

"Get out!" She gave him a hard shove to get him moving.

"Give me back my phone."

"I will when you get outside." It was a lie, but one she was willing to tell to get this kid out of harm's way.

When the kid didn't move fast enough, she gave him a not-so-gentle shove in the right direction.

The two men had separated now. The naked one ripped up a stool that had been bolted into the floor near the bar and swung it at Dalton's head.

He ducked, but the stool hit the wall behind him and slammed right through several two-by-fours, snapping them like toothpicks. While naked guy was busy with that, Dalton dove low, driving his shoulder into the other man's stomach to shove him away from the last of the gawking bystanders.

Sue grabbed the next phone someone was using to record the event and dropped that one in her pocket. "Outside. *Now*."

The woman she'd stolen from was no longer watching the tiny screen on her phone. Now that she saw the kind of mayhem going down in living color and full size, she seemed to realize that this wasn't as much an opportunity to be the next Internet sensation as it was to get her skull crushed in.

Dalton roared. Sue turned just in time to see him lift the soda machine over his head and toss it into naked guy. Liquid sprayed everywhere. A loud hissing filled the air.

The man staggered back under the weight, but flung the machine right back as if it had been a beach ball that had hit him.

Whoever this guy was, he was superhumanly strong.

Luckily, so was Dalton.

Sue managed to clear the restaurant of customers. She saw no one left behind the counter, so she jumped over it to find the surveillance devices she knew had to be recording back here somewhere. Everyone had security systems these days, if only to spy on the cash register.

There were a few employees cowering in a walk-in fridge. She shoved them out through the rear exit.

Dalton's body flew over the counter and took an industrial coffee maker with it as it went. His shoulder crushed a stainless steel cart filled with straws, napkins and paper cups. Everything exploded into a white bomb that fluttered onto his still body.

She had been too busy to feel much of anything other than surprise up to this point, but seeing him lie there, unmoving made a streak of fear light up her spine.

"Dalton?" Her voice shook as she called to him.

Naked guy hopped up onto the counter and looked at her. She'd never seen eyes so empty of warmth as his. She knew without a doubt, that he was the kind of man who could kill her and still sleep like a baby tonight.

The urge to back away was almost uncontrollable. But if she did that, Dalton would be left there, vulnerable.

She'd vowed to protect him. Sure, that was mostly all about keeping his statue safe, but her mind couldn't seem to find the line that separated the man's two forms.

Sue stepped over Dalton's paper-covered body and blocked naked guy's path. "Stay back."

He tilted his head at her warning, as if hearing a new noise for the first time. "I cannot. Thyra's will compels me."

Sue didn't know who Thyra was, but if she was anything like Pyrenia, then things had just gone from bad to worse. "To do what, exactly?"

"Destroy him."

Behind her, Dalton groaned. She didn't dare look back, but just the sound of his voice was enough to make her sag with relief.

"Now?" she asked. "Do you have to destroy him now?"

Naked guy stared at her for a second, confused. "When else?"

"Oh, I don't know. Next month is good."

"Stand aside, human."

Dalton's voice came from higher up now, telling her he was back on his feet. "Do what he says, Sue. You'll only get hurt."

Charlotte's warning not to get in their way gonged in her brain.

She risked a quick glance over her shoulder. Other than a few bruises and scrapes, he seemed to be in one piece.

"I'm your curator. I'm supposed to protect you."

Dalton's tone was apologetic. "She hasn't read the manual, Tristan. Forgive her."

Before she could ask what that meant, Dalton shoved her aside and launched himself at Tristan.

By the time she'd surfaced from under the cushion of napkins where she'd landed, the two men were brawling again.

Clearly she was no match for Tristan's brute force, but there was still the matter of the surveillance recordings and her duty to keep these guys a secret.

They weren't exactly making it easy on her.

She had to break a window to get into the manager's office, but she was able to rip the recording device from the wall just as the faint sound of sirens started squealing in the distance.

"The police are coming!" she yelled over the sound of harsh male grunts.

Dalton was on top of Tristan, pinning the man to the floor and repeatedly slamming his fist into the naked man's head. The blows were so hard, Tristan's skull left a cracked crater in the tile floor and still he didn't relent.

"We have to go. Now!" she yelled.

One second Dalton's fist was flying toward Tristan's head. The next the man was gone and Dalton's knuckles hit the floor.

There was no time now to ask about what had happened. They had to get out of here before the police came and started asking questions she couldn't possibly answer.

The crowd outside of the restaurant was a madhouse. People with children had started leaving as soon as the fight had broken out. A few people had stayed behind to witness the scene, but even they were starting to flee now that sirens were wailing.

She saw flashing lights coming from both directions on the interstate, so instead, she took the county road leading away from the highway and into the countryside. There was no way of knowing where it went other than away, but that was good enough for now.

The first bridge she crossed over, she tossed the cell phones and surveillance recorder into the water below. The only thing worse than getting caught now would be getting caught with recordings of what had gone down.

Finally, after a few miles, her nervous system started to behave itself enough she could form a coherent sentence. "Care to tell me what the hell that was about?" she asked.

"Tristan was sent to gut me."

"Why?"

His answer was a clipped, "Because his mistress ordered him to."

"Did you piss her off or something?"

"Not that I remember, but that doesn't mean a damn thing. Those women don't think right when it comes to logic."

"What women?"

"The sculptors. You met two of them earlier."

"There are more?"

"Too many. Tristan belongs to Thyra."

"And she's some kind of psychotic stoneman killer?"

"I've only seen her in action a few times. That was enough to know that I'd hate to be in Tristan's place."

She glanced his way. "You're wearing his blood."

Dalton started unbuttoning his shirt. "Poor man. I can only imagine what kind of pain he must suffer."

"What do you mean? He seemed okay to me when he was tossing you across the room."

"His statue has been damaged somehow. Every time he turns to flesh, those wounds are in his skin. They won't ever heal unless his statue is repaired."

"Why doesn't his curator take some spackle to him, then?"

"I heard a rumor that he killed his curator and no longer has one." Dalton stripped the shirt off, baring his torso.

It was all Sue could do to keep her eyes on the road, rather than on the man. She hadn't really taken the time to appreciate him when she'd had the chance. Not that she had one now, flying down a poorly paved road at well over the speed limit.

Instead of gawking, she gripped the wheel tighter and pretended that she wasn't missing a fantastic show.

He leaned over the seat. She heard the zipper on his suitcase open. A few seconds later, he was back in his seat, pulling a clean shirt over his head.

She had no idea where she was going, so she started working her way east on the back roads, hoping to connect with the interstate again. "Tristan just popped in that restaurant with no warning. What's to keep him from appearing in the back seat?"

"That was Thyra's doing. We stonemen aren't able to transport ourselves like that. Only our sculptors have that power."

"Okay. So can she plop him down wherever she likes?"

"Yes."

"Any idea why she pulled him out when she did?"

He shook his head. "I figure she didn't want him seen by the police. The sculptors' father gets angry if they let humans find out about us."

"How many of these sculptors are there?"

"I've only met four. I've heard the names of three more."

"And they all have statues like you?"

"Some more than others. It's a bit of a bone of contention between them. Apparently, she who dies with the most stonemen wins."

"Assuming they can die. With powers like theirs, who knows?"

"I've spent more than a few years asking that very question."

"Hearing Charlotte talk, I assumed you were normal men once, right?" she asked.

"That's right."

"Then why do they call themselves sculptors? They didn't sculpt anything, did they?"

"I suppose they didn't. I wouldn't suggest you bring this to their attention, though. Except for Alethia, they all seem a little crazy to me. Different flavors of crazy, maybe, but still off their rockers."

"Yeah. Power and crazy all in one neat little package. Fun times." Signs guided her back to the interstate. There was no hint of police nearby, but that didn't mean no one would be on their tail. All it would take was one person back there to be smart enough to write down her car's description or license plate, and they were screwed.

"How much farther do we have to go?" he asked.

"Another hundred miles or so. We should be there in less than two hours."

"Amazing. I don't think I'll ever get used to how fast technology progresses while I'm imprisoned. I wonder what else will have changed by the next time I'm allowed to walk around in the flesh."

"Maybe by then someone will invent an early warning device to tell us if some deranged stoneman is going to appear on the hood of the car."

He cupped her shoulder. "Try not to worry too much. He's not after you. Just me. As long as you don't stand in the way again, you won't get hurt."

"I'd really prefer if you didn't get hurt, too."

"I can take a hit."

"I noticed. Sadly, so can he. That poor restaurant will never be the same."

"I'd pay for the damages if I could."

"Don't sweat it too much. Between the insurance and the publicity that place will get on the news, they'll be fine. And if not, I'll set aside some of the money Uncle Herman left me to make it right."

"I'm not used to depending on a woman financially."

"Welcome to the twenty-first century."

Sue found the address they were searching for just after midnight. It was a little house in an old part of town. The homes were small, but built in a time when quality construction still mattered more than profit. The lots were large, the trees huge. The windows were mostly dark, reminding her that it was really too late to be knocking on doors.

"We can't wake these people up," said Dalton.

"It's not like we have a whole lot of options. Your giant, bleeding friend could pop in at any minute. If we don't find that puzzle box soon, it could be too late for you."

"I was raised with better manners than this."

"Screw manners," she said getting out of the car. "I want that box."

CHAPTER 7

Thyra summoned Tristan, then forced him to wait while she finished eating.

Blood dripped down his limbs to form little pools at his feet. He said nothing. All he did was stand there, staring straight ahead, as still as if in his stone form.

"Do you want to eat?" she asked sweetly.

He refused to answer. She could have compelled him to do so, but what fun would that have been? It was so much better to grind him down to the point that he was willing to do whatever she wanted.

She licked the juicy roast from her fingers, urging the air to waft in his direction and bring the succulent scent with it.

When he didn't so much as lick his lips, she grew bored.

"You were almost caught," she said. "If I hadn't pulled you from that place when I did, the human authorities would have seen you."

She expected him to make excuses, but none came.

"You've failed me. I should send you back to your stone shell for another hundred years."

His black eyes narrowed so slightly, she wasn't quite sure she'd seen it.

"Do you think you'll survive another hundred years in the elements?" she asked. "Already water seeps into tiny cracks, freezing each winter. Those cracks will expand soon, and when they do, your parts will begin to break off." She gave a pointed glance at his penis, knowing how fond men were of such things.

Tristan stared straight ahead. "You can't hurt me."

"I already have, as the blood at your feet so loudly states."

"That's just pain."

"Pain is usually such an effective teacher with most men." She ran her finger over his shoulder, tracing a line between the trickles of blood. "Why are you immune?"

He looked at her then, and the potent force of his gaze was enough to make her forget to breathe. "I'm not. You simply aren't powerful enough to hurt me."

That piqued her anger enough she felt her power rise, seething with the desire to be unleashed. "You think me powerless?" she asked from between clenched teeth. "Dance, puppet."

Tristan's body lurched into motion, moving as it was compelled to do. He didn't fight her attempts to control him, simply relaxed and let her do whatever she wanted. He twirled through the dining hall in a decidedly feminine display that would have humiliated most men.

But not Tristan. His face was emotionless. There was no fury, no embarrassment. He might as well have been in his stone form, his face was so impassive.

When Thyra realized she wasn't going to win the prize she sought from him, her attention shifted to another.

She brought him to a full stop in front of her. "I want that puzzle box. Find it before Pyrenia's stoneman does, or I'll shove you back into stone form and break your manhood off with my bare hands."

Before he could anger her further, she flung him to Earth to do her bidding.

Dalton had to hurry to catch up with Sue as she went to the front door of the dark house. By the time he reached her side, she was already ringing the bell.

A dog started barking nearby, then another. By the time she'd rung the bell a third time, lights had come on in this house as well as one across the street.

Slow, shuffling footsteps sounded from inside. The lock clicked open, and a short, fuzzy-haired woman peered out from under the chain securing the door. She was eighty if she was a day. Stooped with age, she glared up at them for interrupting her sleep.

"What in the world is going on?" she asked.

"I'm so sorry, ma'am," said Sue. "I hate to wake you like this, but it's important. Can we come in for a minute?"

"At this hour? I don't think so. Whatever it is, it can wait until morning."

"I'm afraid it can't. Please. Will you just hear me out?"

The woman said nothing but didn't shut the door.

Sue pulled the photo from her purse. "We're looking for this. It's incredibly important that we find it right away."

The old woman adjusted her glasses and peered at the photo. "I can't help you."

"I can pay. I don't have much, but I'll gladly pay whatever the box is worth."

"It's not the money, dear. I don't have the box anymore. I sold it months ago."

Dalton felt his stomach drop with disappointment and only then realized just how far he'd let his hopes rise.

Sue was seemingly undaunted. "Who bought it?"

"Some hoity-toity art dealer from St. Louis. He bought a bunch of Mom's old things, including that box no one could ever open. Poor woman went to her grave not knowing what was inside."

"What was the name of the art dealer?"

"State something."

"Do you have his card? A phone number?"

"If I give it to you, will you let me get some sleep?"

"Yes, ma'am," said Dalton.

"Hang on." The woman shut the door and locked it.

Sue must have seen his disappointment on his face, because she put her hand on his arm as if to comfort him. "Don't worry. We'll find it."

"I've already had more hours of freedom tonight than I've had in a century."

"Chasing after a puzzle box because your 'mistress' tells you to is not freedom. Lounging on a beach in Costa Rica, being served drinks by busty, bikini-clad women is freedom."

"It's all relative, but I'll take this little treasure hunt of ours over being trapped inside that cold stone any day of the week."

She gave him a look that reeked of pity. "You never did tell me what got you turned to stone in the first place. Charlotte said I should check the archives to find out about you, and now I'm regretting not listening to her."

He didn't want to talk about that. Not now. Not ever. Nothing she could do would change his path, and nothing she could say would make him sorry that he'd taken it.

The door opened again. The little old woman handed Sue a small slip of paper. "Take this and try not to wake anyone else up tonight, okay?"

"Yes, ma'am."

"Thank you," said Dalton. "Sorry we bothered you."

She shut the door just as that cold, tingling feeling hit Dalton's spine. Dread trickled through him, spurring him into motion. He didn't waste time looking around, he simply grabbed Sue's hand and pulled her into motion.

"Tristan's coming back for another round. *Run.*"

CHAPTER 8

Tristan appeared in the middle of the old woman's lawn, his face expressionless and dripping with blood.

Dalton could not let the man hurt Sue.

He gave her a gentle push toward the car. "Drive away."

"I'm not leaving you behind," she said.

"You can't help me. Just go."

He didn't wait to see if she obeyed. There was no time. Tristan's muscles were shifting and coiling as his body prepared to charge.

Dalton moved first. The more distance he put between Sue and what was about to happen, the better.

Just as he was about to hit the other stoneman head-on, Tristan jumped straight up and grabbed onto one of the bare tree branches overhead. Dalton skidded to an awkward stop and turned around.

The broken end of a branch as thick as a telephone pole was in Tristan's hands. He held it like a bat and swung it right for Dalton's head.

Dalton tried to jump out of the way, but he was already off balance from his earlier miss. The wood slammed right into his chest. The cracking sound that rose up from the impact was loud. The searing pain that streaked across his lungs told him that more than just wood had broken.

The thick branch landed on top of him, crushing his broken ribs.

In the distance, Sue let out a loud cry. He looked up to see her running toward him, wielding her purse like a weapon.

He worked to find enough breath to warn her away, but the blow to his chest had knocked every bit of air from his body.

Tristan turned toward Sue. He took a slow step in her direction, which made her skid to a full stop. Her expression turned from fierce warrior protector to frightened rabbit. Her purse fell from her limp fingertips.

Dalton shoved the branch off and picked it up. No one was going to hurt Sue while he still drew breath.

Before he could cross the distance, Tristan poked one finger against her forehead, leaving a smear of blood behind. "Dalton was right. You should have run."

"Why are you doing this?" she asked.

"Because I must." That was all Tristan had time to get out before Dalton slammed the branch into his back.

Sue jumped out of the way as Tristan went flying sideways. The man landed hard enough to dig a furrow in the old woman's yard.

Dalton gave Sue a push toward the car. "Get out of here before you can't."

She scurried off, but by the time he turned to face Tristan again, the man was already back on his feet.

Pain streaked through Dalton's chest like chain lightning. Each breath was an exercise in agony. He felt the broken ends of bones shifting against each other with every step, but there was no way he could stop and rest now with Sue still in reach.

"Ready for more?" he asked Tristan.

Dirt stuck to the man's naked body, clinging to the blood dripping along his skin. One of his arms hung wrong, but that didn't seem to slow him down.

He picked up the winterized concrete birdbath decorating the yard and flung it at Dalton.

Dalton batted it away with the branch, but all the move did was splinter the wood and rob him of his weapon. The birdbath slammed into his broken ribs and cracked something in his hip.

He went down, sailing back several feet from the blow. His head hit the sidewalk hard enough to crack the cement. Stars exploded above him, and it took a second for him to realize they were only from the hit to his head.

He tried to stand, but the dizziness spun his world until he couldn't tell which way was up. Still, he pushed against what felt like the ground only to find it wet and sticky.

Blood. He could smell it now, feel it cooling on his clothes.

He looked down and saw that a chunk of the birdbath had broken off and was sticking out of his gut. Blood poured from the wound so fast he knew he didn't have much time left.

Across the lawn, Tristan stalked toward him.

This was it. Dalton couldn't get up, and even if he could, it would only make him bleed faster. He only hoped that Sue had done what he'd told her and gotten the hell out of here.

The sound of a car's engine revving blasted in his left ear. He could smell the exhaust and feel the vibration of the engine through the ground.

Headlights splashed across Tristan's bleeding, muddy body.

Dalton looked over his shoulder just in time to see Sue's car careening toward him. The blow knocked Tristan down and sucked him under the car. It bobbed as it rolled over him, coming to a stop only feet from Dalton's head.

A second later, Sue was at his side, dragging his heavy ass into the car. He helped her as much as he could, but only one of his legs was working. Each inch sent pain frolicking through his chest and abdomen. His blood was everywhere, making her grip on him slick.

"I'm getting you to a hospital," she said. "Just hang on."

"No time." Was that frail, breathless sound his voice?

"Don't you dare die on me." She got him in the car and closed the door.

"Gotta turn back to stone. It's the only way." He didn't know if she'd heard him or not, but he couldn't wait any longer.

Dalton ripped the chunk of cement from his gut. The second the blood started gushing out, he willed himself to stone, praying he hadn't waited too long.

Sue had never been more freaked out in her entire life. Blood was everywhere. She was covered in it. So was her car.

There was no way Dalton could survive long enough for her to get him help. There simply wasn't that much blood in the human body.

She saw her car shift as she raced around to get in. The right side dipped low as if something heavy had just gotten in.

A little spurt of fear had her looking around. Tristan's body was still pinned under the car. She could see one of his naked legs peeking out near the tire.

As long as he was still down, they had a fighting chance to get away. She only hoped Dalton could make it that long.

Her tires sank into the lawn, spinning for a minute before she gained the traction she needed to get back onto the street.

"We'll be at the hospital in a minute," she said, reaching over to offer him what little comfort she could.

Her hand hit something cold and hard. She looked over and saw that the flesh-and-blood man who'd been there a second ago was now frigid stone covered in blood.

She hit the curb, which reminded her to focus on her driving. A quick glance in the rearview mirror showed her that Tristan was back on his feet, but only barely. Broken bones were visible in one leg and both arms.

He wasn't going to be running after them, at least.

Sue was shaking so badly she knew better than to keep driving. She found a self-service car wash a few miles away and pulled into one of the bays.

Dalton was still there, his face frozen in a mask of agony. His blood was smeared everywhere, pooling on the carpet at his feet. His clothes were soaked with it, adding to the mess in her car.

She rolled down the windows to get rid of the metallic stench. The cold air hit her face. She sucked it in. Within a few seconds, those gasps turned to sobs.

All the fear she'd felt rolled out of her, hollowing her out as it went. She had no idea how long she sat there crying, but she stopped somewhere around the time she started freezing.

Her clothes were soaked with blood, too. She had to get out of them—get rid of all the mess before she could think straight.

She found a box knife in the toolbox she kept in the car and used it to cut Dalton's clothes away. After purchasing about a hundred dashboard wipes from the vending machine, she managed to clean away enough blood that her car no longer looked like a slaughterhouse. Next, she stripped out of her own clothes and started up the sprayer with a few quarters.

It was, without a doubt, the coldest, most public shower of her life, but there was no way she was walking around wearing Dalton's blood.

By the time she got back in the car, her teeth were chattering behind blue lips. She cranked up the heat and found her cell phone in her purse.

"It's way late," said Charlotte. "Are you okay?"

The floodgates threatened to bust open again, but Sue managed to hold back the tears through sheer force of will. "I'm never going to be okay again. Neither is my car."

"What happened?"

She relayed the story as fast as she could. There was still no way to know if Tristan was going to come limping around the corner at any minute to finish her off.

"Dalton is stone again. I think he's dead."

"He's not dead," said Charlotte. "If you'd read the manual, you'd know that. I kept telling you to read it, but did you? No. Of course not."

"Charlotte. A lecture is the last thing I need. Just tell me if he's okay."

"He's fine. He just got hurt bad enough that he had to return to his stone form to heal."

"Are you sure?"

"Positive. Give him some time and he'll be as good as new."

Relief pulled her in and gave her a bone-crushing hug. Her head spun and she had to anchor herself against the headrest so she didn't puke. "You have no idea how glad I am to hear that."

"Your shaking voice kinda gives it away."

The heat from the vents started melting the ice around her toes. "How long do you think I'll have to wait?"

"Depends on how bad he was," said Charlotte. "So, I can't believe you ran over a stoneman. Who knew you were so ruthless?"

"I didn't enjoy it." Even the reminder was enough to make her queasy.

"I bet he enjoyed it less."

"Why the hell won't he leave us alone?"

"He has no choice, Sue. I know you did what you had to do to defend yourself, but this little setback isn't going to stop him. If he was ordered to destroy Dalton, he will, or die trying."

"So what do I do?"

"It's after two in the morning. I think you should get some sleep."

Sue snorted at how ridiculous a notion that was. "Yeah, right. I'll just pop into a motel for a little shuteye while Dalton chills in my car." She glanced at his face again, hating the pain she saw there. "No one will notice a six-foot stoneman riding shotgun."

"You can't keep going without rest. You sound wrecked."

"I am. As soon as the adrenaline wears off, I'll be lucky if I can sit up on my own."

"You can't stay at the car wash. Someone will come by and see the bloody clothes."

"I can't leave him. Not like this."

"Hang on." Charlotte's bracelets jangled and her rings clicked as she typed. "There's a motel not far from you. I'll text you directions. Go hang there until dawn. Throw a blanket over Dalton, and if anyone asks, tell them you're an artist transporting your work to a buyer."

"I suppose that will work."

"It will. Just lie like you mean it. People will believe anything."

"Is that what you just did to me when you told me he's going to be okay?"

"Guess you'll have to read the manual to find out. And by the way, when you're back, we're going to have a long talk about every little detail. It's not every day a curator gets to spend time with her stoneman, you know. You're one of the lucky ones."

"Yeah. So lucky."

"Stop whining and get moving. I'll check in with you later."

Sue pulled out and headed for the nearest coffee. No way was she going to be asleep if Tristan decided to pop in and ruin all her lucky fun.

Dalton had never before counted the seconds of his imprisonment like he did now.

Even in his stone form, he could feel the pain of his ruined body. The damage was healing, but not nearly fast enough to suit him.

Each cracked bone had to mend, each severed blood vessel needed time to heal shut. He wasn't sure the exact mechanics of it all, but he could feel it happening.

Way too damn slowly.

Sue was driving. He could see out the window as the miles passed. She followed the signs pointing toward St. Louis, getting him closer and closer to the key to his week of freedom.

Every few miles, he felt her hand on his arm or thigh. She offered a few quiet words of comfort and encouragement. Proof she hadn't written him off.

Between reassurances, she shared little stories from her childhood with him. He learned about her family and friends, including the ones she'd left behind to come be his curator.

As the miles passed, a picture of the woman she was started to form. And as his body healed within the stone and he searched for a distraction from the pain, he began thinking about just what he wanted to do once he was made flesh again.

That kiss he'd given her had only been enough to whet his appetite. He wanted more from her than that. So much more.

She fell silent, giving him time to consider just how he'd touch her if given the chance. He knew it was foolish for him to yearn for a woman—to want something he could never truly have. It was the kind of thing that drove men like him mad. He'd seen it happen with other stonemen enough times to know it was possible.

The desire to possess something out of reach made them angry, hostile. With no free will and very few ways of venting that frustration, the anger would build until it was a living, breathing creature of its own. Stonemen spent a lot of time in solitude, with only their thoughts to keep them company. It was easy to let a stray idea bloom into something more—a repeated series of thoughts that circled in one's head over and over again until it was all consuming. When there were no thoughts beyond possessing a woman they couldn't even touch—nothing to distract them from their lust—their minds would crack under the strain, turning them into something dark and feral.

Dalton hadn't strayed down that dangerous path. He'd stayed true to the man he'd been long enough now that he knew what it took.

Acceptance.

How in hell was he going to be able to accept his imprisonment when the woman of his fantasies was walking around his home, tempting him with her presence?

Worse yet, how was he going to feel once she found a man who could make her happy and moved him in with her?

Dalton would have to watch them fall in love, get married, have babies.

He'd already done that once with June, and it had nearly killed him.

He wouldn't fall for a woman and do that to himself again. Not ever. This trip with Sue could be no more than an interesting distraction from the monotony of his life. She didn't care for the job of curator, anyway. After what she'd been through, she'd probably call it quits the second they got back.

And he wouldn't blame her a bit.

"I think I have to pull over for a while," she said. "I'm going to kill us both if I keep driving."

Judging from the angle of the sun, it was afternoon and she hadn't slept at all last night.

"I hate to do this to you, but you're going to have to tough it out on your own for a few hours while I sleep."

She pulled into an old motel and checked in. When she came back to the car, she was carrying an ugly blanket.

"Sorry about this, but if people see you, it's going to cause a stir. I'm going to have to cover you up so you look like laundry or something."

It took her a while to do the job. His vision was blocked, his hearing muted. He could feel the scratchy texture of the blanket on his skin and smell the faint hint of bleach clinging to it. Once she'd arranged the blanket, she stacked something on top of him—luggage, he guessed.

"That'll have to do," she said. "I'll come check on you as soon as I can."

Dalton sat trapped inside his ugly cocoon, unable to do anything but will his injuries to heal faster.

CHAPTER 9

Sue hated leaving Dalton alone. Even though he was parked right outside and she'd parted the plastic curtains enough to see him, she still worried what would happen if Tristan showed up again.

It was her job to keep Dalton safe. Protect him.

She needed to sleep so she wouldn't drive off the road, but even the thought of closing her eyes was too much stress. She was certain that once she opened them again, Dalton would be gone.

She tried to relax with a hot shower, but once she was out from under the spray, her muscles clamped right back up again.

She turned on the TV. Local news reports from the ruined diner and the old lady's destroyed yard where the stonemen had fought made the horror of the battles come rushing back. The police were still searching for the *vandals*, as they called them. Minor injuries were reported at the diner where people got hurt rushing from the violence.

If she'd known what was going to happen, she never would have taken Dalton into a place filled with people. Maybe if she'd done what Charlotte said and read the manual...

As exhausted as she was, sleep eluded her in the face of guilt and worry. She lay on the stiff mattress, propped up so she could see outside. No one so much as walked by. Finally, as the room began to darken with the oncoming dusk, she drifted off into a fitful sleep. She woke up every few minutes, terrified that something horrible had happened to him. No amount of seeing him safe seemed to calm her frayed nerves.

She must have drifted off again, because the next thing she knew, there was a knock at her door.

Panic jolted her upright so fast her head spun. She glanced outside and saw Dalton missing.

Had someone stolen him? Had Tristan come back and pounded Dalton to gravel?

By the time she reached the door, a hundred different catastrophes raced through her mind. She didn't even think to ask who was there or look through the peep hole. All she could think about was finding out what fate had befallen him.

Dalton stood there, the ugly blanket cinched around his waist. There was no visible sign of his injuries—not even a scar. He was covered in smooth, whole skin and so beautiful it made her heart lurch in her chest.

Relief took over her body. She flung herself at him, forcing him to drop the blanket to catch her. She hit him with a solid thud, but he didn't so much as rock under her impact. Instead, he caught her up in one arm and walked her into the room, kicking the door shut behind him.

Sue hugged him tight as her relief coursed through her. She was shaking so hard she worried her knees wouldn't hold her up if she let go.

She pressed her face against the side of his neck, unable to even form words. She still couldn't believe he was safe.

"I've got you," he said over and over as he rocked her slightly.

Words weren't powerful enough to break through her denial. She was still quivering on the edge of sleep, uncertain if she was dreaming this, too.

Finally, she got a grip on herself enough to look up at him. His blue eyes were dark, and a faint smile toyed with the corner of his mouth.

Sue kissed him. She didn't know why, but in that moment, there was simply no other choice. It was either kiss him or fall apart again.

Dalton kissed her back, tightening his hold on her body. Her feet no longer touched the ground, but she didn't care. As his kiss turned from one of surprise to comfort to something hotter and darker, all she cared about was getting more.

Her pulse pounded through her limbs and heated her skin. A deep aching void began expanding low in her belly, quivering with need. Everywhere his skin touched hers, there was an answering tingle, as if her body recognized some long-lost, vital component.

His taste went to her head. She couldn't seem to get enough air. Every breath was laced with the scent of his skin, and she began desperately sucking in as much as she could take.

His kisses turned greedy, almost frantic. His tongue played with her mouth, making her hungry even as he fed her.

Thick, hot fingers splayed across her ass as he lifted her higher. The wall pressed against her back as he pinned her there, pulling the curtains closed. "I'm not sharing you with the world. You're all mine."

Sue hadn't intentionally signed up for the position of *all his*, but the sound of his voice, all low and sexy, was more than convincing enough to get her on board.

The world tilted as he laid her back onto the bed. It had felt cold and hard only a moment ago, but now, with Dalton atop her, she was grateful for the cushion. His weight pinned her there, while at the same time, he managed to slip right between her thighs.

The instinctive need to relax and make room for him took over. Her hips bucked toward him in welcome, and the hard ridge of his erection rubbed against her clit. With only the thin, stretchy cotton of her clothing between them, there was no masking his obvious arousal.

His mouth moved down her body. She wasn't sure how he did it, but he took her clothes off so easily, they seem to evaporate as he passed. By the time he was pressing hot, open-mouthed kisses across her abdomen, her shirt was open, baring her to his questing hands.

Rough, strong fingers moved over her with exquisite care. He stroked and massaged, making her squirm with the need for more.

Sue let herself go, giving herself free reign to touch and grab him in all the ways she'd been craving since she'd first seen his naked body on display in her living room.

Each new swath of skin was hotter than the last. The feel of his muscles shifting beneath his skin as he stripped her naked was enough to make her abdomen clench and her pussy slicken. She'd always had trouble heating up with other men, but Dalton seemed to know just how to touch her to make her burn.

He pulled away, kneeling over her. As the cold air hit her skin, she realized that she was completely naked now. Just as he was.

He stared down at her, his blue eyes so dark they were nearly unrecognizable. A flushed stain of lust painted his cheeks, and his mouth was open around a heavy pant.

Normally, Sue would have balked at having a man stare at her so blatantly. But this was far from normal. There was so much raw lust in his gaze that there was nothing she could do but melt under his stare.

In one smooth move, he grabbed her knees and pushed them high and wide. His dark head lowered, and in the next instant, Sue's world dissolved in a haze of pleasure.

He kissed her pussy like he did her mouth, with greedy hunger and hot, wicked strokes of his tongue. Her belly hollowed out with every one of her heavy breaths until she simply forgot to breathe. The things he could do with his tongue were so good she had to count it as a superpower. When she was certain he couldn't make her even one degree hotter, go one inch higher, his lips fastened around her clit, giving her nowhere to go but where he led. He eased two thick fingers inside, instinctively finding that one secret place that her previous lovers missed without careful instruction.

The combination of sensations was more than she could take. Her body shrank down to a tiny point of feeling, then exploded in a fiery blast of pleasure. The orgasm went on for half of forever, holding on and refusing to let go. Whatever he was doing kept her flying high until the very last ounce of delight was coaxed from her body.

She hadn't even had time to pull in a full breath before he moved up her body and slid the tip of his cock inside. His mouth covered hers, giving her his breath when hers was nowhere to be found.

The aftershocks of her orgasm shook her, each one gaining her another sweet, searing inch of his erection. The taste of her release on the tongue of the man who'd given it to her hit her like a drug. It wasn't the kind of thing that normally worked for her, but with Dalton, everything worked. And then some.

His fingers plucked at her nipples, making delightful chords go off in her belly. The shimmering contractions he caused made him suck in a breath and rock deeper into her.

Sue's body strained to keep up with the demands he was making on her. Each fluid retreat of his body made her desperate for his return. Each time he moved back inside her, the intense stretch made her go weak and give him the room he needed to work his dark magic.

Dalton pulled his mouth from hers and stared into her eyes as his hips continued to move. She gripped him with her legs and wrapped her hands around his neck, holding on for dear life. Her eyelids were heavy, her limbs languid. The slowly coiling pressure he was building in her abdomen was beyond her control, so she simply let go and gave him what he wanted.

"I never thought I'd have this again," he said.

"Sex?" she asked, proud she was able to form the single coherent word.

He paused, his erection deep inside her. The move made sparks dance at the corner of her eyes and heat seep from her pores.

"Human touch," he said, correcting her. "The feeling of being connected."

They were definitely connected. In fact, she was certain he couldn't have been a bigger presence in her world right now if he'd tried. Every one of her senses was filled with him, making him seem larger than life. "Connection's good."

He smiled at her breathless response. With a tight grip on her waist, he lifted his hips and forced her to take him as he moved.

The change in angle hit a whole new and exciting set of nerve endings and rubbed her clit with a sweet kind of torture. Sue splayed her hands across his pecs and held on for her life. Her breasts bounced as they moved, and the hot stare Dalton gave them was enough to make steam rise from her skin.

Suddenly, he jackknifed up, pulled her against him in a crushing hug and took her mouth like a man on a mission. Within seconds of his siege, her body surrendered and she released her cry of completion in his mouth.

As the second wave of her orgasm hit, she felt Dalton's cock swell and pulse as he came. His grip on her was so hard she could barely breathe, but who needed air when she had a man like him coming right along with her.

She collapsed inside his arms as the last few spurts of his release filled her. Sweat made their bodies slick, but he seemed to have no trouble lifting her enough to ease her down to the mattress. Only then did he slowly withdraw from her body.

They lay side-by-side for a while, holding hands. She didn't know how long, but it was long enough for her to catch her breath, cool off, and thank God she'd kept up with her birth control pills despite her recent lack of a sex life. She didn't know if Dalton had been toting around any STDs with him when he'd been turned to stone, but based on the way his body had healed in just a few hours, she wasn't too worried. Maybe she would be once the sexual high wore off, but right now, she was feeling too damn fine to let anything harsh her buzz.

He rolled on top of her again, holding his weight off her body. The position made his arms flex in a mouthwatering display and reminded her of just how glad she was that she was the curator for such a hot stoneman.

Dalton swooped down and kissed her mouth. Slowly. Thoroughly. By the time he was done, she was starting to heat up again.

This man had a way of going to her head and making her forget that the rest of the world was even a thing she had to worry about.

"You keep kissing me like that and we're never going to make it to St. Louis," she said.

"It would almost be worth it to stay here and take you again if not for the fact that I could spend an entire week doing so if we find that box."

A whole week? Her poor heart would never survive it intact. She wasn't one of those girls who could fuck and run. She cared about the men she slept with, and that wasn't something she could safely do with Dalton.

She had to remember who he was. *What* he was. There was no such thing as long term for them. No matter how much either of them might want it.

She pushed away the thick layer of emotion settling over her with a forced smile. "You have an excellent point. If you're all healed up, then we should go." She felt his cock graze her thigh, still hard enough for them to go another round. "And you're definitely all healed up."

He gave her one more soul-stealing kiss, then rolled away. A few smears of dried blood marred his back, but other than that, he was still a sight to behold.

Who knew a man as old as him could have such a world class ass?

"You should shower while I grab your clothes. There's still some blood on you."

He nodded. "I'm sorry about your car. If I had a way to pay for the damage, I would."

She waved the offer away. "Don't worry about it. I'm just glad you didn't bleed out entirely."

"Me, too." He went into the bathroom and shut the door.

Sue cleaned up in the sink outside the bathroom, dressed and fetched a new outfit from the car. She came back in just in time to see him exit the bathroom with a cloud of steam curling around him.

Every thought drained from her head. He looked like some kind of ancient god, all wet and golden. It was no wonder someone had wanted to capture him in stone. Looks like his were far too amazing not to immortalize them in solid rock.

A trickle of moisture seeped into her panties, making her wish she'd brought another pair inside. The clothes in her hand slipped from her fingertips.

Dalton picked them up and pulled her against him in a one-armed hug. "If I kiss you again, I'm going to take you again."

Sounded like a good idea to her. "Okay."

"I love how you respond to me, Sue. I love the way you sound when I please you. I love the way you taste."

She trembled. He had no idea what all that talk of love was doing to her. She was normally a stronger woman than this, but he seemed to blow all of that away with a few little words. "You're pretty tasty yourself."

He let out a low growl of approval, then took a long step back. The damp towel around his waist thrust out obscenely with his arousal.

She wanted to fall to her knees right then and there and see if she could make him squirm as much as he had her.

Dalton must have seen her thoughts cross her mind. He covered his erection with the pile of clothing and gave her a hot grin. "Let's find this art dealer. If there's still time before our deadline, then you and I can find a nice, quiet place to do whatever is on that sweet mind of yours."

Right. Art dealer, then sex. She could do that. "Okay. But you should get dressed now. If you stay naked, I can't be held responsible for what I might do to you."

He gave her a wicked smile. "I think I can live with that."

CHAPTER 10

Alethia knocked on the door of her sister's study. She hated coming here, but Pyrenia had left her no choice.

Lalia looked up from the book perched in her lap. Her exquisitely tailored suit hugged her slim frame. It was the exact shade of the deep sapphire glasses she wore. Not that she had any need for corrective lenses.

Her mousy brown hair was pulled back in a tight twist that left not a single strand free. As Alethia entered the room, Lalia's disapproving stare pinned her in place. Eyes the color of old parchment peered at Alethia over the rim of her glasses.

"I'm occupied," said Lalia in a quiet voice meant for churches and libraries.

"I'm sorry to disturb your studies. I know you're busy, but there's a matter I thought you would like to know about."

"Another human matter?" she asked, disgust clear in her tone.

A direct answer to that question was going to get Alethia thrown out, so she hedged. "It's come to my attention that one of your contractual clauses may be triggered."

Lalia sighed. "I don't have time to monitor them all. I'm pursuing other interests now."

Alethia glanced at the book. "You're reading a romance."

"Yes."

There really was no delicate way to put this. "You hate men."

"I don't hate them. I've simply not yet found any use for them."

"So, why the book, then?"

"I'm studying what it is that makes women become stupid when an attractive penis is around. And for that matter, I'm seeking to discover what, exactly, makes one penis more attractive than another."

"It's not just a man's sexual organs a woman is after when she falls for a man."

Lalia frowned in confusion. "But that's the only thing a man has that a woman doesn't. What else would hold her interest?"

This was clearly a conversation that was going to take more time than Alethia had. As it was, Sue and Dalton were speeding toward a trap. If Alethia didn't warn them, they were going to walk right into it and possibly reveal what he was in a very public way.

That was not going to please Father.

Alethia took a deep breath and tried to find some sliver of logic sharp enough to lodge itself into Lalia's dense brain. "There's the matter of companionship, compatibility, laughter, emotional support, and many other things I don't have time to list."

"Those are only things that weak-minded people need."

"No, those are things that normal people need. You're…special."

"I know."

Alethia resisted the urge to groan. "You should keep studying. I'm sure you'll find that elusive pattern soon enough. In the meantime, please review your contractual clauses."

"I told you, I've let that all go in my intense pursuit of knowledge."

"I promise, this specific clause will support your study."

That seemed to pique her interest. "Which contract?"

Oh, no. She wasn't going to step into that mess again. Meddling in her sisters' affairs was one thing. Calling attention to obvious points of contention was another. The last place she wanted to be was between Lalia and Pyrenia when they butted heads. "All I'll say is that you should look up from your studies long enough to see what's happening on Earth. There's a stoneman on a mission, and watching him and his curator interact may be far more informative than any novel could ever be."

Lalia marked her place and closed the book. "If you're wrong about this, the only contracts I'll be reviewing are yours. And you really can't afford to lose any more of your stonemen, can you?"

Alethia had to keep up pretenses. If she didn't, her sisters would learn too much, and they'd never again respect her. Without that respect, she wouldn't be able to do nearly as much.

"You're right, of course. I'm simply trying to cut down the number of stonemen the others have. Even the playing field."

"At least tell me which of our sisters has earned your interest this time."

She hesitated. Telling Lalia would speed up the process, but it would also put her at more risk of being discovered. "Let's just say that Thyra has gotten involved."

Lalia waved her ink-stained hand. "That hardly narrows it down. She loves to spread chaos in her wake. Tell me who or I go back to my book."

It was a risk Alethia was going to have to take. She could already feel the minutes on Earth ticking by. If she didn't get there in time, things were going to end badly. "Pyrenia. I don't think she even remembers that you added a clause to this particular contract."

Lalia's parchment colored eyes narrowed in speculation. "I will find this contract and use it to destroy her fun."

"That easy? I don't even have to talk you into it?"

Her smile barely shifted her mouth. "Not at all, dear sister. She deserves whatever she gets."

"Why? What did she do this time to anger you?"

Lalia stood and smoothed out her tailored skirt. "She interrupted me."

Just as Alethia had. "I'll go now."

"That's the smartest thing you've done since before you knocked. Don't think I'll forget it."

Alethia knew she wouldn't.

Dalton was playing with fire. He knew that, but he couldn't seem to keep his damned hands to himself.

Sue made him forget every reason he shouldn't strip her naked and take her right here in the car. Even the sight of her hands on the wheel was enough to make him wonder how it would feel to have her stroke him.

He'd taken her too fast. There were so many thing he still wanted to do with her. Do *to* her.

He had no business having sex with her at all, much less figuring out how he was going to get some more. What had he been thinking?

He hadn't been. That was his mistake. He'd only meant to find her so he could be sure she wouldn't get caught by Tristan if Thyra ordered him to hurt her.

But then she'd thrown herself at Dalton with relief shining in her eyes, hugging him tight, and he'd forgotten all about danger.

He stared out the car window, watching the miles pass by. He couldn't look at Sue and not want her, so it was best to not look. Even without his eyes, he could still smell her. He still knew she was right there, only a short reach away.

He needed to get used to that. For the next several years— if she stayed on as his curator—she was always going to be just a short reach away and still completely lost to him. She would move around the old farmhouse, maybe even talk to him or touch him, but he'd never be able to bed her again. He wouldn't even be able to hold her.

How was he going to suffer through her life's journey as a spectator without going mad? When she brought men home, he'd be there to bear witness. Even if he didn't see them do anything, he'd still know what was going on—that another man was taking his woman.

His woman.

Since when did he think of her like that? And how the hell was he going to stop thinking that way?

Sue was under his skin, sure enough. He wished he knew how to get rid of his desire for her. Should he keep his distance so he didn't get any deeper? Or should he scratch his itch as hard and fast as he could for as long as he could?

She stopped along the way and bought them breakfast at a fast food place. The taste of coffee hit his tongue like an old friend, easing some of the tension riding at the base of his skull. He wolfed down a few of the little sandwiches and finished off his coffee. By the time he was done, the traffic around them had thickened.

He had seen bumper-to-bumper traffic on TV, but he'd never thought to witness so many people in one place. As amazed as he was by the sight, all he could think about was how many people would get hurt if Tristan showed up now.

"The art dealer's place is close," she said. "We can sit in the car while we wait for him to show up."

"You don't think he'll be home?" Dalton asked.

"His card had his business address on it. My guess is he won't show up for work until after ten. We'll have a few minutes."

As they moved onto narrower streets, Sue slowed to a crawl behind a small truck. Behind them, more cars lined up.

Up ahead, a large woman pushing a grocery cart blocked the street. She stopped at a white van and knocked on the side door. It opened just enough for him to catch a glimpse of two men sitting in back.

Sue nodded toward the woman. "Those are cops."

He looked but all he saw were men sitting in cars. "Are you sure?"

"Positive. And they're not alone."

He saw the second pair of men now, sitting in a plain black car a little farther down the block. "There might be more. We can't stay."

"You got that right. That lady who gave us the art dealer's card must have called the cops when we tore up her yard and told them where we were going. I saw the news. The police are searching for us. Between the yard and the restaurant you and Tristan destroyed, the police must be hoping to stop us before we do any more damage."

"What do we do? I can't get taken to jail."

"I know. Just scoot down and try to stay out of sight."

He did as she asked. She kept driving, keeping her coffee glued to her lips to hide her face. She turned a few corners and finally said, "Okay. You can get up now."

They were sitting in an alley behind a line of buildings. "Did they see you?"

Her eyes were on the rearview mirror. "So far, so good. They must not have had a great description of my car."

"You have to get out of here. I'll go back there on foot and try to sneak in."

She snorted at his idea. "You're too big to sneak anywhere. Besides, what do you know about picking locks?"

"I know enough to simply smash my fist right through them."

"I see. You're a stealth kind of guy."

"Do you have a better idea?"

"I do. But we're going to have to go shopping to make it happen."

Alethia abandoned her grocery cart in an alley and altered her appearance to match that of a business man, complete with suit and tie. She wasn't sure if her timing had been good enough to warn Sue and Dalton that the police were looking for them, but the fact that there were no lights or sirens going off made her feel a little better.

Now all she had to do was get back home and make sure that her studious sister Lalia had done her homework.

If Alethia pulled this off, she would be one soul closer to making up for what she'd done.

CHAPTER 11

Two hours later, Sue looked nothing like herself. Her hair was hidden beneath a paint stained handkerchief. Her clothes looked like they'd been used to mop up after a bull fight inside an art store. The large canvas she had spray painted was so far from fine art it might almost pass as some.

Armed with her canvas and the hippiest clothes she could find at the thrift shop, she walked right down the sidewalk past the first set of cops. Dalton was several paces ahead of her.

He looked different, too. Even she had trouble recognizing him.

Gone were his jeans and flannel shirt. He'd slicked back his hair and shaved his face clean. The raven-colored suit she'd found him fit him like it had been made for that fabulous body. A sleek leather briefcase completed the look she hoped would fool the cops long enough for them to find the box.

He held her phone up to his ear, talking into it as he walked. She couldn't hear much of what he said, but his low, authoritative tone was enough to make her thighs tighten with the need to wrap around his hips and ride him.

Like it or not, Dalton was in her blood. She had no idea how she was going to face his naked statue every day and not want him.

Desperately.

Her sexual frustration was a problem for another day. Right now, she needed to stay sharp and keep her stoneman from being detained long enough to reveal that he was usually a statue. That was her job. She would do it even if it meant abandoning the box.

What good would a week of freedom do him if he had to spend it in jail?

She watched as he cleared the next group of eyes staking out the art dealer's showroom. Next door was a jewelry store, which he went into as if he owned the place.

Phase one complete. So far, so good.

Sue passed the jewelers and fumbled to open the door to the showroom. She was greeted immediately by a woman so classy it made Sue wish she'd been in one of her power suits, rather than paint-stained thrift store finds.

The black dress the woman wore hugged her slim form. She was model tall, model thin, model beautiful. Diamonds dripped from her ears and nestled in the hollow of her throat.

She smiled at Sue as if she didn't even notice how ratty and paint-stained her clothes were and extended her hand to shake.

Sue set the canvas down against her thigh and wiped her hand on her pants before she touched the woman.

"I'm Rachel. How may I help you today?"

"I was hoping to talk to Mr. Statesworth. Is he in?"

"Do you have an appointment?"

"No."

"I'm sorry. He only sees new talent on Tuesdays. If you'd like to set up an appointment next week, I think he has an opening in the afternoon."

"I kinda need to see him today." Sue picked up her horrible painting and started back in the direction Rachel had come from.

"I'm sorry, ma'am, but you're not allowed back there."

"I'm not going to touch anything. I just want to look at your setup. See if it's right for my work."

The electronic bell on the door chimed as Dalton walked in. Rachel's head turned toward him and that warm welcome she'd worn for Sue suddenly seemed like a cold snub by comparison. Rachel looked at him like she wanted to eat him for dessert.

"Stay here," ordered Rachel. "I'll be right back."

The sway of Rachel's hips as she approached Dalton was enticing enough that even Sue couldn't look away. Poor man didn't stand a chance.

He shook her hand. She covered the back of his, lingering a bit too long, leaning in to put her cleavage on as much of a display as any painting hung on the walls.

To Dalton's credit, he didn't even glance down.

Sue kinda loved him for that.

Rather than watch the show, she left Dalton to work his magic while she went in search of Mr. Statesworth.

She found him sitting behind a trendy, asymmetrical, modern desk made from glass and chrome. Looking at it, she wasn't sure how gravity didn't just pull it over.

Mr. Statesworth appeared to be in his sixties, with a full head of white hair and impeccable taste. The soft gray suit he wore was probably worth more than her entire wardrobe. The diamond cufflinks flashing at his wrists could have easily bought her car.

He looked up from his laptop as she barged in. "I only see new talent on Tuesdays."

"Yeah. Rachel said that, but that's not why I'm here."

He rose from his chair. "We don't have an appointment."

"I know. I just need a moment of your time."

He looked past her as if expecting Rachel to come to his rescue. When she didn't, his shoulders fell with acceptance. "Please, have a seat."

"Thanks. I'll get right to it. I'm looking to purchase an antique puzzle box." She took out the picture and slid it across the gleaming desk toward him. "This one."

His white eyebrows lowered as he picked up the photo. "Yes. I remember this piece. It was magnificently complex. To my knowledge, no one had ever been able to open it."

"Do you know what's inside?"

"I don't. I prefer not to unravel such mysteries with X-rays or other imaging technology."

"Don't you want to know what's in it?"

"Not if that knowledge is going to devalue the item, no."

Smart man. "Honestly, I don't care what's in it. I just need to buy the box for a friend. She really has her heart set on it."

"Sadly, the piece is no longer in my possession."

"Who has it?"

He rose from his chair again, his posture one of dismissal. "I'm sorry I can't help you. Rachel will show you out."

Sue dodged his hand as he moved to guide her out the door. "I can't leave until I know where to find it."

"And I never reveal the names of my customers. It's bad for business."

His hand gripped her arm as he moved toward the door. Her choices were to fight him or go along quietly.

With the cops sitting right outside, there was really only one option. It was possible he had already been alerted to be on the lookout for her. As soon as he was out of sight, he could call the police and they'd stop her and Dalton at the door.

She went along like a docile creature. The act grated on her nerves, but she pulled it off without permanently damaging anything.

In the showroom, Dalton stood over a ceramic vessel that looked like something dug up from a mummy's tomb.

Rachel was standing so close she was almost under his arm. "You have exquisite taste. This is one of the best pieces we currently have on display."

"Rachel," called Mr. Statesworth. "A word."

Sue didn't wait for them to talk. She caught Dalton's eye and shook her head. Then she left the building with her painting in tow, hoping he wouldn't be far behind. Putting on a dejected frown of disappointment for any cops watching wasn't a hard thing to do considering she hadn't managed to get what she'd come for.

She retraced her steps back to her car, then drove around the block to pick up Dalton where they'd agreed to meet. That way they wouldn't both be leaving the building in the same way they'd come.

Only he wasn't there.

She sat with the engine idling, waiting for him. Each minute that passed made her neck muscles draw tighter.

What if he'd been caught? What if the police were already taking him in for questioning?

He might have watched a lot of TV, but he wasn't part of her world. He couldn't know all the bad things that could happen. Hell, her uncle hadn't even had Showtime.

Sweat beaded up along her hairline. She lowered the window to let in the cold air and listen for the sound of footsteps.

Or sirens.

More time passed, filling her gut with anxiety. She was just about to get out of the car and go looking for him when the passenger side door opened.

Sue squeaked and held her chest to keep her heart from beating its way free. Dalton's tie was gone and there was lipstick on his collar.

"You okay?" she asked as she caught her breath.

His face was flushed with embarrassment. "She said she wanted to go to dinner with me, but I don't think that's what she meant. I kept her busy for as long as I could." He swallowed hard, his eyes wide. "In my time, women were a little more…subtle."

Jealousy reared its green head, but Sue kept her cool. "You gave me time to grill Statesworth. Way to take one for the team."

"Did you find out where the box is?" he asked.

"He wouldn't say. What about Miss Floosy-pants? Did she tell you anything?"

"Only that she didn't have access to her employer's paper files. He doesn't keep confidential information on his computer. She said he kept all his records locked in his office file cabinet."

Great. Now they had to either convince Statesworth to give up the information, or they had to break in and steal it.

He tugged nervously at his lipstick-stained collar. "We should go. She might have gotten loose."

"Rachel? You talk about her like she's a wild animal."

"The woman had to have had more than two hands." He patted his fly as if to check to make sure everything was where it should be. "And they were…everywhere."

Another spurt of jealousy died a quick death as she saw how the ordeal had upset him.

"She wanted you. And who could blame her? You look totally hot in that suit."

He pulled off the jacket and tossed it in the back seat like it was a bag of live snakes. "Yes, well, I'd rather look cold. I thought I was never going to get out of there."

"How'd you manage?"

"I tied her to her desk with my tie."

Sue laughed. Then she realized he was serious and laughed louder. "You realize you can never show your face there again, right?"

"That's fine by me."

"You can't seriously be that upset. I mean, she was gorgeous."

"She looked like a boy dressed as a woman. No," he cupped his hands in front of his chest, "curves at all."

Sue's nipples hardened as she remembered just how much loving attention he'd given them only a few hours ago. "I can't say I'm disappointed that you didn't like her."

He put his hand on her knee. "You're the only woman I think about like that. Chances are you're the only woman I'm going to think about like that for the next hundred years or so."

She didn't want to dwell on losing him before she had to. For now, they were together, and she was going to enjoy every second of it. "You know," she said in what passed for her sexy voice, "I could strip for you sometime. Maybe put on a little show to keep you warm."

A shudder rippled through his heavy frame. "Tell me more."

She pulled onto the highway, heading south, away from the city. The fewer police there were around, the better. With her bad luck, their faces were on camera from the showroom and were currently being passed around to law enforcement everywhere.

"Well," she said, "I'd probably buy some sexy bit of lacey lingerie and put it on for you. Is there a color you like?"

She glanced at him and saw his face was flushed red and his chest was moving faster. "On you? Any of them."

"Maybe something pink, then."

"Pink is good. It'll match all those sweet spots on you that taste so good."

Now it was her turn to blush. "I'd put on some music with a nice beat, light some candles. Maybe do a little dance."

He made a choking sound in his throat and slid his hand up her knee.

The memory of his hand on her bare skin was enough to make her grow wet and ache for him. She shoved it all away and concentrated on not crashing the car.

"Then what?" he asked.

"I'd take my clothes off, nice and slow, giving you just a hint of what was coming."

"Dear heaven. Something more is coming?"

"Yes," she said, letting him hear her smile. "Me. I'd touch myself for you until I got off."

His grip tightened. "I don't know if I'd survive that without going mad. Trapped in the stone, unable to touch you…I'm not sure I'm a strong enough man."

"Would you rather I didn't put on a show?"

"Hell, no. If I'm going to go mad, that's the way I want to go. Smelling your arousal in the air, seeing and hearing your pleasure. If I can't have you, at least I can have that."

She found a sporting goods store and pulled into the parking lot. Once her seatbelt was unfastened, she turned to him and took his hand in hers. "I wish there was some way we could communicate. It's fun and all to plan sexy games, but what if it really does bother you?"

"It won't." He paused as if deciding whether or not to speak. "Just…please don't let me see you with another man. I don't think I could take it."

She wasn't planning on having sex in the living room, but the walls in that old house were thin. She liked to think that eventually she'd settle down and have someone to keep her warm on those cold, drafty nights. She wished like crazy that the man could be Dalton, but they both knew that wasn't going to happen. "I promise. I don't ever want to hurt you."

He slid his fingers through her hair. "All you have to do is live a happy life, and I'll be fine."

"You don't know that."

He nodded. "I do. You're not the first woman I've grown to…care for who I've had to watch live her life."

She wasn't his first? For some reason, that bothered her more than she dared admit. "You've done this before?"

His fingers stroked her temple, her cheekbone. "No. Never this, but there was another woman once, when I was a real man."

"What happened?"

He looked away, and she lost the warmth of his hand on her face. "It doesn't matter. All you need to know is that I want you to be happy. Your life will go on once I'm stone again, and that's good. It's what I want."

Maybe he didn't care about her as much as she hoped if he could so easily accept that she would move on with her life. She knew that she'd be pissed as hell if he started talking about being with other women when they hadn't even taken the time to see where this could go.

But that was the problem. *This* couldn't go anywhere, and he knew it. He'd been alive a lot longer than she had. And he'd had plenty of time to come to grips with reality.

She might as well have started falling for a stalagmite.

"I'm going to go take a walk. Clear my head," she said. "Can you stay here?"

"If that's what you want."

"Just try not to destroy every car in the parking lot if Tristan comes back."

He pointed to a vacant lot across the street where a piece of land was for sale. "I'll go sit over there. Just in case."

She'd only been half-joking, but he was right. There was no way to know if or when Tristan was coming back for round three.

Which was exactly why she'd come here. It was time Sue armed herself with more than hopes and dreams.

It was well after dark when Sue drove the car back to the art dealer's showroom. The street was mostly empty, and she couldn't see a single sign of any police nearby.

"What do you think?" she asked Dalton.

"I think it looks too easy."

"You only say that because you have the ability to punch through locked doors. I promise you, getting inside is going to be anything but easy."

"You let me worry about that. As you said, there will be cameras inside. I don't want your face showing up on any of them. You'll stay in the car and let me do the thieving."

She didn't like it, but what choice did she have? At least if only one of them got caught, she could bail him out. Or buy him. She wasn't sure exactly what the police would do with a statue if they found one in a county jail cell. Maybe auction it off with the drug dealers' cars and houses.

"Tell me the plan again," she said.

"I'll break in, search Mr. Statesworth's files and find the name of the person who bought the puzzle box. Then I'll come out, and we'll drive off."

She eyed him, wondering how he could look so relaxed. Her shoulders were up by her ears and an army of anxiety goblins was marching up and down her spine. "What if you set off the alarm?"

"I should have at least a minute or two to get what we want and get out. If not, don't wait for me. Just go. I'll meet you at the backup location, just like we planned."

Sue shook her head. "This is insane. Maybe I can try to convince Mr. Statesworth to give us the name. Maybe bribe him."

"And you think that's less likely to get us picked up by the police? You've already asked about the box—the same item that we asked about before Tristan and I tore up that nice woman's yard. I've got to think that after today, Mr. Statesworth will have talked to the police about us. They'll be looking for us. And with all the cameras in that place, they'll know exactly what we look like."

"What if the police are here now?"

Dalton shrugged. "Only one way to find out." He reached for the car door and paused.

"Second thoughts?" she asked, hoping he'd say yes. As important as this week of freedom was to him, she almost wished he'd reconsider just *how* important.

Not that she could truly understand what he felt. She'd never been trapped, her free will stripped away. Though if the cops caught them breaking into the place, she was going to get a front row seat to that kind of torture.

"No second thoughts," he said. "I just need one more thing."

He leaned over and kissed her. Heat flared between them as it always did, but this kiss was different. Sweeter. More precious somehow.

He was kissing her goodbye.

Sue gripped his face and savored every second of it. By the time he was done with her, she could barely open her eyes for the spinning of her head. "You have one hell of a potent kiss, Mr. Thatcher."

"You as well, Miss Sullivan." His fingers trailed over her cheek, and then he was gone.

Since all the doors and windows of the showroom were wired to the alarm, Dalton found another way in. He ripped away a section of stucco and drywall with his bare hands. The insulation came out like a long, pink tongue, giving him just enough room to squeeze through the wooden framing.

He found Mr. Statesworth's office. It was locked. The file cabinet Dalton hoped held customer records sat in the corner, only ten feet away. It had five drawers, and while it wouldn't have been hard for him to haul the whole thing out, he wasn't entirely sure it would fit between the wall studs.

After a careful scan through the glass of the office door, Dalton saw no sign of any kind of alarm sensor. His guess was they were more worried about protecting the art than they were the files.

With a hard twist of the lever style knob, he broke the lock and pushed the door open.

A flashing light began blinking in the corner of the room—one he hadn't seen before. A second later, a loud beep cut through the silent office.

He'd triggered the alarm.

As fast as he could, Dalton ripped open the top drawer where the date labels indicated the newest files were kept. He scanned through starting at the beginning, flipping from file folder to file folder, looking only at the photos stapled inside.

He made it all the way through the top drawer and had started working on the second drawer when he heard sirens getting closer.

A few more files later, he could hear voices inside the building. Someone was telling him to come out.

He couldn't. Not until he found that name.

Sweat trickled down his spine, making him glad he'd left his jacket behind. His mind kept straying to Sue—where she was and whether or not she'd gotten away before the police had arrived.

He prayed she had.

The voices grew louder. He was out of time.

He flipped to the next file and saw the image of the puzzle box right there, in full color. He wasted no time in ripping out the page with the customer information, then took off at a dead run.

He saw a blur of motion to his left as he streaked down the hallway.

"Stop!" yelled an authoritative voice.

Dalton kept going, waiting for the feeling of hot lead digging into his skin.

He slammed through a pair of double doors into a large room he guessed they used for storage. Crates and boxes lined the walls. Smaller boxes stood on sturdy metal shelves. Everything was carefully labeled.

Footsteps sounded just outside the doors. Dalton ducked behind a crate, but he couldn't hide forever. They'd search the room and find him. If he moved, they would find him. There was no other way out.

CHAPTER 12

Sue had never been as terrified in her life as she was when she saw the police storm the building. She hadn't wanted to leave Dalton, but she knew she could be more help to him free than standing next to him behind bars.

She waited at their rendezvous location for as long as she dared before driving away. The backup plan was for her to wait at the donut shop for him to show up or call, but she couldn't bear to go that far away. Instead, she hid her car in a parking garage and walked back through the streets, weaving between buildings, until she found the back entrance for one of the apartments across the street from the showroom.

The old apartment building wasn't locked, even at this hour. As she went inside, she saw why. There wasn't a thing in here worth stealing. Several of the units had eviction notices on them. One was decorated with police tape. Everything in here was dirty, peeling and moldy. And from the smell of it, the sewer lines were no longer working right.

Sue held her nose and moved to the front of the building. She stayed low, peeking out through the window to see what was going on.

There were three police cars here, their lights flashing. Several uniformed men milled around, along with a few curious onlookers. Sue would have joined them, but she was afraid the police would recognize her.

As she waited to see Dalton being toted out in handcuffs, her stomach churned. She was certain he'd been caught, and yet there was no sign of him.

After almost an hour, one of the police cars left. Then another. Mr. Statesworth showed up. The officers spoke to him. Still no sign of Dalton.

She didn't know what else to do, so she went back to her car and drove to the donut shop. On foot, it would take him at least half an hour to get here.

She waited three times that long, her anxiety growing with every second. By the time the donut shop owner pulled in to start doing his thing, she knew Dalton wasn't coming.

Her only choice was to go back to the showroom and hope she found some hint of where he'd gone before the police found her and toted her off for questioning.

Dalton tried to fight Pyrenia's summons, but it was impossible. He was still under her control. Whatever she wanted, she got, and evidently she wanted to watch him squirm.

She was lying naked, face down on a cushion, being held up by the four large stonemen while three more massaged her body. Her skin gleamed with oil so shimmery she looked as though she was covered in gold dust.

"Nice trick," she said. "What better way for you to hide than to pretend you're just one more piece of art?"

"The trick won't work at all if you don't let me go back into my body. That art dealer is going to know I'm not part of his collection as soon as he sees my giant stone ass in his storeroom."

"Your personal problems don't interest me. Where is the box?" She rolled onto her side, revealing a glorious pair of breasts also shimmering with golden oil. All Dalton could think was that he doubted they'd taste half as good as Sue's.

"I'd tell you, but the name of the person who has it is on a piece of paper that is currently balled up inside my fist on Earth."

Pyrenia gave him a pout. "You certainly are getting uppity with me. I'm starting to wonder if this free time you want so much is even good for you. I think you should stay here until you learn better manners."

Dalton nearly strangled himself cutting off the words he wanted to shout at her. Nothing he said in anger would do him any favors, so he kept his mouth shut and bowed his head to hide the rage seething behind his eyes.

"That's better," she said. "Now come and rub my feet."

He'd already started moving forward with her compulsion before she'd finished speaking. "I want to relax a little while before I start to play with you."

Play with him? That couldn't be good. He'd seen what happened to the men she'd played with—the way they'd crumbled under her torment.

But what choice did he have? He was her slave, incapable of refusing her slightest whim. And she would play as long as she wanted. There was no way for him to know how long he'd be stuck doing her bidding. He'd learned from experience that the way time moved here was irrelevant. A few seconds could be a few days on Earth or the other way around. His only choice was to bide his time and hope that when he went back into his body it wouldn't be too late.

Sue waited until the police left and the cleanup efforts had started at Mr. Statesworth's showroom.

She'd been watching for hours for some sign of Dalton, but the binoculars only gave her a view through the front windows. She couldn't see the offices or back rooms where she worried he might be trapped and hiding.

From what she could see, there were only the owner and Rachel in the building. Sue had caught glimpses of them here and there, and neither one looked pleased.

Around lunch time, she called in an order for sandwiches to be delivered. Sue paid a young woman she'd found two blocks away fifty bucks to go into the building posing as a customer at the same time the food delivery showed up. That way, both Mr. Statesworth and Rachel would be occupied for at least a minute.

As soon as both Rachel and Mr. Statesworth were busy, Sue slipped past the police tape, through the hole in the back wall of the building.

There weren't many places Dalton could be hiding. She checked the bathroom, both offices and a broom closet.

Sitting on Mr. Statesworth's desk was a pile of Dalton's clothes—the ones he'd been wearing when he'd come in.

The idea of him running around naked was only thrilling for a second before her mind turned to all the reasons he might have had his clothes taken from him. Maybe they had him held captive somewhere, hidden even from the police. Maybe the police had already taken him away, forcing him to wear one of those awful orange jumpsuits. Or maybe he'd taken his own clothes off for some reason, and they'd kept them so they could use a dog to track his location.

The only room left other than the showroom was the one marked STORAGE.

She went inside, resisting the urge to turn on a light. Instead she used her cell phone's screen to give her enough illumination to see where she was going.

"Dalton," she said in a loud whisper.

No answer.

She didn't know how much time she'd have until she was found, but she knew it wasn't much. As she scanned the rows of boxes and shelves, she searched for a place she could hide if someone walked in. The only area that she thought would shield her from sight was behind a large crate.

Maybe if he'd had to hide, that's where he'd gone, too. If he'd been hurt, he could be back there, bleeding.

Sue hurried behind the crate and nearly ran into Dalton's stone form. He was crouched into a small space, completely naked, hugging his knees. One fist was balled up around a piece of paper she could barely see.

She knelt in front of him, hoping he could hear her. "Time to go. We only have a minute before our way out is blocked."

He didn't turn back into his flesh form. For all she knew, he hadn't heard her at all.

What if he was injured as he had been before and needed to heal?

Sue wrapped her arms around him and tried to scoot him. He didn't even wiggle. He was way too heavy for her to move.

She couldn't leave him here like this, but she couldn't stay, either. If she got caught, there'd be no way to explain her presence. Mr. Statesworth would doubtless call the police and she'd be trapped in the legal system for who knew how long.

She couldn't help Dalton from inside a jail cell.

Rather than stay and wait for him to reanimate, she moved a couple of crated paintings to hide his body. Once that was done, she leaned close. "I'm going, but I won't go far. I'll be waiting for you."

With that, she snuck back out the way she'd come in and ran back to her car.

There was nothing she could think to do now but wait. As every second passed, the dwindling amount of time they had left to find the puzzle box weighed on her. She racked her brain for another move to make, but all she could think to do was wait here.

Dalton would come to her. He had to.

The rest of the day passed in tense silence. She peered through the binoculars, certain that at any second, she was going to see a flurry of activity inside indicating that Dalton had been found.

The sun set. Her stomach rumbled with hunger, but she was too tense to risk putting anything in it.

The surrounding area cleared out as businesses closed and people went home. A few meager, flickering lights lit the windows of the mostly empty apartment building across the street, but other than that, she barely saw any proof of life.

Mr. Statesworth's Porsche sat where he'd parked it earlier today. He was still inside, holding Dalton hostage.

The night closed in around her, weighing down her eyelids. All this stress had left her exhausted, but she didn't dare close her eyes.

Her cell phone rang, making her squeak in surprise. Charlotte's cheerful face showed up on the screen.

"Hello?"

"I tried to reach you to chat all day. Where have you been? I've been worried sick. I even burned my bangs making jewelry today because I was so distracted at the torch."

Sue filled her in on everything that had happened.

"Whoa. You slept with him? How was he? I bet he was nice and hard. I can't say I haven't fantasized about riding the ol' rock a time or two myself."

"Seriously? Dalton is trapped inside a building with police dying to lock him up, and all you care about was how good he was in bed?"

"I like to start with the most interesting bits and work my way out from there. You know, one time I dressed Vincent up in one of those elephant trunk undies, just for kicks." She laughed to herself. "I wish I'd been smart enough to set up a nanny cam so I could have seen the look on his face when he turned to skin and bones. Instead, I was asleep, and woke up with the thong binding one of my wrists to my bedpost. I don't think he was amused."

"I don't have time for this, Char. I need to keep watching and make sure I don't miss him when he comes out."

"*If* he comes out. It could be weeks or even years before he animates again."

"No. He has to come out tonight."

"Stop worrying about him. He's a hot statue in a warehouse filled with art. Worst case scenario you have to buy him back."

Sue hadn't even thought about what would happen if he didn't come back to her soon. "We don't have much time left to find the box."

"Sorry, babe. I think the whole box-finding thing is all you now. If his sculptor has her talons in him, there's nothing you can do."

"I can use that ring again and demand Pyrenia let him go."

Charlotte snorted in amusement. "Yeah. That'll work. It won't get you eviscerated at all."

"I'm not afraid of her."

"You should be. Those women have centuries of ruthless behavior on their records. Some are worse than others, but even the best ones only leave humans alone because they have no interest in our puny lives. Promise me you won't use the ring."

"No. I won't."

"Won't use it or won't promise."

"I'll do what I need to do. I made a promise to protect Dalton. If that means I have to face a snake-toting, beetle-bikini-clad crazy chick, then so be it."

"She could kill you with a twitch of her littlest finger. You can't go messing around with powers you don't understand. Have you even read the manual yet?"

"I've been a little busy."

"You've got some time now. There's only so much I can to do protect you. You need to educate yourself enough to watch you own back."

"Does the manual say how I can free him?" Sue asked.

"Sure. It's got a whole chapter on how to break your stoneman out of an art museum." Charlotte snorted again. "Of course it doesn't tell you that. You're not supposed to get your stoneman in that kind of trouble to begin with.

Hell, you're not even supposed to be hanging out with him. And sex? Totally out of the question."

"No," said Sue. "I don't mean how to free him from the building. I mean how to free him from being…what he is?"

"Ah. You want to break the curse. I see someone's violating the rules already. You're getting emotionally attached."

"He's a person. It's kinda hard not to care about him. *I'm* not made of stone."

"Yeah, well he is. If you don't want to have a complete goatfuck on your hands, I suggest you remember that."

Sue was afraid it was already too late for that. Not that it mattered how she felt if he stayed trapped in that building all night.

"Will you do me a favor?"

Charlotte sighed. "I'll try."

"Call Mr. Statesworth's office. Pretend you're a neighbor and that you saw someone moving around in his house. Maybe that will get him to leave."

"If he has caller ID, he's going to know I'm calling from out of state. The last thing I want is to get wrapped up in your drama. I've got orders to fill."

"There are ways to block your number. Google them. Please?"

"Fine, fine. I'll do this. But the next time I talk to you, you'd better have read the damn manual."

"I will. Once I find this box, I promise that'll be the first thing on my to-do list."

Charlotte hung up. A couple of minutes later, Mr. Statesworth hurried from the building. His tires squealed as he sped down the street.

Sue held her breath, hoping Dalton would come out. After she got dizzy a few times, she realized that her breathing—or lack thereof—wasn't doing a thing to make him human again.

Her only choice was to go in after him and hope that, once inside, there was some means of getting half a ton of stone into her trunk by herself.

She had just slipped around the back of the building into the delivery area when she saw a shadow dart across the pavement.

Her heart tried to curl into a tiny ball and make a break for it up her throat. By the time she could breathe again, she was crouched behind a tall, wooden crate with her fist clutched against her mouth to keep quiet.

The crate stood near the back entrance of the showroom. One side of it had been pried open, leaving splintered bits of wood along the edge. The side panel was propped against the wall of the building. Straw had once lined the bottom of the crate, but was now being coaxed out by the wind. Slowly, she shifted until she was standing inside that crate, clinging to the shadows.

Dalton appeared in front of her, half naked. His shirt and shoes were under one arm. His jeans were open at his waist as if he'd been in too much of a rush to button them.

Relief launched her at him, and she hit his bare chest with a hard thud. He wrapped his arms around her, letting his clothes fall to the ground. His mouth found hers, and for a moment, his kiss drove all the air from her lungs and the sense from her mind.

She breathed him in, savored him. Her tongue slid along his, desperate for more of him. Her whole system rejoiced at his presence, and all she could think about was how close she'd come to losing him.

His hands slid over her back, so wild and hot, she wasn't sure how she'd managed to survive without his touch for as many hours as she had. This man went to her head. He stole all rational thought and left way too much intense emotion behind.

He made her want things she knew she could never have.

His kisses turned darker. She could feel some kind of tension vibrating through him. Each stroke of his hand became more insistent, sneaking beneath her clothes until meeting bare skin.

She pulled away from his mouth to ask him what had happened, but the words died on her tongue.

There was a wild look in his eyes that bordered on desperation. His jaw was set, and a bright stain of color darkened his cheeks and mouth. Even though she'd only seen him a few hours ago, he seemed leaner, harder.

He lifted her up and pinned her against the wall. His thigh slid between hers, and he let some of her weight go so that she was riding his leg. The pressure against her clit sent a stream of sparks up her spine and stole her breath. As she shifted to ease her labored breathing, the motion rubbed her just right until she felt herself drawing tight.

Dalton saw it too, and finally, he smiled. But it wasn't like the ones she'd seen before. This one was darker, more dangerous.

She'd always had a weak spot for bad boys, and the way he was looking at her now, her weak spot was turning into a sinkhole.

"What happened to you?" she asked. No way had he changed this much without something sparking it.

Rather than respond, he covered her mouth with his and kissed her until there was no more air to be had. He shoved her shirt and bra up, baring her breasts to the cold wind. She barely had time to feel the chill before his hot mouth was on her, drawing hard on her nipples, one after the other.

Sue gripped his shoulders, holding on for dear life. She wasn't sure exactly how she'd ended up pressed against a cold, hard wall with Dalton's blast furnace of a body keeping her front warm, but she *was* sure she didn't care. All she cared about was that she was here now, with his hands at her waistband, deftly unfastening her jeans.

His hand slid inside. His fingers glided over slick skin.

He hummed in appreciation. Her feet touched the ground briefly, then he spun her around to face the wall.

Her wet nipples hit the chilly surface, and damn if her whole body didn't clench on the verge of orgasm. The sensation was too sharp, too extreme. She found herself panting in order to stave off the need to come.

More cold hit her skin as Dalton shoved her jeans down just enough to make room for his cock. The heat of his body enveloped her, and she was no longer thinking about the cold wall or the chilly draft crossing her ass. All she could think about was the wide head of his cock pressing against her, demanding entrance.

The slick pressure made her quiver. She couldn't widen her stance to make room for his thickness. All she could do was whimper while he worked his way inside her.

Finally, after an endless series of tiny, clinging thrusts, he entered her the rest of the way with one smooth drive forward.

The breath left her body. There was no room for something as inconsequential as air—not when she was filled up with hot, throbbing Dalton.

He stayed like that for a moment, stealing her ability to do anything but feel. His presence inside her took up all the room in her brain, leaving nothing but pure sensation in its wake.

One big, hot hand wrapped around her and covered her breast. He caught her nipple between his fingers, rolling and pinching with expert ease. His other hand splayed across her belly, hugging her tight so she could feel his erection even more keenly.

Then he started to move.

It wasn't slow and gentle as he'd been before. This time, he didn't coax or cajole. He demanded. Each thrust rocked her body. Each retreat left her dying for more. Her whole body shook as he took her, and she found herself letting go and arching back at him to take whatever he needed to give.

His breathing became ragged. His hold got tighter, practically lifting her up with each hard, rocking motion.

His mouth was right by her ear, and the rough sound of his voice made her knees go liquid. "You're going to come for me while I fill you."

Sue whimpered and clung to the wall. She clenched her thighs together and tried to hold on for just a minute more so he wouldn't think he had as much control over her as he did.

Her plan failed. The pad of his thumb grazed across her clit, and she couldn't hold back anymore. Her whole body gave up the fight, and her instincts took over.

The sound of her breathless cries echoed off the buildings. Dalton's voice joined hers as she felt him throb and spurt between the clenching pulses of her own release.

As her orgasm let go of her, she went loose in his arms. He held her up, but she could feel his powerful body trembling. He eased his erection from her body, then worked her panties and jeans back over her bare ass.

Sue straightened her clothes with one hand while clinging to the wall with the other. She could barely stand, but managed to cover herself against the cold air.

His semen trickled out of her, soaking her panties. The scent of sex was all over them, lingering in the still air between them.

Dalton took a deep breath that made his chest expand in delightful ways. She couldn't help the little thrill she felt at knowing that, for now, he was all hers.

His gaze hit her, and while the fires she'd seen there earlier were banked, there was still plenty of blaze. "We should go. Before I forget myself and take you again."

The idea didn't bother her nearly as much as it should have. "We can't stay here. Definitely time to go."

He leaned down and kissed her again. Deeply, thoroughly. When he lifted his head, all she saw was barely restrained lust riding his features. "I'm going to have you again. Soon."

She was all for it—enough that she was already starting to wonder if it was safe enough to have just one more quickie against the wall. "The car is down the street. I don't know if Mr. Statesworth is coming back or not. I wasn't even sure if you were going to be…you when I found you."

He frowned as if confused. "Mr. Statesworth? How long have I been gone?"

"It's after ten."

"Of what month?"

She blinked at that. "It's still Saturday. The day you left. You've only been stone for a few hours."

His mouth went slack in disbelief. "Hours? She did all of that in a few hours?"

"She who? How can you not know how long you've been gone?"

"I wasn't inside of my stone form. I was…with Pyrenia." Something about the way he said it gave her pause, but before she could ask, he picked up his clothes and ushered her away from the building with a firm hand at the small of her back.

They got in the car, and she started driving. It didn't matter where. The more distance between them and that building, the better.

He was quiet as she drove. She kept glancing over, wondering if he was okay. As the minutes passed, he seemed to be getting a better grip on himself.

"I found an address before I was forced to hide," he said as she made a left.

"What address?"

"The man who bought the puzzle box."

"Where is it?"

He pulled a crumpled piece of paper from his pocket and smoothed it out before reading her the address.

She knew the place. "That's a little town not far from here. Maybe half an hour."

"We should go there. Find the box."

"Not now," she said. "It's too late. The last thing we need is to draw more attention from the police. We'll have to wait until the first thing tomorrow. I'll get us a room for the night."

He fell silent, and she could see his shoulders creeping up toward his ears.

"What?" she asked. "We still have most of a day before our time is up. And honestly, I really don't think I should be driving when I'm this tired."

"I understand. Do what you need to do."

She pulled into the next hotel she saw and parked. Dalton made no move to get out.

He didn't look at her when he said, "I think that I should go after the box alone."

"What's that supposed to mean? We're a team. Aren't we?"

"Can you drop me off near the address? I'll walk the rest of the way."

"I thought you were all about getting me into bed again. Why are you so eager now to go out on your own?"

"After what I did to you, I really think we're both better off if we part ways."

"What did you do to me?"

"I took you. I didn't even stop to find out if you had another man in your life now or if you even wanted me. I just wanted you and took you."

"Another man in my life? I already told you I was single."

"That was before."

"Before what?"

He didn't answer.

Sue wasn't sure what was going on, but she was sure as hell going to find out.

CHAPTER 13

Dalton was still shaking when Sue shut the hotel room door behind her. He knew what was coming—an interrogation.

He tried to brace himself for it, but he doubted it was going to help.

"Are you going to tell me what happened while you were with Pyrenia?" she asked.

Dalton settled in a chair on the far side of the room—as far away from the bed as he could get. "It doesn't matter."

"It seemed to matter to you a little while ago." Sue knelt in front of him and took his hand in hers. "You can tell me anything, you know."

"Are you sure? Pyrenia's not a kind woman. She has utter and complete control over me. There's no limit to the things she can make a man like me endure."

"You thought you were gone for longer than a few hours. Let's start there. How long did you think you were gone?"

"Months," he admitted. "I was so jarred to find out that I came back to the same day that I'm still having a hard time dealing with it."

"What were you doing while you were away?"

"Watching you. Or so I thought."

"I don't understand."

What point was there in lying? He was only going to have a few more hours with her. Maybe if he could tell her what she wanted to know, she'd let him take her again. Heaven knew he couldn't think of a single thing he wanted more. Except for his freedom, which he would spend as much of as possible inside her sweet body.

Dalton sucked in a fortifying breath. "I thought I was back in my stone form in your house. I thought you were mad at me."

"Mad?"

"You ignored me. Most of the time."

"I'd never do that."

"I know that now, but it seemed so real."

"What did?" she asked.

"You went on with your life. Saw other men. Brought them home. I saw you…" he had to clear his throat. "With them."

"You mean sex?"

He nodded. "That's the only time you ever acknowledged my existence. You'd smile at me while they took you, like you were taunting me."

She moved onto his lap, and damn if she didn't feel perfect there. She looked right into his eyes. "That's not the kind of person I am. It was just some cruel trick Pyrenia played on you."

"I know that now, but at the time it felt real. I kept getting angrier and angrier. That's when I realized the truth."

"What truth?"

"She wants to destroy me. It's not enough that I'm her slave. She wants to break my will, too. She wants to twist me into something unrecognizable." He couldn't look Sue in the eye. "I've seen her do it before. I was stupid enough to think I was immune—that my will and character were too strong—until today."

"We're going to find that box. Maybe if you have a little vacation, you'll be able to resist her tricks better."

"And if not?"

She cupped his face in her hands and forced him to look at her. "I'll be there for you. I'll remind you every day of the kind of man you really are. I won't let you forget."

Sue was so sweet, she made him wish for impossible things. If he'd been a real man, she was exactly the kind of woman he'd take as his wife. Kind, sexy, beautiful inside and out.

He didn't know how he was going to find the strength to watch her die of old age and not go mad with grief.

Rather than ruin what little time he had, Dalton forced a smile. "With you in my life, I could never be weak."

She beamed and gave him a kiss so full of hope it broke his heart. When she pulled away, her eyes shining and bright, her mouth rosy, he knew he'd never again see a sight half as pretty as she was now.

"You know," she said. "We have the whole night before we need to leave. I can think of at least a couple of ways we could spend it."

He stroked her cheekbone. "You said you were tired. You should sleep."

"I'll call in sick to work on Monday and sleep then. Right now I want you."

There was no point in resisting her. Of all the women on the planet, she was the most enticing. He'd be a fool not to revel in her while he could.

Dalton let his smile warm and threw himself into living out every fantasy he could with her. With any luck at all, they'd live on in his memories and remind him that for a few brief days, he was almost a real man again.

Sue woke slowly. Every inch of her body was delightfully sore. She had beard burn all over, muscles that screamed from intense use, and an array of love bites across her chest, belly and thighs. The intimate reminders of last night's debauchery made her smile as she stretched.

Walking today was going to be interesting.

She opened her eyes, expecting to see Dalton lying beside her. Instead, all that was left was a dent in his pillow and a note.

Forget the box. A week of freedom will only make me want what I can't have. Thank you for reminding me what it feels like to be a man. I'll never forget you.

With love,

Dalton

Her heart sank as the meaning of his words set in. He'd left. For good.

She flew out of bed, rushing around the room to get dressed and gather her things. He'd very obviously gone through her purse. There was a note where her cash had been, apologizing for taking cab money.

She had no idea how long he'd been gone, but she was determined to find him again before he disappeared out of her life forever.

She couldn't stand the idea of losing him. Not yet.

Morning rush hour traffic clogged the streets, frustrating her to the point of screaming. As she came to a dead stop for the tenth time, she dialed Charlotte.

A groggy voice answered. "What?"

"He left me."

"Who left you where?"

"Dalton. I woke up this morning, and he was gone."

"Where did he go? After the box?"

"No. He said he doesn't want it anymore."

Charlotte sounded more alert now. "He's lying. You need that box. He may not think he wants it now, but once he'd trapped again, he'll resent giving it up."

"*I'm* not giving it up. I'm going after it."

"He's trying to protect you."

"You don't know that."

Charlotte sighed. "Yeah. I kinda do. Did you ever go look him up in the archives?"

"No. There was no time."

"Well, I did."

"What did you find?"

"Basically, your stoneman is a hero. The man traded his free will and enslaved himself to save the woman he loved. That's not the kind of guy who will let a woman take unnecessary risks for him. And I promise, playing with those sculptors is definitely risky."

Sue felt her body go still. Of course saving someone was what had earned him a seat at Pyrenia's wacky table. He was exactly the kind of man who would give up everything because it was the right thing to do.

It's why Sue loved him so much.

That love terrified her, but she let it spread through her, strengthen her. She wouldn't have chosen to love a man she could never have, but he was more than worthy of the feelings she had for him. And he deserved his week of vacation.

"Tell me more," said Sue. "Everything."

"He lived in Nebraska, farming his father's land. He was a young man, eager to make his own way in the world and create a life for himself and his family. He met a local woman, fell in love, they got engaged. Then she got sick— some kind of fever. The archives aren't specific. All we know for sure is that she was going to die, so Dalton prayed and went to every church and doctor in the county. No one could help. The archives say that a witch sought him out and told him there was a way to save his love. He was desperate enough to try anything, so he went against his Christian upbringing and took the witch's advice. The old scroll he read was a spell designed to summon Pyrenia. She offered him a deal to save his fiancée."

"And he took it," guessed Sue.

"Yep. His fiancée lived and became his curator."

Sue's heart broke at the story. It seemed like something out of a fairy tale, only the hero was doomed to be a statue in her living room. "That poor man."

"I haven't even gotten to the rough part yet."

Sue wasn't sure she wanted to know, but she was burning with curiosity. "What is that?"

"His fiancée ended up marrying another man and having kids. Since she was his curator, she kept him close to protect him. They lived in that old house of yours, before the extra rooms were added on. Dalton must have seen…everything."

He'd asked her to never be with another man where he could see it happen. Now that she knew his story, she understood why he'd been so intense in his request.

Sue's heart wept for him.

Tears clogged her voice. "He had to witness the woman he loved live her life without him—the life he was supposed to have had with her."

"Looks like," Charlotte said.

No wonder he freaked out so bad when Pyrenia fooled him into thinking that Sue had moved on, too. He may not love her, but he was still a good enough man to care about her. And even if he didn't, he certainly wouldn't want to watch her getting it on with other men.

Pyrenia was a complete and total bitch for pulling his strings like that. If it weren't for the fact that the puzzle box was going to give Dalton a week free of her, Sue would have found it and smashed it where she stood, just to spite the hell-bitch.

"I need to see him again," said Sue.

"Why? To tell him you'll stop living your life now that you've met him? You can't do that."

"How do you know? You have no idea how I feel about him."

"It doesn't matter how you feel. I get that he's a good guy and probably rocked your world a little, but he can't be what you need. You might as well fall in love with your vibrator."

"I'm his curator. It's my job to keep him safe."

"It's your job to keep his statue safe. From the damage I've seen on the news, you have no business being anywhere near him in his flesh form—not while that other stoneman is on his ass."

"I have to go, Char. He needs me."

"You're going to get hurt."

"I know. No getting around that." No matter what happened, even if she got the box and he spent his entire free week with her, she'd still feel ripped apart when he had to go.

She'd fallen in love with a man she could never have. There was no way this wasn't going to end badly.

CHAPTER 14

Alethia found Dalton walking along the highway. She pulled her car over and waited for him to reach her.

"You look like you could use a ride." Her voice creaked with age thanks to the old woman disguise she'd cast over herself.

"Cabs cost more than I thought."

"Where are you headed?"

"Nebraska."

"Just so happens I'm going that way. Get in."

He did, and the instant he was inside, she could smell anger and sadness clinging to him.

"You look like you've been through it," she said.

"You could say that."

"What happened?"

"Long story. One I'm not inclined to tell."

Alethia shrugged. "Suit yourself."

A few miles passed. The whole time he studied her. "Do I know you?"

"Maybe. Ever lived in Montana?" she asked as she altered her license plates to match that state's.

"No. I could swear I've seen you before."

"Anything's possible. I was in love with a man in Nebraska for a while. Spent some time there before I realized it wasn't going anywhere."

"Was he no good?"

"No. He was very good. Too good. But he lived there and I lived in Montana, and it just wasn't ever going to work. I broke it off and broke his heart."

"You did the right thing."

She let out a gusty snort. "I was an idiot. He died a year later, and I realized I could have spent all that time with him. Instead I threw it away so I wouldn't get hurt. Got hurt anyway."

"Life is pain."

"Listen to the wise, learned thirty-year-old. You're hardly even toilet-trained. What the hell do you know about pain?"

"Plenty."

"Is that why you're walking along the highway alone, sulking?"

"No. And I'm not sulking."

"Fine. Pouting, then."

"I'm not pouting, either."

"Could have fooled me. I have seven grandkids. I know pouting when I see it."

Dalton fell silent. She was almost sure he was done talking when he surprised her by speaking again.

"I met someone," he said, his voice quiet, as if he didn't want it to carry too far.

"A woman?"

"Yeah. One hell of a woman."

"And she's in Nebraska?"

"No."

"Don't tell me you left her."

"It's really none of your business."

"I know. But the drive is long, and you're not paying me anything. The least you can do is entertain me."

Anger poured from his tone. "My pain is no one's entertainment."

How wrong he was about that. Pyrenia loved to make her stonemen suffer. Almost as much as Obelia did.

"Indulge an old woman," said Alethia. "Maybe I can even help."

"I doubt that." He let out a long sigh. "I have to leave the country for a long time. I'll probably never see her again. What point is there in prolonging something that isn't going anywhere?"

"I see. You're worried you're too weak to handle loving and losing."

"No. I know I can handle it. I just don't want to."

"So she's not that great. Not worth the pain."

"Wrong again. She's fantastic. She's worth a hell of a lot more than mere pain."

"Then it was her idea. She doesn't want to get hurt."

"I never talked to her about it. I just left."

"Ouch. And here I was thinking you were a decent man."

"I *am* a decent man."

"Decent men don't walk away without at least talking things out. You just disappeared. She's probably convinced it's all her fault. We women are good at that, you know."

He turned around and looked behind him as if he could actually see her. "You think I hurt her?"

"From what you've said? Absolutely. But you can write her a letter from wherever you're going. Explain everything."

"Stop."

Alethia hid a smile. "What?"

"Stop the car. I need to get out."

"You're going to go back to her?"

He nodded. "She's probably still in the hotel. She was exhausted."

"You left her in a hotel? Oh, honey. That *was* low."

He spoke through gritted teeth. "I'm starting to see that. Are you going to pull over?"

"Nope. I'll drive you back, though. If we hurry, we might be back there before checkout time."

"Wait. I know where she's going." He pulled a crumpled piece of paper from his pocket and handed it to Alethia. "Do you know where this is?"

"No, but my phone does. I'll get you there." Alethia hit the accelerator. There wasn't much time left before the window to find the puzzle box closed. And if she missed that, all her carefully laid plans were for nothing.

Sue pulled onto the property at the address Dalton had given her. The place was outside of a small town—too far away for anyone to complain about the fact that the front yard was basically a junk pile.

Old cars, refrigerators and appliances sat in a strange pattern, each one gutted for parts and rusting. Last year's weeds stood between gaps in the chunks of metal, nearly as tall as the appliances. Neat, linear rows were mowed clean. As she drove up a slight slope, she got enough of a view of the junk to see that it was arranged in the shape of a maze. A tall fence surrounded the house so that the only way to the front door was through the maze.

Lovely.

Sue paused and made a mental note of which way to turn to get to the door. By the time she parked and began traversing the maze of junk, her focus was so completely on remembering the series of turns that she barely noticed the odd house until she was standing in front of it.

The windows were stained glass depicting jigsaw puzzles. The front storm door appeared to be one giant sliding number puzzle with the free space used as an opening for a mail slot.

Instead of a doorbell, there was a panel with four colored squares. As she pressed one, lights flashed and beeped. When she didn't hear the doorbell ring inside, she pressed another button. The same pattern of lights and tones repeated.

That's when she realized this was also some kind of convoluted puzzle.

She pressed the series of buttons to match the pattern, and was rewarded with the sound of the doorbell ringing. It was the music used on the game show *Jeopardy*. Of course.

A tall, thin woman in her mid-fifties answered the door. She wore a T-shirt that boasted "I do crosswords in pen." Her pajama bottoms were covered in jigsaw pieces, and a pair of tiny ring puzzles dangled from her ears.

She propped her hands on her hips. "Whatever you're selling, I'm not buying."

"I'm not selling anything," Sue hurried to say. "I'm looking for something." She pulled out the picture of the wooden puzzle box and handed it to the woman. "Do you have it?"

"I do."

"This is going to sound strange, but I really need that box. Is there any chance you'd be willing to sell it?"

The woman narrowed her eyes. "You sound desperate. Why is it so important to you?"

Sue hated lying, but what other choice did she have? She couldn't exactly tell the woman that she needed it to give a half-man, half-statue a week of vacation from the hedonistic demigod who enslaved him. "It's for a friend."

"Right," said the woman, clearly not believing a word. "It's for a *friend*."

"It is. He's been dying to get his hands on it for a while now. His birthday is coming up, and I just can't stand the idea of disappointing him."

The woman blinked a few times. "Um. Okay. To each his own, I guess." She crossed her arms. "I want thirty thousand."

"Dollars?" squeaked Sue.

"It's an antique. Some would say priceless. It took me years to get my hands on it."

"But you're willing to sell it?"

"I solved the puzzle. Opened the box. It wasn't really my thing."

"What was in it?"

"You don't know?" she asked.

"No. How could I? No one seems to have been able to open it."

The woman beamed. "I'm just that good. Now, did you bring cash?"

Sue had enough money in her account to cover it, thanks to her uncle's inheritance, but she'd earmarked those funds to pay for repairs on the house. If she spent it all, she was going to be living in a rundown, leaking, drafty home for years to come.

But at least she'd be free, unlike Dalton. How much was a week's worth of freedom worth to him? How much would she spend for even a day with him?

"Show me the box," Sue said.

The woman shut the door in her face, then came back a few minutes later holding the box. In person, it was easy to see the joints in the wood where the pieces slid together. She swore it looked like there were at least twenty different sections. Each was a slightly different shade. There were areas that were darker, obviously from years of being handled, and a few scratches and gouges where someone had tried to pry it open.

The woman held it in a firm grip. "The only way to open it is with the right sequence of sliding segments. It took me two weeks to crack it."

"I'm sure your record is safe."

"So, do we have a deal?"

Sue nodded. "Yeah. We do."

She transferred money to the woman's bank account via her phone. Once the funds were moved, the woman wrapped the box up in a piece of cotton and put it in a plastic sack. "Keep it away from moisture or the pieces won't slide right."

"I'll remember that. Thanks."

The woman went back inside and locked the door. Sue went back out through the maze. She got lost a couple of times. As soon as she hit the next dead end, she turned around.

Tristan stood right in front of her, naked and dripping blood. He held out his hand and said, "Give me the box or I'll have to take it."

CHAPTER 15

The old woman driving Dalton went stiff next to him.

"Are you okay?" he asked.

"Tristan is back," she said, her voice tight with fear. "He found Sue."

Dalton had no idea how the woman knew all that, but it hardly mattered. "Drive faster," he ordered.

"It won't help. There isn't time. You have to go now."

Before he could ask what that meant, she laid her hand on his arm. One second he was sitting in the car, the next he was standing outside of a junk pile.

A woman screamed from a few yards away. It was Sue's voice, and she was terrified.

Dalton leaped on top of a washing machine and saw her pressed back against a refrigerator with Tristan only a few feet away and getting closer. She clutched something against her chest as if it were precious.

The box. She'd found it. And if Dalton didn't get to her in time, she was going to forfeit her life for it.

The shortest path to her was a straight line. Without hesitation, he barreled through the junk, sending metal, earth and weeds flying. As the frame of a rusting plow cleared his path, he saw Tristan's bloody body turn to face him.

Dalton slammed into him, grabbing him hard enough to carry him into the next row of junk. Metal sliced along his skin, but he ignored it.

"Run!" he yelled to Sue.

From the corner of his eye, he saw her flee. Now he could fight without fear of her getting hurt.

He balled up his fist and hit Tristan square in the jaw. The man's head snapped back, but his stoneman's frame held strong. He bared his teeth and came at Dalton with the force of a battering ram.

Dalton flew back into a wheelbarrow, which gouged a deep furrow in the ground and kept going until it hit the trunk of a large tree. Branches cracked. Sticks rained down. His head spun and something black fogged his vision.

When it cleared again, Tristan was coming for him, hefting the trenching blade of an old tractor like a scythe. He pulled it back as he closed in to strike. His eyes were empty, dead. For a split second, Dalton felt pity for the man. Tristan took no joy in attacking a fellow stoneman. He would kill Dalton, but only because there was no other choice.

He regained his feet, pushing away the blackness through sheer force of will. Tristan's muscles flexed as he began his strike. Dalton tried to move out of the way, but he was too slow, too dizzy. He misjudged the distance and could see the blow coming for him.

In that instant, blood bloomed across Tristan's chest and sprayed out behind him. A loud boom thundered in the air. A look of confused shock and pain tightened his brow.

Because of his compulsion, he couldn't stop. He had to do as he was ordered and kill Dalton.

He took another step forward. Again there was a loud boom of a shotgun, only this time, Tristan's body turned to stone just as the impact hit.

A chunk of stone about the size of Dalton's hand flew out of Tristan's side. It was a fatal blow. The instant the man turned to flesh again, he would bleed out in seconds.

Dalton turned to see Sue standing with a shotgun in her hands. Her face was covered with a mask of horror, and tears flowed down her cheeks. "I had no choice," she whispered. "He was going to kill you."

His heart broke for her. He knew exactly how she felt. How helpless and trapped. How terrified.

He pulled her into his arms and kissed the top of her head. She smelled so damn good. Felt even better. She clung to him, heedless of the blood and dirt sticking to his clothes.

He never wanted to let her go.

That's when he realized his mistake. He'd fallen for a woman he could never have. And now he was going to have to spend the next several decades seeing her every day without ever being able to touch her.

A woman's angry voice rose up from the house. "I've called the police. You're not going to get away with ruining my property like that."

"We have to go," said Sue. "I have the box. We have to find a way to get it back to Pyrenia before the deadline."

"There's something I have to do first." He picked up Tristan's stone form and carried it to Sue's car. Then he returned for the pieces of rock littering the ground. He couldn't get every bit of shattered stone, but he hoped he'd gathered enough to save the man's life.

"What are you going to do with that?" she asked.

"Can you find someone to glue him back together? If he's whole before he becomes flesh again, he may survive."

She glanced at his pitted, cracked statue. "He's beat up really bad, isn't he?"

"Looks like he's been left out in the elements for years. His curator should be hanged."

"If he even has one."

There was a watery flash of light. An instant later, Alethia appeared in front of them wearing the same clothes the woman who'd given him a ride had been. Her skin was bleached with worry, and her voice held a frenetic quality of urgency. "I'll take care of the mess here," she said. "You two have to go to Pyrenia. Now."

"What?" asked Sue.

"Has something happened?" asked Dalton.

"Yeah. Thyra's pissed at what you did to Tristan. She's coming for payback, and if you're here when she finds you, you won't survive."

Sue grabbed Dalton's arm. "Where do we go?"

"Home," said Alethia.

The next thing he knew, he and Sue were standing in front of Pyrenia in a sea of downy feathers. The sculptor dismounted the stoneman she'd been riding, leaving his erection stiff and gleaming. She scowled so hard it made her eyes go red. "No one interrupts my fun and lives to tell."

CHAPTER 16

He had nowhere to look but at the blatant sex act they'd interrupted. Everything here was white. White sky, white ground, white bed with white pillows. The only sources of color were the flush of arousal in Pyrenia's cheeks and the slick purple head of the man's erection.

"We're sorry for interrupting," said Dalton, shifting to stand in front of Sue. "We found the box and didn't want you to wait for it a second longer than you had to."

Pyrenia's scowl softened. "Give it to me."

Sue handed it over, glad to have the thing in the woman's hands where no more angry stonemen could show up and try to take it from her.

Pyrenia began moving sections of wood in an effort to open it. When she didn't get it right on the first try, a table appeared in front of her. She smashed the wood to splinters with her fist and picked up what was inside.

It was a length of ivory, carved with curving sinuous lines and protruding, smooth flowers. The ivory had yellowed with age, but there was no mistaking the purpose of the object once she held it up in plain sight.

"It's a dildo?" asked Sue. "We nearly got killed for a *dildo*?"

"No. You nearly got killed for a week of Dalton's freedom. Don't pretend otherwise."

A low burn of anger began heating beneath her skin. "I could have gone to any one of a hundred sex toy stores and got you one of those."

"I wanted this one. At least I thought I did. Now that I have it…" she held it up next to the rather impressive erection of the man lying on the cushions. He hadn't moved since they'd arrived, not even to cover himself. "…I see that it's too small." She tossed the piece of ivory behind her, where it disappeared into nothingness.

"I'd like to begin my week now," said Dalton.

Pyrenia pouted. "That little thing was hardly worth a week. I'll give you a day."

Sue opened her mouth to scream at the woman, but Dalton's hand tightened on her wrist—a clear warning to stay quiet.

"Then I'll take my day," he said, completely calm.

The scenery around them shifted. Clouds burned off and the sea of feathers at their ankles blew away on a strong, sudden wind. Walls solidified around them, and each one was filled to the rafters with books.

A beautiful woman in a tailored suit and glasses sat at a writing desk. She held a quill poised over a piece of parchment that was the exact same shade of her eyes. "You may not go back on your bargain, sister."

Pyrenia crossed her arms over her naked chest, forcing her breasts to bulge upward. "Stay out of my business, Lalia. Dalton has agreed to the new terms."

Lalia held up a piece of parchment. "The document is clear. I recorded it exactly as it was spoken. You owe this creature his week of freedom."

"Fine," said Pyrenia on a pout. "It doesn't matter anyway. Once his week is over, nothing will have changed. He'll still be mine. Only this time, he'll stay here with me like Sergei." She waved to the naked man who was still sprawled out and erect, waiting for her to mount him again. Only now he was on a leather couch, rather than a feather bed. The change of scenery hadn't done a thing to improve his situation.

Just as Dalton's week of freedom wouldn't improve his.

A deep, mournful ache clenched under Sue's ribs. She couldn't let a man as good as him suffer. He'd given up his life to save the woman he loved. He'd spent decades imprisoned and enslaved, all for the crime of loving someone else more than himself.

Sue knew what she had to do.

She stepped forward, pulling her hand from his. She forced herself to look Pyrenia right in the eyes. "I want to take his place."

"No!" shouted Dalton.

"Silence," Pyrenia barked.

In that instant his lips clamped shut and his body went immobile. He sucked air in through his nose and strained against the invisible forcing holding him in place.

"Go on, dear." The woman's smile was like slow, sweet poison. By the time she'd closed the distance between them, Sue already felt her life draining away. "What are you offering me, exactly?"

"When his week of freedom is over, I'll take his place. I'll…serve you and you'll free him to live out his life."

"You think I'll just let him go?" Pyrenia asked. "I've grown quite fond of him. We made plans."

"Now you can make them with me." Just saying the words made Sue's skin crawl, but she forced herself to stay strong.

Lalia lifted her quill and glanced at Pyrenia. "Are you considering this?"

"I am," said Pyrenia as she made a slow circle around Sue, studying her. "I have so few women in my collection."

"Whom will you choose for a termination clause?" asked Lalia.

The air in the room shifted, throwing books and papers around. As soon as the windstorm died down, another woman was present. She had long, black hair down to her knees and wore a tight, sleeveless dress that showed off an array of tattoos. As she glanced at Sue, her striking tri-colored eyes narrowed. "I will. These two nearly destroyed my Tristan."

"So you seek to help them, Thyra?" asked Lalia.

"No. I want to make sure this bitch can't possibly escape. And if she does, then I get her."

So this was the woman who had sent Tristan after them. From the looks of things, Sue had chosen the wrong woman to piss off. "I'm sorry we hurt him, but you did send him to kill us."

"You tried to take my toy."

"It was *my* toy," Pyrenia nearly screamed. Her face darkened to a mottled red as she faced Thyra.

"And you didn't even want it," Sue reminded her before realizing how stupid that was.

Thyra's long black hair shortened and lightened. The strands wove themselves into a tight braid, which then disappeared beneath a suit of armor. Her voice came out as an echo from inside the full metal helm. "I want her."

Pyrenia ran a finger across Sue's arm. "You can't have her. She's mine."

Sue had to work hard not to jerk away from the woman's touch. "Not unless you free Dalton."

"What does Dalton have to say about this?" asked Thyra.

His mouth worked, but nothing else did. He was suspended above the ground, unable to move. "I won't let her sacrifice her life for mine." He looked at Sue, his blue eyes pleading. "Don't do this. You have no idea what it means to let them control you."

She went to him and took his hands in hers. His fingers were stiff, and she didn't know if he could feel her or not, but she had to touch him. "You've given up enough of your life. It's your turn to live now."

"I can't let you do this. I refuse your offer," Dalton said.

"It's not yours to accept or refuse, stoneman," said Pyrenia. "It's mine."

"But," Thyra told Dalton, "if you want to belong to me, I'll see what I can do to ease your guilt. Perhaps give you a new plaything to occupy your time."

The veins in Dalton's neck throbbed. "If you think another woman could replace Sue, then you're so far beyond humanity you're unrecognizable."

Thyra beamed. "Thank you. That's the sweetest thing anyone's said to me all day."

"Sisters," said the woman with the quill. "I have matters to attend. Will there be a contract or not?"

"Yes," said Sue, as Dalton said, "No."

"Ignore him," said Pyrenia. "He's merely a meat puppet."

Dalton strained against his invisible bonds. "Just as you'll be if you make a deal with her, Sue."

That's not what she wanted, but she knew this was the right thing to do. She might never get another chance to free him. "Please try to understand that I need to do this. I could never again look at myself in the mirror, knowing the man I loved was suffering and I could have ended it."

The whole room fell silent.

"Loved?" asked Dalton in a quiet voice.

She guessed the cat was out of the bag now. She really hadn't wanted to bog him down with her girly emotions, but this might be the only chance she ever had to tell him how she felt. "Yes. I love you, Dalton. You're the kind of man I'd always believed existed but had never found. You're good and kind and selfless. You deserve a chance to find happiness for yourself. It's what I want. More than anything."

"You can't want it more than your freedom."

"I do." She looked into his eyes so he'd see the truth. "This is what I want."

"Then it's done," said Pyrenia. "I accept the woman's offering. They'll have their human week together, then she will be mine." Her smile widened as she glanced at the naked man on the couch. "I think Sergei is going to enjoy her. I know I'll enjoy watching him break her in."

Sue's stomach heaved, but she forced herself to stay calm. What happened next week would happen. It was a done deal. For now, she would spend a few days with Dalton and then say goodbye to the people she loved.

The sister in the prim suit lifted her quill and began to write. "The party of the first part." She looked at Sue. "That's you." She continued, "agrees to release her will to the party of the second part—that's Pyrenia—for an unspecified period of time immediately following one human week of freedom. The party of the first part agrees to this in return for the release of one stoneman, previously called Dalton Thatcher from Pyrenia's control, henceforth and forever. This agreement is considered legal and binding to all parties involved unless and until the party of the third part—as yet unnamed and unknown—executes an act— highly unlikely—that constitutes the dissolution of this agreement as set out in clause 16B of the Sister's Original Agreement as witnessed by Father or until such time as the game is concluded." She looked up from her writings. "Do I have any sister present who seeks to claim possession of this poor creature's exit clause?"

Pyrenia rolled her eyes. "Booorrriiing."

Thyra stomped her combat boots and pouted. "I keep hearing *party, party, party,* but I'm not having any fun. Where are the Jell-O shots?"

Lalia tapped the quill impatiently. "The contract must be complete before it's filed."

Pyrenia gave Lalia a menacing glare. "Do you think anyone would notice if I shoved *you* in some dusty old file box for a century or two?"

Thyra beamed. "You know what Father did to you two the last time he caught you fighting. I would love to see that again. Please continue."

Sue cleared her throat. "Excuse me, but can we please get on with this?" she rushed forward so Dalton wouldn't have a chance to stop her and scrawled her name at the bottom of the document. It didn't matter what flowery words or legal speak they used. The situation was still the same.

"I agree," Sue said. "My slavery for Dalton's freedom."

"No," bellowed Dalton. "I won't let you hurt her. She doesn't know what she's saying."

"Too late," said Lalia as she scribbled something onto the parchment. "We are all bound by contract."

Everyone in the room fell silent and stared. Dalton's eyes welled with tears. Grief lined his face and bent his spine in defeat.

Sue couldn't stand seeing him like that, but what choice did she have? She couldn't let the man she loved spend another day as a slave to such a twisted bitch—not when she could save him.

Even if it cost her freedom.

The sisters all looked up at the same instant. Sue felt a powerful presence sweep down over them. She saw nothing, but there was no mistaking the pure, godlike power that poured down over them.

Even the sisters seemed to shrink in the midst of that presence.

The air around Sue shifted. A bell rang, but it that wasn't really a sound—more like a wave of pressure thrumming against her. All she knew for sure was that something important had just happened.

Words without sound shimmered in her head, bypassing her ears entirely.

It is done.

Then, as quickly as the powerful presence appeared, it was gone.

Pyrenia snarled at Sue, hatred plain on her face. "I'm going to kill you for this, human."

CHAPTER 17

Dalton's body was released from its invisible prison. He fell to his knees, grief and fury at war for control over him.

Sue had given her life to save his. Even as he was terrified for her and angry that she refused to listen to him, he couldn't help but love her for her selfless gift.

She'd traded her freedom for his. Without hesitation or condition for her enslavement.

A gong sounded in his head, followed by the powerful echo of the words, *It is done.*

He didn't know who spoke, but the words were clear enough. Sue's life was over, and it was his fault for dragging her into Pyrenia's games.

She glared at Sue with naked hatred in her eyes and bared her teeth. "I'm going to kill you for this, human."

As Pyrenia stalked toward Sue there was only one thing he could think to do: Kill Pyrenia before she could hurt Sue.

He charged, surprised when he didn't run into a brick wall of compulsion. His shoulder barreled into her stomach, taking her down to the floor. He pinned her there, his hand gripping her throat.

There was no way to know if a creature like her could die, but he was going to find out.

From the corner of his eye he saw Thrya's appearance shift and morph into that of a cheerleader. She waved her poms and jumped up and down with glee. "Fight, fight, fight!"

"Violence will get us nowhere," said Lalia in a calm tone. "Father has spoken."

Dalton tightened his grip, watching Pyrenia's face turn red.

A fist of pressure slammed into his chest, sending him flying back through the air. He hit a shelf filled with books, which cascaded down on top of him.

"What the hell are you all doing?" demanded Alethia, who had just poofed into existence nearby.

"Dalton was trying to kill Pyrenia," said Thyra with a wide smile. "It was adorable."

Lalia rolled her eyes. "Yes. Absolutely precious."

"You have to forgive him," said Sue. "He's just upset with me."

"Upset?" he nearly bellowed. "You're throwing your life away. No way am I letting the woman I love sacrifice herself for me."

Alethia hauled Dalton to his feet and grabbed Sue by the hand. "No one is sacrificing anything." She glared at the other women in the room. "What none of my sisters have told you is that Sue's willingness to sign that contract and trade her freedom in the name of love triggered the termination clause in Dalton's original contract. You're both free to go. I suggest you do so before anyone else does anything stupid and winds up in a new contract with Thyra."

Thyra's cheerleader skirt lengthened and turned into a nun's habit. With a pout bowing her full mouth, she said, "Everyone is always blaming everything on me."

"He tried to kill me," said Pyrenia. "He should give me another century of service for the insult."

"You'll get over it," said Alethia.

"What just happened?" Sue asked.

Lalia pushed her glasses up on the bridge f her nose. "Every contract we sisters make to claim a stoneman has a termination clause. Father insisted."

"Termination clause?"

Thyra nodded. "It makes the game way more fun."

Lalia rolled her eyes. "That's not why Father insisted we use them. It's to ensure that we're keeping tabs on one another, so that no sister breaks the rule of law."

"I don't understand," Dalton said. "I didn't know anything about a termination clause."

"It's not your right to know, human," Pyrenia spat. "And I didn't choose to tell you. The last thing I want is a bunch of my property living in hope and thinking of ways to free themselves when they should be thinking about ways to better serve me."

"So this termination clause in Dalton's contract was his get-out-of-jail-free card?" Sue asked.

"Not free," Alethia said. "It had a high cost—a sacrificial act of love—but it was one Sue was willing to pay."

"And all stonemen have these escape clauses?" Dalton asked.

"No fair!" Thyra shouted. "No telling! He's going to ruin the game."

Lalia let out a longsuffering sigh. "I realize you're not as bright as the rest of us, but do try to consider it as a challenge, will you? Besides, even if he wanted to tell every stoneman out there, he has no access to my files. All the contracts are protected."

Thyra started forward, malice clear in her eyes. "I'll show you a challenge."

"Sisters!" Alethia shouted to be heard over the growling. "Enough! Go, all of you. The show is over."

Thyra and Pyrenia disappeared in a huff, but Lalia lingered behind.

"What now?" demanded Alethia.

"It was my clause that freed him. I'd like a moment with them if you don't mind."

"Fine. Just be fast. I want them home before they do anything stupid."

Lalia tilted her head to the side as she stared at Dalton. "You loved a woman enough to enslave yourself." She turned to Sue. "And you loved him enough to do the same to free him. Now he loves you enough to fight a creature who could slay him with a mere thought. May I see what that feels like?"

"Love?" asked Sue, perplexed. "You don't know what love feels like?"

Lalia blinked her parchment colored eyes and held out her hand. "Why do you think I created the termination clause? I've been studying this affliction you humans have for one another. It intrigues me."

"Go find a boyfriend, then," said Dalton.

"I just want a brief glimpse. I promise it won't hurt."

Sue took her hand. Tears shimmered in her pretty brown eyes. "Everyone should know what it feels like to love. And be loved, don't you think, Dalton?"

There was one more reason to love Sue—one more to add to the growing mountain. That she would have such sympathy for people who toyed with humans the way the sisters did was humbling.

He nodded. "You're right."

Sue took Lalia's hand. She gasped. After a moment her eyes also filled with tears. She looked at Dalton, and he swore she gave him that same look of love Sue did.

Lalia held out her other hand. Dalton gripped it, but felt nothing.

She, on the other hand, broke down sobbing. "So beautiful. Books don't do it justice. The two of you are going to be so happy together."

Lalia disappeared, leaving them standing with Alethia.

"I'm going to send you back now. And don't worry about the police or the mess you and Tristan made. I repaired everything and undid the events in the minds of those who saw them. You're free. No looking over your shoulder. Even Tristan has no reason to hunt you now."

"You can do that?" asked Sue.

"Cleaning up after my sisters is something I've gotten quite good at doing lately."

"Why did you help us?" asked Sue.

"Because none of my sisters can win the game. It's too dangerous for humans if they do. My sisters each think they are the most worthy of the prize, but not one of them has felt what I have."

"What's that?" asked Sue.

"Pain. Loss." She closed her eyes. "Grief."

"I don't understand," said Sue.

Alethia nodded. "That is because you are mortal. Powerless. You have no idea what my sisters are capable of. I do. And I am the one who must keep them in check."

"Thank you," said Dalton as he took Sue's hand. "We may not understand why you helped, but we are grateful."

The next thing he knew, they were standing in the farmhouse. Alone. The base of his statue was gone, leaving only a dust-free square on the floor to mark where it had once stood.

He pulled Sue into his arms and kissed her until they were both breathless. When he lifted his head, he could hardly believe that she was still here. And that he was real, made flesh and blood once again.

"You saved me," he said. "Your love saved me."

"You saved yourself by being so damn easy to love."

He shuddered with emotion. He still couldn't believe that a woman as beautiful and kind as she was could love him. He'd always tried to be a good man, but no man was truly good enough to deserve a woman like Sue. "I love you, too."

She grinned and gifted him with a kiss so hot it nearly singed his eyebrows. "So, what do we do now?"

"I don't know about you, but I'm going to spend the rest of my life proving to you that you didn't make the wrong choice in freeing me."

A sexy light glinted in her eyes. "I can think of some ways you could get to work on that."

"Oh, yeah?"

"Yeah." Her voice went all soft and sultry. "You can start by repairing the roof and working your way down."

He laughed and kissed her again. "That can wait for tomorrow. Today I'm going to start at your mouth and work my way down."

"That has promise, too." She melted in his arms, and he knew that as long as he lived, he'd never grow tired of the way she was looking at him right now—so full of love and happiness he didn't know how to hold it all.

He may have spent the last one-hundred-sixty years made of stone, but for Sue, he was putty in her hands.

The End

THE
STONE MEN
SERIES

BOOK 1
    Rock Hard — Kathy Lyons
    Made Flesh — Anna Argent

BOOK 2
    Rock Candy — Kathy Lyons
    Heart of Stone — Anna Argent

Kathy Lyons

Kathy Lyons is the wild, adventurous half of USA TODAY bestselling author Jade Lee. A lover of all things fantastical, Kathy spent much of her childhood in Narnia, Middle Earth, Amber, and Earthsea, just to name a few. "There is nothing I adore more than to turn around on an ordinary day and experience something magical. It happens all the time in real life and in my books." Winner of several industry awards including the *Prism—Best of the Best, Romantic Times Reviewer's Choice*, and *Fresh Fiction's Steamiest Read*, Kathy has published over 50 romance novels and yet says she's just getting started. "It's the love story that gets me every time. There's magic powers and then there's the magic of love. The first is cool. The second is life."

Check out her latest news at www.KathyLyons.com, Facebook: JadeLeeBooks, Twitter: JadeLeeAuthor

Anna Argent

After spending years working in corporate America as an engineer, Anna traded it all in for a quiet life in the country. She lives with her husband on a small cattle ranch in the Ozark Mountains, penning stories filled with love, lust and a healthy dose of magic. She loves to hear from her readers at www.AnnaArgent.com.